MOMENT OF LO[

While she was being driven out of the suburbs
toward the West End in the beautiful Rolls,
Christa couldn't even enjoy the luxury of it,
nor glory in the notion that this was to be her
way of life from now onward. No more
queueing for buses or strap-hanging in the
underground. She would always have a Rolls,
and everything else she wanted, as the wife
of the Director of Parfum Joyeux. She would
adore her husband, too. But just supposing
for one moment that Barby was right and that
it was not the best thing for Stephen.
This idea thrust itself like a dagger into
Christa's heart.

Moment of Love

Denise Robins

CORONET BOOKS
Hodder and Stoughton

Copyright © 1964 by Denise Robins

First published in Great Britain by
Hodder and Stoughton 1964

Coronet edition 1967
Second impression 1969
Third impression 1976

Printed and bound in Great Britain for
Coronet Books, Hodder and Stoughton, London
by Cox & Wyman Ltd, London, Reading and Fakenham

ISBN 0 340 02474 7

FOR CHRISTINA FOYLE WITH MY ADMIRATION
AND AFFECTION

"Each in another's eyes finds light,
The Light of compassion.
This is the moment of pity, this is
The Moment of Love."

From *The Desolate City*
by Wilfrid Scawen Blunt

1

Golling & Nash had closed down for the night.

The big departmental store in Oxford Street had suddenly become a great silent monument to all the good things of life that can be bought or sold. The long counters were shrouded; dust sheets flung over the dress models on their stands; lights extinguished; lifts 'grounded'. Night-watchmen came on duty. Hundreds of employees, chattering, scurrying to get home, had left by the staff entrance. The huge glass doors all along the front of the block were locked. Nothing of the day's clamour remained. Nothing but the brilliant, still-lighted windows displaying new summer dresses, coats and gay hats; gloves and stockings, bags and costume jewellery; linen; and all the variety of household furnishings.

What of the girls who worked in that vast establishment – the clerks, the shop assistants, the models, the buyers, the juniors, the dozen and one members of the staff? What of their personal lives, now that they had been released from the bondage of the long tiring day; from the necessity to serve the public, to be polite and patient in the face of continual frustration. Those who all day continue to smile and assist, no matter how weary or bored, can relax now and become individualists again. They can think of themselves – instead of customers. Their personal lives and joys and sorrows can once more become of paramount importance. Golling & Nash – the great gilded monster-god that devoured them all day, demanding perpetual sacrifice – can be abandoned.

Christa Coombe and Barbara Lane, friends from their schooldays, were both employed by Messrs. Golling & Nash. Christa as a typist in the cashier's office on the top floor; Barbara in the hat department where she did a certain amount of modelling. She was a particularly beautiful girl with a warm white skin, brown lustrous eyes and dark auburn hair which she wore long as a rule, but which today was brushed high up on her head. She was slim and graceful. She had a good following of admirers among the male members of the staff.

Christa was one of her most loyal friends and generous admirers – without a trace of jealousy. She, herself, was a Devon girl, whose father had been a not very successful farmer and whose mother had had Scandinavian blood in her veins. Christa was on the small, thin side, with too high a forehead, and too wide a mouth. If she had any beauty it lay in her dazzlingly fair hair – thick and wavy, and eyes which were of a light fascinating grey with big black pupils. They held a soft, melting expression. Barbara often teased her friend about her 'softness'. She was very sentimental.

"You're a romantic little soul – you'll have to be careful or one day'll you'll get badly hurt," Barbara would warn her.

Barbara was a vain, pleasure-loving, rather greedy girl. There was nothing soft about her. She was as calculating as Christa was the reverse. She even had a cruel streak that she concealed, and a quick, passionate temper. Men were carried away by her physical perfection. They were the opposite of one another. Nevertheless they got on well, mainly because the gentle, reserved Christa adored and admired her flamboyant friend.

On this warm summer evening as the girls walked arm-in-arm down Oxford Street, they both felt on top of the world. They were facing an exciting holiday; going abroad next week.

"I'm getting so thrilled, I can't bear it," Barbara announced, looking slantways, provocatively into the eyes of a boy who almost stopped in his tracks and turned to gaze longingly after the brilliantly beautiful girl. "Tomorrow – then Sunday – then over to the other side of the Channel. To my beloved, divine Paris!"

Christa smiled. Barby called it '*her* Paris'. She seemed to think of the French capital as *hers*. But she had never been there. It figured only in her dreams and imagination. Neither girl had so far set foot on the Continent. Their holidays, shared or apart, were usually spent in rather dull coastal resorts – in England (often with Barbara's mother). In such places, a cheap boarding-house and more often than not, poor weather, spoiled any chance of a 'wonderful time'. But during this year, the two girls had been saving rigorously. Now at last they could afford to go abroad. They had bought their tickets from a Sloane Street Travel Agency. They had their passports.

8

They were going across from Newhaven to Dieppe – the cheapest route.

What fun it had been planning it all, Christa thought, as she waited with Barby at the bus stop for the one that would take them both to Wood Green.

Barbara lived with her widowed mother. Christa had a 'bed-sit' in a house in the same road. But since she had lost her aunt and only relative in Devon, five years ago, she spent most of her time in the Lanes' home, and ate with them during the week-ends. Mrs. Lane was like a mother to her – Barby, a sister. They had as good as 'adopted her'. Without that small, shabby but comfortable little house where there was always a meal and a welcome, Christa would have been very lonely and miserable.

She felt that she owed the Lanes everything; there was nothing too much she could do for them in return. She loved Mrs. Lane who was a kindly, simple woman in her early fifties. Barby, beautiful Barby, with all her 'boy-friends', her party evenings, was often out. Christa felt such affection for her that she prayed quite passionately that she would one day find the right man and settle down. Her passionate nature and lack of stability often frightened Christa. Barby was so restless and discontented. Some of the girls in the shop called her spoiled. Christa knew that she was selfish, even to her own mother, and often traded on Christa's adoration. But Christa forgave her as her mother did, and bore her no ill-will.

Christa rarely went out to parties. She was painfully shy. She suffered from an inferiority complex, possibly because she was too much with Barbara. She was certain that she would never make the grade with the boys and would be an 'old maid', although Mrs. Lane never stopped telling her that she was sweet and charming and would one day find some man to appreciate her.

Christa wanted desperately to be loved . . . and to fall in love. She had a store of deep sympathetic feeling . . . a great deal to give. Once when Barbara was modelling new hats, Christa watched her and said:

"You look terrific, Barby – you always do! But at least I'll know that if any man falls for *me*, it won't be for my glamour. It'll be *for myself alone!*"

Barby raised a cynical eyebrow and grinned.

"Or for your pay-packet, honey-chile – men generally want *something* in return."

9

Christa sighed and smiled.

In the bus going to Wood Green this evening, she clutched her bag tightly between her hands. She said breathlessly:

"My eyes are like X-rays – I can see straight through the plastic to my Traveller's Cheques."

Barbara smothered a giggle.

"And I can see my little packet of French currency. Oh, lord, I wish I had your head for figures! I can't count. It's about thirteen new francs to the pound, isn't it? I *must* try to remember. Ten bob is roughly six and a half francs."

"That's right," said Christa.

"You know that boy who works in the Men's Ties and Socks – the tall fair one —"

"Yes?"

"He was in France in April. He says everything's crashingly expensive."

"Oh, well, we've got enough for our fortnight."

"And the hotel these agents booked us into is comparatively cheap, they say."

"Oh, I want to see Notre Dame and the Louvre and the bridges over the Seine," said Christa.

"You're too intellectual for me, duckie. I just want the shops in the Rue de la Paix and the Eiffel Tower!"

"I want to see them, too, of course."

"We must both buy a hat – you *can't* leave Paris without buying a hat," said Barbara, her large eyes shining greedily.

"Okay by me," said Christa.

A well-dressed business man, carrying a brief-case sitting opposite the two girls got off the bus. As he passed he glanced down at them. The romantically-minded, humble Christa thought:

"He's looking at Barby – everyone does."

She might have been surprised if she had known what the man with the brief-case was thinking. He had noticed the tall dark-eyed, auburn-haired girl, judging her to be a model. Then he saw the small slight one with the fair hair and serious face. He thought:

"Auburn-hair's a beautiful girl. Yet I prefer the little fair-head. The other might be difficult. Damned conceited, too. Knows just how attractive she is. The small one has a very sweet smile. H'm!"

But he departed – never to see either of the girls again.

In the Lane household at Wood Green that evening, Christa

and Barby were busy pressing, folding and packing. Barbara's mother – a thin, tall woman with greying hair, sat with one eye on the girls, the other on television, and a cigarette between her lips. She was an inveterate smoker. She fanned herself with a paper. It was a close night and the little house was stuffy.

"You both look very pleased with yourselves," she teased them. "I wish in a way you'd gone on one of those conducted tours. I don't altogether like the idea of two attractive girls like you, who don't speak one word of French, being alone in Paris."

"Oh, we'll be all right, Aunty Cath," said Christa.

"Don't be so old fashioned, Mum," said Barbara impatiently. "Are you picturing us being robbed and left for dead in a back alley? I assure you we can take care of ourselves."

"We can take care of *each other*!" added Christa, vigorously pressing a blue and white linen suit (three years old). It had creased a bit since she had last worn it.

"We'll call in Maigret if we get into trouble," added Barbara, borrowed her mother's box of matches, lit a cigarette and flung herself into a chair. "Finish my dress for me, Chris, you're so much better at ironing than I am."

Catherine Lane, who had never been out of England in her life (Barbara'a father had been a typically insular Englishman, preferring his regular annual holiday in Bournemouth or Brighton), sighed, then shrugged her shoulders. No use counselling the young today. They were too independent, and they were sure they knew everything. However, she was glad her 'adopted daughter' was going with Barby. Barby was so excitable and wilful. Christa was much more reliable, the mother had to admit that. Dear little Christa looked quite pretty tonight, if she but knew it, her cheeks flushed from the heat and exertion of ironing; her naturally wavy hair tossed back from her forehead. A pity she was so thin – so pale, as a rule. Rather insignificant perhaps compared with Barby. But she was a sweetie and *most* unselfish.

"I hope you'll have a glorious time, my dear," the older woman sighed. "If I were ten years younger I'd come with you."

"Are you threatening us?" her daughter grimaced at her.

But Christa, always terrified of hurting anybody's feelings, quickly added:

"I wish you could come, Aunty Cath."

Barbara certainly did not wish anything of the kind. She loved her mother, but she loved herself more. She didn't want the maternal eye upon her or anybody with her in Paris except Christa, the adopted sister and friend who was always ready to say 'yes' to any of her propositions.

On the Saturday morning before Golling & Nash closed down for the week-end, the two girls were given a 'send-off' by their friends, all wishing them "happy holiday" and teasing them.

"I bet you two'll get into some sort of scrape."

"Wait and hear what the *Monsieurs* say when they see our Barbara strolling down the Boulevards."

"Gosh, don't I envy you going to *Paris!*" exclaimed one girl who worked in the Hat Department. "*Chapeau* shops in the Rue de Rivoli. *Think* of it!"

It was exactly what Barbara *was* thinking about when at last she and Christa leaned over the rails of the Cross Channel steamer on their way to Dieppe. It was a French boat. The chatter of the French staff made the girls feel that their holiday had already started. It looked like being a perfect crossing. The June morning was cloudless. The sea was calm. The boat was crowded.

The girls were immensely thrilled. Christa wore a pale blue thin wool suit with a white sleeveless blouse. Barbara was in a delicate shade of yellow linen with a wide belt and carried a white jacket. Tall and graceful, as usual attracting a great deal of attention.

They were to be ten days in Paris and the last three were to be spent in Dieppe where they had booked a double room in a small hotel. Both wanted sea air and swimming as the finale to their holiday.

They went down below to eat lunch. They could hear the French language being spoken on all sides. Now and then Christa felt uneasy.

"Shall we ever manage – not knowing a word," she murmured.

"Of course. Everyone seems to speak English over there."

All the same, even Barbara privately wished that *one* of them was a bit more travelled and competent to deal with a crisis, if one should arise.

It was in the dining salon that they first noticed *HIM*; the tall, dark-haired young man who sat alone, eating his meal. He spoke to nobody, He had segregated himself. While he ate, he wrote busily on a sheet of foolscap and kept examining papers which he extracted from an attaché case.

His appearance attracted Barbara. She whispered to her friend:

"Isn't he gorgeous? . . . that figure . . . those strong features . . . those marvellous eyes? He's a film star."

"He's certainly very handsome," said Christa.

"I wish he'd look at us."

"Oh, Barby, you are awful —" began Christa.

Then the handsome young man actually turned his head and glanced in their direction but immediately looked down at his work again. The girls grimaced at each other.

"A woman-hater, huh?" muttered Barbara.

"No – just reserved, I'd think. Shy, like me," Christa bit her lip and smiled. "He's rather dignified," she added.

"Wonder what he does . . ."

They ruminated. He was a diplomat . . . he was in the Secret Service . . . he was going to Paris on important business . . . he was wealthy and successful, of course. Look at his well-cut light grey suit . . . his pale yellow and white silk tie. He was a baronet, perhaps an earl, or even a duke. He spoke to the waiter in perfect French, adding a few words in English. He was definitely an Englishman. The 'old school tie' . . . and now the two girls, fascinated, watched him draw an English passport from his attaché case.

"I'm mad about him —" Barbara rolled her eyes heavenwards, lit a cigarette, and smoked it dreamily.

Christa smoked but was less of an addict than her friend. She sipped her coffee and with her soft eyes watched the handsome stranger. The stories they were weaving around him were probably the absolute opposite of the true facts. But it was during the few seconds in which he had glanced toward them that she had noted how blue his eyes were, and how tanned his face – a curiously attractive face with high cheek-bones. And she liked his well-bred hands . . . noted the signet ring on his little finger. He was the kind of man a girl could fall very much in love with, she thought. And there followed the sadder thought that never would such a man look at Christa Coombe.

Suddenly Barbara smothered a laugh.

"I've made up my mind what he is," she whispered. "He's married and running away from his wife and children. I saw him start like anything just now when a woman appeared with two little girls in the doorway. All hope is lost, Christa, let's turn our attention elsewhere."

She laughed at her nonsense, but Christa continued to think

13

about the sun-tanned stranger with the wonderful eyes and the aloof personality. Somehow she did not *want him* to be a married man.

2

At last they were in Dieppe. As they stepped on to French soil, the girls broke into mutual sighs of rapture.

"We've made it!" sighed Barbara, "I can *smell* France. Garlic, and coffee, and quite a different brand of cigarettes."

Christa nodded. She stared excitedly around her. Jostled by the crowd as they stepped off the boat into the Customs shed, she began to wish again that she had gone to night classes at the Polytechnic and learned to speak French. It seemed to her that now she and Barbara were separated from everything and everyone English. It was a French world that screamed and gesticulated about them. They passed through the Customs easily, but while still in the Customs shed (the Paris train was waiting for them on the track), they were confronted by a blue-bloused man with a peaked cap who smilingly seized their two suitcases.

"Wait!" began Christa.

"Hi!" said Barbara, "we can carry those ourselves . . ."

The man disappeared. So did their suitcases. Other porters were trundling piled-up trolleys towards the train. Barbara said in a slightly doubting voice:

"Everyone's doing it. I suppose we'll see the stuff again on the train itself. I'm jolly glad we labelled everything."

But once they reached the train, the girls searched up and down the corridor and saw no sign of the smiling porter or their luggage.

Christa began to feel anxious. Every porter they spoke to answered by shrugging a shoulder and letting loose a flood of rapid French. It was a warm day – warmer here than across the Channel. Tendrils of hair clung damply to Christa's forehead. Even the impeccable Barbara looked hot and bothered.

"This is a *nice* start," she said in a grumbling voice.

'Our luggage has been nicked. That fellow wasn't a porter at all."

Then suddenly she turned. There stood *The Man* . . . the dark-haired, blue-eyed 'ambassador' (or whatever he was). Barbara seized her opportunity.

"Oh, please can you help us," she began.

He looked politely at the tall beautiful girl in yellow.

"Of course, what can I do?" Christa thought his voice as attractive as his face. She plucked up courage and put in her say.

"A porter seized our suitcases and we just can't find him."

"Did you take his number?"

Barbara shrugged. Christa felt ashamed and small.

"No, we didn't," she admitted.

The Man's expression suggested disdain and an ineffable air of boredom.

"He thinks us idiots, so we are," thought Christa.

But Barbara had decided to make the usual attack with her beauty and charm. He listened to her explanations, then went off. He returned with the porter *and* the suitcases. The fellow, it appeared, had been looking for *les deux jeunes dames*. They followed him towards a second-class carriage.

"Thanks terribly —" Barbara began, flashing her big brown eyes at their rescuer.

"Not at all," he said in his cool voice, turned and jumped into a first-class carriage near by.

The girls, laughing a little, seated themselves in their own carriage which was already half full.

"There you are," whispered Barbara, "He *is* married and too terrified to stay talking to us. Can't you tell."

"He was very nice," said Christa.

And that was the beginning of the adventure and of a train journey which was to end in tragedy. Until they reached the outskirts of Paris all went well. Christa and Barby had tea on the train, and an early dinner washed down by a cheap bottle of *vin du pays*. They enjoyed every minute of it. They found the unfamiliar countryside vastly interesting. England . . . Wood Green . . . dear Mum and the house in Nightingale Avenue . . . all seemed so far, far away.

Then came the accident. Suddenly the Dieppe–Paris express began to sway and lurch. There was a screeching of brakes, the whining of broken metal, the splintering of wood. The dangerous swaying and rattling brought the two girls on their feet, white-faced and terrified. The other occupants of the carriage shouted and grabbed at seats or luggage-racks. Then they were all hurled together in a sobbing, screaming tangle of bodies, legs and arms, as the Paris express met an outgoing suburban train moving at full speed.

For months afterwards, Christa remembered that dreadful moment. It was as though she had been hurled from a pleasant gentle dream into a ghastly nightmare. She heard her own voice screaming and Barbara calling:

"*Christa*! ... *Mum*! ..."

After that, silence and darkness. Christa's forehead had hit the window-ledge, violently.

She was one of the first to regain consciousness. She had been only temporarily stunned. Her awakening was a continuation of the nightmare. The lights had gone out. She found herself in a dim ghastly twilight in which she could see little but could hear the screams and moans around her. She pushed a suitcase off her legs and struggling up, she saw, to her horror, the figure of her friend opposite her. Barbara lay trapped under a pile of jagged woodwork. Her beautiful face was a terrible mask. Blood ran down from her head. Her complete stillness struck chill in Christa's soul. She cried out frenziedly:

"Barby, *Barby*!"

To her immeasurable relief, Barbara's heavily-lashed eyelids lifted. At least, thought Christa, that meant she was still alive.

Christa began to laugh and sob hysterically. She managed to stagger on to her feet. She, herself, had escaped miraculously – she realized that. Her injuries were little worse than a few odd cuts and bruises. But what of the others? She could hear that terrible screaming still going on along the line. People were shouting, rushing along the track. Now also, she could hear the sinister siren of fire engines, rising above the other grim sounds in the night.

She began to pray as she used to do when she was a little girl.

"*Please God don't let this be true ... !*"

But it *was* true, and Barbara did not stir again, and the dreadful sights and sounds went on until suddenly two hands, strong and warm, lifted Christa's shivering body clear from the wrecked carriage and set her on her feet. A man's voice asked:

"Are you all right?"

16

She looked up at his face dumbly. She saw that it was *Him*. Save for stains on his suit and his dishevelled hair, he appeared to her as debonair, as cool, and controlled as ever. He touched her gently. He seemed suddenly like an old friend . . . the only English friend she had in this dark shattered world . . . in this alien land in which she had landed only a few hours ago, full of joy and gaiety.

Christa burst into tears and clung to *The Man*. He looked down at the fair head . . . at the tangled waves of hair grey with dust and splinters of wood . . . then at the grimy young face. Her soft grey eyes were tragically frightened. He felt a sudden tenderness toward her. He wanted to comfort this poor young girl. She was obviously too shocked to think for herself.

"There, there," he kept saying, patting her shoulder, all right. It's a grim show, but you're all right."

"My friend . . ." sobbed Christa, "my friend . . . Barby."

"Where is she?"

Christa pointed a shaking finger at the half-buried girl behind them. With a shocked exclamation, the man left Christa and started to pull aside timber and metal tearing at them – trying to extricate Barbara. After that, it seemed to Christa that things were taken out of her hands and passed in to those of the unknown Englishman. He was in complete control now – the wonderful blessed control of a strong resourceful person who could speak perfect French, give orders, and see that they were carried out.

In less than a quarter of an hour, he had pulled Barbara clear of the wreckage. She was unconscious but still breathing, so he assured Christa. An ambulance would soon take them to a Paris hospital. He could not go with them. He must stay, he said, and help along the line. A business friend, who came from Dieppe and had been travelling with him, was unhurt and already assisting the stretcher-bearers. Christa looked at *The Man* with frightened eyes.

"We can't speak the language . . . we're absolute fools, I'm afraid. Must you leave us alone . . ."

Then he smiled. Christa thought she had never seen anything so comforting and understanding as that smile.

"Here's my address," he said. "It's my sister's apartment. She lives in Paris." He wrote rapidly on a piece of paper and gave it to Christa. "Go straight to her when they've finished with you. I expect they'll keep your friend in the hospital, but you'll be discharged, I'm sure. Do you understand? Go to my sister. She'll help you."

"Yes," Christa nodded. "Thanks terribly," and she held on to the piece of paper as though it were a mascot to which she must cling at all costs.

The ambulance moved swiftly through the outskirts of Paris to the Hôpital St. Georges. It was a Convent for the sick run by nuns. Christa's gaze rarely left the pale still face of her friend whose hand she held all during that drive. An attendant had temporarily bandaged the wound on Barbara's forehead. But the injured girl did not stir. The French ambulance man – speaking broken English – tried to reassure the weeping Christa. *Mademoiselle's* pulse was quite strong, he said. There was no fear of death.

It was a grim entry into the gay French capital for the girls who had set out from Newhaven so happily this morning!·

Christa was too dazed to take much interest in the handsome brightly-lit streets through which they were now being driven; she barely saw the parks or boulevards or the crowds sitting outside the cafés, drinking and chatting; yet she had so often dreamed about Paris – those wonderful chestnut trees in the Bois – the silver waters of the Seine – the old, lovely bridges – the spires of Notre Dame.

Then, high on a hill in Montmartre, they came to the St. Georges. White-robed nuns with winged caps received the patient. Barbara was wheeled into the theatre for immediate examination and X-rays. Christa was taken to a casualty reception ward.

3

ONE hour later.

Nine o'clock. Christa was now allowed to leave the hospital. She felt considerably better. The terrible sensation of cold and sickness had gone. The nuns had given her food and coffee and she had enjoyed both. A bespectacled young doctor had dressed the minor cuts and abrasions on her left arm and told her she was fit to go home. She had seen Barbara, who was back from the theatre and in bed now in one of the women's wards. A nun who spoke English convinced Christa that her friend's condition was not critical, and suggested that Christa returned to the hospital to see her friend tomorrow. By then Barbara should have recovered consciousness. The wound on her head was nasty but not dangerous. Her face was unmarked.

"*Quelle jolie fille!* What a beautiful girl!" Even the old nun had made this exclamation when she spoke of Barbara. Christa left the Convent warmed by the feeling that her friend's beauty had not been impaired. She also took the precaution of wiring her adoptive aunt in case news of the Paris express disaster should be announced over English radio or television and come as a shock to Mrs. Lane.

"*In train accident but both safe writing*," Christa worded her telegram.

Now she stood on the steps of the hospital gazing at the lights of Paris – seeing for the first time the outline of Sacré Coeur, loveliest of churches, etched against a luminous sky on this perfect moonlit night.

The nuns had given her the name of a small hotel where she would be safe for the night, and, also enough money for her bill. They had lost both handbags and suitcases. Christa intended to take a taxi to the hotel, but dreaded dealing with the foreign driver. After the first hysteria had died down, she realized to her dismay that she and Barbara had absolutely nothing left. Tomorrow, of course, she could go to the British Consul. He would doubtless make arrangements to issue new passports and advance them a loan. The doctor at the Hôpital St. Georges had told her, too, that they could claim compensation from the railway company. But that would take time. Meanwhile . . . what a holiday! As soon as poor Barby could travel, they would have to return to England.

Then Christa remembered the address *The Man* had given her.

"*Go at once to my sister's apartment*," he had said.

She felt so utterly lonely and wretched, she was seized suddenly with an overwhelming desire to take advantage of this kindness. She was about to hail a passing taxi when a car drew up before the entrance of the St. Georges Hospital. Out stepped *The Man* himself. Christa, thrilled and delighted, hailed him.

"Oh, hello . . . *hello!*"

He recognized the slender fair girl and greeted her quite warmly in return.

"*Hello* there! I was just coming to ask after you two," he said.

"How good of you!" exclaimed Christa and the tears rushed to her eyes.

"The professional rescue chaps are down there at the wreck now, and they don't need my help any more. Fortunately there are not many dead. Most of the injured seem okay. And your friend —"

"Still unconscious but they say she is going to be all right," said Christa.

"Good. And you?"

"Oh, I'm not hurt – only the odd cut and bruises on my left arm. And of course I'm a bit shaken," she smiled.

It was that courageous smile and the way she looked – so small, so fair, so child-like in the soft summer moonlight – that went straight to the man's heart. A heart that had for a long time been armoured against feminine seduction of any kind. But there were no wiles here he thought – no artificiality – this girl was only a child whose holiday had been ruined. She looked pathetic. He said:

"I'm just in time – I'll drive you to my sister's apartment." The colour rushed to Christa's cheeks.

"There's no need. The nun gave me the name of a hotel . . ."

"You won't like being alone in a strange Paris hotel tonight after that accident," he cut in. "Look – here is my card. You can place your trust in me. I am well-known in Paris. My sister and brother-in-law, Monsieur Claude Roché, are directors of a big perfumery business. You may have heard of Parfum Joyeux. I also am a director. I handle the English side of the business. I was on my way over for a week or two to stay with my sister, and to meet a business contact in Dieppe. That is why I was on that train. I usually fly."

Christa recognized the name Parfum Joyeux. One of the most popular perfumes in the world. It was Barby's favourite scent. Christa had actually bought her a tiny bottle of it last Christmas from the Perfumery Department at Golling & Nash.

The Man continued:

"Will you come with me and let Madame Roché – my sister, Julia – look after you?"

Christa looked down at the card.

20

Mr. Stephen Harrimay.

So *that* was his name. Stephen. He seemed to have two addresses; one in St. James's Street, London, and one in Paris, c/o Parfum Joyeux, Faubourg St. Honoré.

She raised her head and looked at him.

"I'd love to be with – English people – I admit I – I *am* rather miserable," she said in a choked voice.

Once again he found her extreme youth and inexperience and the candid humility that went with it – touching.

A few moments later Christa and Stephen Harrimay were driving downhill and across the bridge to the other side of the river. The Rochés' apartment was at the top of a huge block in the Boulevard Suchet.

On the way the man asked a few questions. He learned the girl's name, and Barbara's; where they came from; what they did. He might have guessed it, he told himself. Two young business girls from London . . . of course he knew Golling & Nash . . . who didn't? A second Selfridges. He had shopped there, himself.

This shy unimpressive child was a typist. The more beautiful one who had flicked her long eyelashes at him, a model in the hat department.

Poor darlings, thought Stephen. Rotten show . . . this accident on their first day in France. But they were lucky (all of them) to be alive. What a collision! A ghastly pile-up on the line! Damn good thing they'd got that fire out so quickly. The unfortunate driver of the express, poor chap, had died.

As Stephen talked to Christa, she felt her nerves quieten and her spirits rise. He no longer seemed the frigid, haughty 'diplomat' of hers and Barby's imagination. He had become quite human – kind – friendly.

Stephen sat back in his corner of the car, smoking a cigar – he liked the thin French cigars, and conscious that his own nerves were jangled after the shock of that accident. He was exhausted, too. His clothes were dishevelled and dirty. He would be thankful for a hot bath.

He was very attached to his sister Julia. She was a woman of thirty-five – a year older than himself. A bit possessive – always had some beautiful girl lined up as a future wife for him and at the moment wanted him to marry a young pianist – a friend of hers. Her husband had plans for moving their home from Paris to Cannes, thus settling near their main factory which was at Grasse. It was Julia's idea that they could then leave the Paris business entirely in Stephen's hands. He would have to live part of the time here, and part in London. But he needed a wife – the right sort of wife, Julia kept saying – the sort to help him in his career.

But Stephen was in no hurry to find a wife.

He had already had one unfortunate experience – a youthful attachment to a young girl who had changed her mind on the very eve of their wedding and married the 'best man'. Stephen had adored her – his beautiful honey-fair Dorella. She was a Canadian whom he had met on a business trip over there. He had been twenty-four at the time, full of ideals and believing in loyalties. The cruel sudden jilting and betrayal by his fiancée and his best friend, overnight turned the idealistic boy into a cynic. At first he felt that he no longer cared much about Dorella or any girl in the world. But lately, there had been Julia's latest discovery – Felise. Half-French, half-English, Felise Markell had come to Paris to study music at the Conservatoire. She was wonderful to look at, and had money, too, inherited from her English grandfather on her father's side. With her not inconsiderable musical talent, she had much to offer a man; and Stephen loved music. Julia stated openly that she thought Stephen would be mad not to take advantage of the fact that Felise was deeply in love with him. But so far, Stephen had not committed himself.

"If I fall in love with Felise eventually – I shall marry her. *Nous verrons*. Wait and see, Julia," he had said.

That was as far as things had gone, although he had to confess that he had sometimes considered an engagement.

He missed Felise, her vibrant, exciting personality and her music, when he was away from her. He admired her musicianship. Now as he drove with little Christa Coombe to his sister's home, he thought about Felise. Already he had spoken to her on the telephone. He had got through to the Roché apartment to explain why he was so late. They had known he was not flying this time as usual, because he had arranged to interview this business associate who proposed to build a new perfume factory near Dieppe. Monsieur Proust had been talking with Stephen when the collision occurred. Proust, like himself, had escaped injury and had gone on to his mother's home in Passy.

Felise happened to be with the Rochés when Stephen phoned. She had seized the receiver from Julia's hand.

"I was terrified when I heard the news on the radio," she

22

had exclaimed. "Oh, come home quickly – let me look at you – let me make sure you are all right."

He could be sure of a dramatic welcome from Felise. He could so easily picture her vivid face with the green-gold, almond-shaped eyes, and their long black, painted lashes. Felise loved an exotic make-up. Her mouth was always brightly rouged, her dark hair, cut with a fringe low on her forehead rather like Elizabeth Taylor's in style. But somehow his attention kept turning in this moment to Christa's thick fair 'schoolgirl-mop' of hair. Of whom did this funny, shy, rather badly-dressed little thing remind him? he asked himself frowning. She was really so unlike the chic women in his own circle in Paris or London. As for those light grey eyes —

Now his pulses jerked; remembrance played its part. *Dorella.* Of course. The fair-haired faithless Canadian whom he had been so near to making his wife – yes – *she* had had hair just like Christa's, and even the same pale grey eyes – deceptively soft eyes.

Abruptly, almost crossly, Stephen turned his attention from Christa. To hell with her and her sad childish type – all a snare and a delusion as well he knew.

"We're here," he said.

Christa stepped out. Stephen paid the taxi. She looked around her. This then was the Boulevard Suchet. A beautiful broad street with trees on either side.

"Tomorrow when you have recovered, you must see more of Paris," he said trying now to forget Dorella and to be kind again.

Christa was humbly grateful. She had already fallen in love for the first time in her life, quite deeply in love, with this stranger. Since the accident he had become her rescuer, her hero, the most marvellous man in the world.

Now they were in a lift, going up to the top of the big block. The Rochés occupied the Penthouse which, Stephen told Christa, had a superb bird's-eye view of Paris.

Stephen had his own latch-key. He opened the front door. Christa caught a vague impression of a wide handsome hall full of fine colourful tapestries. A bronze figure on a marble and gilt stand held aloft a candelabra in which six electric candles burned goldenly. On one side of the hall stood a marble-topped Louis-Seize table; on it stood a huge jar of mauve carnations and pale pink roses. The floor was of black marble. It looked tremendously new and exciting to Christa – the home of

23

wealthy, artistic people; the kind she had hitherto only seen in films, or the stage, or in pictures in expensive magazines.

She stood shyly behind Stephen. Then a tall woman with a perfectly made-up face, and wearing faultless black, rushed into the hall. One glance at her told Christa that this must be Stephen's sister, Madame Roché. She had the same very blue eyes.

"Steve – my *dear* – are you all right?" she began in a breathless voice and shot a terrified look at his weary face and dishevelled clothes. She did not seem to notice the young girl hiding behind him. He answered:

"I'm fine, Julia – absolutely unhurt – no need to panic, my dear."

"*Grâce à Dieu!*" she sighed in French. "Felise and I have been worried out of our wits."

Stephen moved aside.

"I have brought you Miss – er – Christa Coombe," he said, "One of the English girls I told you about over the phone. Her friend is in hospital still unconscious. This poor child has no money, no luggage, and as I said, I felt sure you'd give her a bed and look after her tonight. It would be a kindness, Julia – she is a stranger to France. A hotel would be very unnerving for her."

"Of course – I am delighted," said Julia Roché with exquisite bland courtesy and immediately held out a hand which Christa gratefully clasped. But Christa felt that Madame Roché had already retreated behind a wall of caution – even disapproval.

"I – I *can* still go to a hotel – I told your brother so," Christa began to stammer.

Julia, however, whatever she felt, was also a kind woman. She broke in:

"Oh, definitely not – you must stay with us tonight. You are English and if you are a friend of my brother, I would not dream of letting you go to a strange hotel. I have a spare bedroom here. Come along and have a drink – you must be very upset."

She paused. She was thinking:

"What on *earth* has Stephen found? She's very suburban and gauche and *so* badly dressed. Oh, how *like* Stephen to do a thing like this! As a small boy he used to bring home every stray child or animal around the place. He is *too* quixotic."

The shy Christa was further intimidated by the sudden arrival of another person on the scene. A most attractive girl wearing a white sleeveless dress, its severity relieved by a glittering aquamarine collar, bracelet and ear-rings to match. Christa stared at the much made-up face, with the almond shaped green-gold eyes and 'Cleopatra' hair-style.

"Stephen . . . oh, *mon Dieu* . . . how worried I've been!" she exclaimed, speaking in English with a faint accent. Then she burst into tears and held out both hands to Stephen who took them and kissed them both.

"I was *terrified* you might be dead!" she added and clung to him, shuddering.

"There, there, Felise, *soyez tranquille, chérie* – I'm all right," he murmured with some embarrassment.

Christa stood motionless, thrust back into darkness, into her own cold terror of loneliness – of shyness.

Felise – '*ma chérie*' he called her! – this beautiful dark foreign girl named Felise must, then, be a fiancée whom Stephen had not mentioned. Perhaps *The Man* was engaged. He hadn't been running away from a wife, as she and Barbara had imagined . . . but *running to* his wife of the future.

4

CHRISTA stood silent, watching, half-fascinated, as Stephen Harrimay tried to soothe Felise. She held on to him but finally broke away, dabbing her eyes with a chiffon handkerchief and trying to laugh.

"*Grâce à Dieu!*" she said as Julia had done, but with theatrical fervour, "you are all right, *mon cher*."

"Now," Stephen said, pulling at his tie, "let's all go into the salon."

Julia turned to Christa.

"Come to my room – you would probably like to tidy," she murmured.

Christa began to stammer:

"Really – I ought to go – to a hotel – I don't want you to put yourself out —" she broke off and her large soft eyes filled with tears of sheer exhaustion and nervousness.

Madame Roché was touched by the sight of the tears. She began to feel a slight, even scornful pity for the young timid girl. Certainly Julia was less troubled now about her brother's interest in Christa. It was only a 'poor little thing' he had picked up – no glamour-girl. Nothing to cause Julia a moment's anxiety. Stephen had more taste than this, she thought.

"Stephen dear, take Felise into the salon," she said lightly, "I'll join you with Miss Coombe in a moment."

Christa's gaze followed Stephen as he led Felise away. She felt ready to sink through the floor. It was as though with him, her anchor departed. She began to flounder in waters too deep for her. She had always been painfully nervous with strangers. This chic, distinguished woman, Madame Roché, with her easy grace of manner, and all the wealth and luxury surrounding her, was enough to strike dread in Christa's soul. She knew that she was foolish . . . that such a chance as this would have delighted the more sophisticated Barbara . . . but Christa would have given anything to turn and run out of the flat; to find a more homely place, and someone like Aunt Cath . . . at the kitchen sink . . . the ironing-board . . . or the sewing-machine.

She was bewildered by the turn events had taken, and the shock of the train accident. In the bedroom she looked so pale as she turned to Madame Roché that Julia felt genuine concern.

"My dear – you're not well. I think you had better lie down."

"Yes, for a moment, perhaps —" began Christa.

"I'll tell Yvette to prepare one of the guest rooms. Meanwhile stay here and I'll fetch you a cognac," said Julia. She thought: "What a bore this all is, but the poor child really looks dreadful. One must be charitable!"

Christa sank on to the brocade-covered stool in front of the long white and gold painted dressing-table.

She went suddenly limp. With a deep sigh she put her face in her hands. After a while she looked up and stared around her. She was alone. She heard Madame Roché calling her maid. What a *magnificent* bedroom! Christa had never been in one like it. Here was all the grace and dignity of a Paris apartment at its best. Perfect taste; pale yellow carpet with curtains of grey frilled taffeta, wide-shaped pelmets with gold tassels. The low double bed was covered in grey lace over a foundation of yellow satin; at the head lay a pile of taffeta cushions and against them lay a life-like French doll with powdered hair, dressed as Marie Antoinette in a magnificent satin crinoline.

Here were built-in cupboards . . . satin-panelled walls . . . gilt and crystal electric candlelights . . . an intriguing perfume lingering in the air. Over the dressing-table hung a large photograph in a white leather frame. It was of Stephen Harrimay . . . a much younger Stephen, wearing riding-kit, holding a crop under one arm. It was inscribed: *"From your devoted Steve."*

Christa's eyes, magnified by tears turned to this photograph and did not move away. It fascinated her. She thought: *"What a marvellous looking boy he was . . . she must be proud of such a brother!"*

Madame Roché was very kind – Christa quite liked her – but that girl – Felise – there was something about her that had made Christa shrink. She prayed that she would not have to meet her again tonight. She was so conscious of her cheap clothes, her lack of polish, her inferiority to Felise and all these people.

She mustn't be ill now and put them to a lot of trouble, she thought. If that happened she would feel bitterly ashamed. Barbara would be furious. If she were given such an opportunity as this, then flung it away, Barbara would say she must really be stupid.

Gradually Christa recovered, she felt the strength returning to her limbs and the courage to her heart. She took off her coat and combed back her thick tangled hair. The whiteness of her own face frightened her but the colour began to steal back. Julia came in with brandy. Christa took one or two sips then returned the glass with a faint smile.

"Thank you. I'm not used to it but it does make one feel better, doesn't it?"

"Yvette is making your bed. How do you feel now?"

"Absolutely fine. Please don't worry about me any more," said Christa with forced brightness.

"Good," said Julia. "You've had a terrible experience. Stephen told me it was chaotic on the line. All those poor injured people! So tragic! How lucky that you escaped."

"Oh, I know! But my poor friend, Barbara, didn't. She is still unconscious."

"Don't worry too much. It is like that with concussion. Stephen as a boy in our English home, was thrown from his horse, one day, riding in a Point-to-Point. He was quite insensible. We were all petrified for him but he recovered within twenty-four hours.''

Christa's gaze moved to the photograph above the dressing-table.

"Mr. Harrimay has been terribly kind," she whispered.

"Stephen is always very nice to people," said Julia. "Especially those in some kind of trouble."

Christa sat silent. She took it for granted that Madame Roché wished her to realize at once that she had not been personally singled out for Stephen's favour. After a moment Christa said timidly:

"My friend Barbara is very beautiful – she's a model – I'm terribly glad her face was not hurt."

"So am I. But now tell me about yourself," said Julia kindly.

Christa gave a brief account of her life in London. The older woman half-listened, thinking that this respite would give Stephen and Felise an opportunity of being alone together. Poor darling Felise! She had almost fainted when she had heard about the accident. She was so passionately in love with Stephen. Julia felt hopeful that Stephen would shortly see how foolish he was not to realize that the talented, attractive girl would make him an ideal wife.

So this young English girl was a typist from Golling & Nash in Oxford Street. Julia remembered having shopped there at some time or other. She had thought it rather a 'cheap' type of store. But then over here, Julia had the finest shops in Paris at her disposal.

She did not find Christa interesting. The girl was just one among thousands of other 'little things' who earned their living in shops and offices. Quite unremarkable – although those large light grey eyes were attractive. She was not what Julia would call 'top drawer' but she had a sweet voice. Certainly she did not push herself forward.

"I have no family. Barbara's mother is like my own aunt," Christa told Julia.

"How sad – for you to have no parents," murmured Julia.

"But Mrs. Lane is so good to me and Barbara is like my sister," added Christa.

"Have you Scandinavian blood in you?" asked Julia, not because she was particularly interested but because she wanted to mark time and leave Stephen and Felise alone a little longer. "Where does the 'Christa' come from?"

"My grandmother was Norwegian but lived in England and my parents came from Devon. I was born in Exeter," Christa explained.

"Ah – yes," said Julia, "it is from Norway you get your very fair hair, perhaps. Have you ever been to Norway?"

"No. This is the first time I have been abroad in my life."

Madame Roché pulled a shoulder strap into position, glanced sideways at her slim silhouette in the long mirror and decided that she must go to her *couturier* in the Fauboug St. Honoré tomorrow and tell him that this dress did not hang as well as it should. It was a disgrace – and she had paid over a hundred thousand old francs for it, too! Everything in Paris was shockingly dear; but thank goodness Parfum Joyeux was a world-winner. They had had a fantastically big turnover last year. Taxed out of existence, of course, but one could still retain *something*.

Julia brought her thoughts back to her uninvited guest.

"What a shame – that your very first trip abroad should be so ill-fated," she said. "Now if you feel better, and do not wish to lie down, shall we go into the *salon* and join the others? Have you eaten?"

"Yes, the nuns at the hospital gave me something."

The sight of the *salon* further overwhelmed Christa. It was a room about thirty feet long with three balconied windows. The curtains were not drawn. She could see the stars and below, the glittering lights of the capital. What a wonderful view of the silver Seine, winding its way under bridges, old and new. It fascinated Christa. Her eyes widened with interest as she noted the Rochés' antique furniture; gorgeous satin-brocaded covers, and valuable china. The lamps were pale pink alabaster with huge black shades. There was an Aubusson carpet on the polished floor. A baby-grand piano in a French painted case stood with lid open at the far end of the room. Everywhere there were glorious flowers, and over the carved walnut mantelpiece hung a magnificent painting. Christa did not know it but it was an original Corot.

Stephen who was seated on the sofa beside Felise, rose to his feet as his sister and Christa entered. He smiled sympathetically at the young girl.

"Feeling better now?"

"Yes, thanks," she answered. "This is all so thrilling for me," she added with a deep blush. "It is enough to make anybody better. I wish Barbara could see this glorious place."

"I'm sure she soon will," said Stephen, "I'll telephone the hospital for you later tonight and find out how she is."

"Thanks awfully," breathed Christa.

"Come and take a look at Paris from the balcony – it's a splendid night and you must try to forget what a poor welcome you have had from our French railways, and admire our city," said Stephen.

He took her arm in a friendly way and led her on to one of the balconies. Leaning over the wrought-iron railings, soothed and charmed, Christa looked down at the glorious panorama. Stephen pointed out the Arc de Triomphe, the Eiffel Tower, the floodlit spires of Notre Dame, the sparkling fountains in the Place de la Concorde.

Inside the *salon*, Julia and Felise whispered together rapidly in French.

"Who in heaven's name is she? What on earth did Stephen bring her here for?" Felise demanded fiercely.

Madame Roché assured her that there was nothing for her to worry about. Christa was just a little English typist on holiday but because Stephen had spoken to her and her friend on the train, he had taken compassion on them after the accident and invited Christa here.

"We'll get rid of her tomorrow. I must just give her a bed for the night," Julia ended.

Felise looked relieved.

Madame Roché then said:

"The girl-friend who was injured, works in the same stores. Apparently she models hats, and is very attractive."

"Then let's keep *her* away from Stephen," said Felise with a slight laugh.

"Oh, my dear, as if you have need to worry, when you know that Stephen never looks at girls and that you're the only one who ever interests him."

A warm rapt look came into Felise Markell's eyes. She was very emotional. The French half of her nearly always came to the fore. She had inherited nothing in her nature from the English Markells who once lived in Leicester, and belonged to a hunting circle. Until she met and fell in love with Stephen (Julia had then been a guest at her home in Leicester and, later, introduced her to Stephen), she had had no other passion but music. Now, living in Paris with one of her French aunts who had an apartment in the Rue St. Roch, she was becoming more French than the French. Lately she had gained immensely in chic and poise. At twenty-four, she was at her very best. She had tremendous charm when she chose to exert it but she was possessive and jealous with a curiously ruthless streak for one so young. She went on whispering to the woman who had become her greatest friend and whom she knew to be utterly on her side over this question of marrying Stephen.

"He has been so sweet to me tonight . . . I swear I'll pull it off soon, Julia. And I'd better be nice to his protegée hadn't I, or he'll think me unkind."

Julia agreed. So, under the guise of friendly concern, Felise set herself out to dazzle Christa and watch the impression it made on Stephen.

She seated herself beside the English girl and while they were drinking coffee (only Christa ate one or two of the little cakes), Felise was tactful and sympathetic. She suggested that she would go with Christa tomorrow to the hospital to visit Barbara.

"After all I'm half English and we British must stick together," she said with a light laugh. Then looking at Christa's hair, clapped her hands together and flicked her long silky lashes at Stephen.

"Isn't she *blonde*? How wonderful to have such fair hair. I've always hated being so dark," she exclaimed in her artificial way.

"I don't know what's wrong with your own hair," put in Stephen, as she had intended him to do.

"Exactly," put in Julia, "as if Felise should worry, with that marvellous black hair of hers – it's like those pictures of Elizabeth Taylor as Cleopatra. And you ought to hear her *play*, Christa. We must call you Christa – Miss Coombe is so formal."

"Please do," said Christa who was beginning to feel that Felise was really very nice. "I wish I could hear Miss Markell play."

Stephen flung himself into a chair, stretched out his long legs and lit a fresh cigar.

"Yes, play to us, Felise," he said.

At once she got up and walked to the piano. A moment later the *salon* was filled with the rich sound of a study by Rachmaninoff. Certainly she played with brilliance. Christa sat lost in respectful admiration. She shut her eyes and relaxed. Her nerves were soothed and quietened. She began to feel more at home. The atmosphere in this sumptuous flat was a bit rarefied for her but she knew a little about music. Her mother used to play the piano in her spare time. She had been quite a good pianist. Christa preferred listening to a good concert on Aunt Cath's radio to watching television.

Sometimes when Barbara was out she took herself to a 'Prom' concert at the Albert Hall. When Felise stopped playing, Christa surprised everybody by asking for a Chopin Polonaise to which she gave a name. Stephen turned to her, his eyes surprised. So the little typist from Gollings was not wholly ignorant outside her job, after all.

Christa's hair shone with a peculiar lustre against the scarlet studded satin of the high-backed chair in which she was sitting. It was the devil, he thought, how that wretched hair kept reminding him of Dorella; how the memory assailed him with bitter-sweet pangs. What tricks the mind could play on one. He was almost shocked by the quite unreasonable longing that seized him to get up and go across to that insignificant little thing and thread his fingers through the thick gold waves of her hair. Suddenly Christa looked straight at him. Those light grey eyes were unmistakably grateful. He imagined they mutely begged for his approbation. He did not return the smile. Instead he got up, walked to the piano and looked over Felise's shoulder, watching the swift movement of her strong young fingers over the ivory keys.

Could he ever love *this* girl? *Would he ever marry her as Julia wished?* One side of him wanted to . . . the practical side, agreeing with what Julia so often pointed out. It would be a sensible marriage. And earlier this evening when she had flung herself into his arms, overcome by her fear for him, he had known how much she wanted him to make love to her. But there was always that other side . . . the cautious cynical Stephen that Dorella had made of him. The Stephen must, if he ever married, be wholly in love and quite sure, this time, of his woman. Such a love might he supposed, grow after further association with Felise, but it had not done so yet. When she finished playing, he thanked her warmly and asked her to play again. She looked up at him with pride and delight in his nearness.

He avoided looking towards the fair-haired, lonely little figure in the red-satin chair.

5

CHRISTA spent that night in the blue and silver guest room which had its own bathroom and where everything had been 'laid on' for her. She had been lent one of her hostess's satin, cyclamen-pink nightgowns, and a velvet tailored dressing-gown of the same colour. English magazines and books were put by her bed – the most exotic Christa had ever slept in, with filmy curtains looped from a gilt crown, draped on either side.

Christa slept badly, pursued by nightmares, re-living the scene of the train accident. She awoke several times bathed in sweat, calling Barbara's name. Nobody seemed to hear her.

She rose early, took a hot bath, and finding the apartment deserted, crept out and down in the lift to the street. She needed a walk in the fresh air. She felt restless and ill at ease in Madame Roché's apartment. And she was very worried. When Stephen telephoned to the hospital late last night, they had given him no better news of Barbara. She was still unconscious.

Christa walked down the handsome boulevard on this sweet summer morning and gradually felt better. Paris woke early; she enjoyed seeing the old women in their black shawls, and the errand boys with their berets and blue blouses riding their cycles, carrying baskets of long fresh loaves. The cafés were being washed and garnished for the new day. The traffic was stirring.

Christa walked for a mile or two. When she got back to the apartment, she found Stephen standing outside the entrance of the flats, a newspaper under one arm. He was looking somewhat anxious. His brow cleared as he saw her.

"Hello, there! My sister went into your room a few moments ago and found you had gone. We were quite alarmed."

Christa coloured and apologized. She told him that she had needed the walk.

"Yes, I expect you had a bad night," he said. "So did I, as a matter of fact. One is naturally shaken after such an accident. Now you'd like me to phone the hospital for you again, wouldn't you?"

"You really are most kind," she said, "but I can't stay in

your sister's place. I must leave after breakfast. It would be an imposition for me to remain."

"Indeed, no – I'm sure Julia will want you to stay on," said Stephen carelessly and not very tactfully. "My brother-in-law is away for the moment so there is plenty of room, and Julia has two servants eating their heads off and doing little."

Christa said nothing, but she had made up her mind to leave. A call to St. Georges brought more cheerful news. Barbara had at last recovered consciousness, but the doctor considered it unwise for her to be moved for at least a week. After that, she would quite certainly be on her feet again, he had told Stephen Harrimay. Her condition was not for the moment one hundred per cent, and because of that head injury he considered careful nursing and quiet essential. Christa could see her today for a few moments only.

"Now," said Stephen, having translated all this for Christa, "you can be happy again."

"Yes, it's *wonderful*," she said and her large eyes shone.

"I have business to do, but Felise – Miss Markell – says she will drive with you to the hospital. She must first do some practising but her teacher is away, ill, at the moment, so Felise can come round here soon after eleven. My sister says you can borrow her car and chauffeur."

"Oh, I don't want to be a nuisance —" began Christa.

"My dear child, we are all delighted to do what we can," broke in Stephen.

After breakfast, Christa spoke to Madame Roché who had remained in bed with a headache. She must move to an hotel, Christa said; the one which the nuns had recommended. But Julia had already discussed this matter with her brother.

"Let her go to an hotel, Steve," Julia had said. "There is really no need for you to interest yourself further."

But he had argued:

"I'm not particularly interested, I assure you, but I just haven't the heart to banish that little thing to a strange cheap hotel. She's painfully shy and she doesn't speak one word of French. She's having a hell of a holiday – why, just think, Julia, you've got the space – why not let her stay in the flat until Claude comes back?"

"Certainly Claude won't want her here," said Julia coldly.

Finally, to please her adored brother, she consented to keep Christa here for a few days more. She now issued the invitation.

34

"I can never thank you enough," Christa gave way overwhelmed at last.

Stephen had work to do and Julia went to an appointment with her hairdresser. Before he left, Stephen said to Christa:

"Miss Markell has very kindly offered to pilot you to the British Consul before you go on to St. Georges. You must, you know, see at once about new passports for yourself and your friend and an advance of money. Meanwhile if you are in financial straits, I will gladly lend you what you need."

"I seem to do nothing but say 'thank you'," came from Christa, her eyes looking up at the man's handsome face with almost agonizing gratitude.

"Well, don't," he laughed briefly. "I'm only too glad to be of help – Felise feels likewise."

"Miss Markell is wonderfully beautiful, and she plays terrifically well," said Christa with a sudden childlike enthusiasm which Stephen found naïve but refreshing.

He had met few girls in London or Paris as *ingénue* as Christa. But it pleased him. He was something of an idealist; deep in his heart he craved for a better world; a finer type of existence. To him, modern life – the machine and scientific age – was cold and unrewarding. He made money – his business prospered. He had all and more than a man could want; but associating with a girl like Christa Coombe brought him sharply to the realization that what his sister spent on her shoes and gloves, might keep those two shop-girls for a year.

He remembered suddenly that Christa had just made a remark about Felise. Hastily he answered:

"Oh, yes – Felise is extremely talented and attractive."

After he had gone, Christa pondered over those words. What would it be like to be a girl whom Stephen Harrimay found 'extremely talented and attractive'? She recalled the way he had stood behind Felise while she played the piano last night; his serious expression and the girl's beauty, and definite spark of genius. Christa once again became forlornly conscious of her own shortcomings.

"I must not allow life to push me into the background," she mentally chided herself, "I must try to be more like Barbara. She would not have been shy with these people or afraid to open her mouth. She would have made a hit – as I can never do."

Christa determined to overcome her feelings – especially for

35

Felise. It seemed obvious that Stephen was going to marry her.

When Felise came to pick her up, Christa thanked her warmly for coming to her aid.

But now that Stephen was not there to watch, Felise no longer acted a part. She was subtly but definitely unkind. She took Christa to the British Consul – arranged for fresh passports to be issued to her and Barbara, and arranged a small loan. But on the way to the hospital, she spoke disdainfully to Christa:

"It is a little awkward for you being in Paris without luggage. I mean your clothes . . ." she broke off, her brilliant eyes searching Christa's figure, making her painfully conscious of the difference between her own appearance and that of Felise.

Felise wore a black and white striped silk suit essentially 'Paris', a chic white hat on her dark head, long white gloves, and exquisite Italian shoes. Christa's suit, although it had been pressed by Yvette, still bore the marks of yesterday's travel and accident. She had no gloves. Her dark blue sandals looked out of place.

Felise went on:

"All such very bad luck for you. I'm sure you'll want to get back to London with your friend as soon as possible."

"Yes," said Christa, crimsoning.

"You aren't very different in size from myself," added Felise grudgingly. "We are both slight. I could give you an outfit I've finished with, if you wouldn't take offence, and perhaps a bag and a hat, too."

But Christa's blood seemed to rise in revolt. She hated the idea of taking charity from this particular girl. She could no longer feel gratitude or show it. A wave of pride made her forget her manners.

"I don't want anything, thank you," she said stiffly. "I can manage. I've got some money now. I'll buy what I need."

Felise opened a gilt and enamel powder-compact and glanced at her reflection. Her lips twisted into a half-smile. She felt a little ashamed of what she had done, but in a vicious way was also pleased. She bitterly resented this English girl whom Stephen had brought home. Having reduced Christa to a 'state', she added fuel to the fire.

"Stephen – is rather impressionable. Your friend is a model – glamour-girl, isn't she? Was he very taken with her?"

36

Christa's heart beat fast, acutely aware of the claws behind the velvet glove extended to her by this young woman.

"Yes. Barby is marvellous, but I don't think Mr. Harrimay was particularly impressed. He was just very kind to us both because he saw how helpless we were after the accident."

"Ah, then it must have been *you* he fell for," said Felise with a rasping laugh that fell upon Christa's sensitive nerves like the rattle of hail stones. She made a sharp retort.

"Not at all. There was nothing like that. He certainly did not fall for me anyhow. You and he are practically engaged, aren't you?"

"Practically," agreed Felise in a pleased languid voice, and sat back in the car and looked out at the green trees in the Bois through which they were driving.

Christa, too, looked at the trees and at the people strolling with their children or smart poodles. There was a mist in front of her eyes. Felise had brought back the old frustration; the hateful sense of inferiority.

Then suddenly Felise altered her mood again. She could not have been more helpful to Christa than she was once they reached the Hôpital St. Georges. She made a charming impression on everybody there.

At last, when Christa sat alone beside Barbara's bed, she knew that she should have felt grateful to Felise. It would have been difficult for her to have found her way around or managed things so smoothly on her own. *Yet she hated Felise.* For some reason which she knew to be both inexplicable and absurd she also hated the thought that one day Stephen and Felise were going to be married.

6

BARBARA looked wan and white, a bandage around her forehead, one arm in a sling. She clutched Christa's hand. Gone temporarily, her self-assurance, her poise, her conceit. Tears rolled down her cheeks.

"Oh, Christa, isn't it *ghastly* . . . when I came to, and realized

I was in a French hospital, and all that had happened, I wanted to die . . ."

Now Christa forgot herself and became strong, and dominant in the effort to comfort her adored friend.

"Nonsense, darling – you're going to be quite all right. The doctor says you'll be out in a week, and none the worse. Why should you want to die? You must be thankful you weren't killed. And think how lucky *I* was, too!"

"And *The Man* . . ." now Barbara's lips curved into a wan smile. "Fancy *him* being so nice to you."

Christa described the Rochés' apartment . . . Julia . . . Felise . . . the whole set-up. Barbara exclaimed:

"I say! I can't wait to go and see it all for myself."

"I can't wait for you to do so, darling," said Christa. Tenderly she leaned down and adjusted the woolly dressing jacket that had been loaned to Barbara. "You really don't look too bad at all – not a mark on the old face," she said cheerfully.

"Thank the Lord. I might have been killed, and awful facial injuries would have been worse," admitted Barbara with a shudder. She touched her bandaged forehead. "The nurses say this will heal eventually without a scar."

Curiously, Christa glanced around the ward. The nuns in their voluminous robes and big winged caps, moved solidly, quietly around, carrying basins or pushing trolleys, placidly smiling, bent on their charitable mission. It was a bare austere cold-looking ward with a large crucifix on the whitewashed wall at one end. Under this stood a table covered with flowers which lent the only touch of much-needed colour.

"You are being well looked after here, aren't you, darling?" whispered Christa.

"Very, though the food is grim – too much garlic. But they couldn't be more kind. It's awful not being able to speak the language. I make signs," Barbara giggled weakly. "One sister speaks English and translates what I can't understand, and she gives me the things I want, and one woman over there speaks English, too, and we gossip together."

"Mr. Harrimay said he would look in and see you to-morrow," said Christa.

At this, the doleful expression on Barbara's pale face altered to one of pleasurable anticipation.

"Then I must put on the glamour for *him*," she said. "Buy me some things, Christa, there's a sweetie. Make a list. Lipstick – my red – you can get that Revlon one I use, over here.

Foundation – you know my kind – eyelash black and silver-blue shadow."

Barbara became quite alert and cheerful as Christa wrote the list to dictation. They had received enough money from the Consul to last them for the moment, anyhow. When Christa told Barbara that Stephen had offered to lend them as much as they needed, Barbara said:

"Okay – take him at his word."

"But we *can't* – we couldn't possibly take such advantage –" began Christa.

"Oh, don't be so pious," broke in Barbara peevishly. "He's a wealthy man, isn't he? Think of the gallons of Parfum Joyeux sold all over the world. It's as popular as Chanel or Worth. He and this sister of his must be worth a fortune."

"I hate borrowing, no matter how wealthy they are," said Christa, rather sullenly. On such occasions as this she and Barbara did not see eye-to-eye.

"We can repay him in London," Barbara argued. "If you're too sensitive, *I'll* borrow from him when I see him. Bet he'll want to shower *me* with francs . . ." and she began to laugh and flutter her eyelashes wickedly.

She made Christa laugh, despite herself. Barby could be unscrupulous when she wanted her own way but so amusing.

"Oh, well – all right," Christa gave way.

"Tell me more about *The Man's* background," said Barbara.

Christa did so, and could not hide from her adopted sister the strange repugnance she felt for Felise – the half-French, half-English pianist whom he was supposed to be thinking about as a future wife.

Barbara put her tongue in her cheek.

"Poof – watch me cut *her* out!"

Christa laughed but with a curious pain in her heart. She looked into Barbara's lustrous eyes; at the magnolia skin; the rich curving mouth; the swan-neck; the auburn tendrils of hair peeping from the bandages. Lovely Barbara – pride of Golling & Nash – much more beautiful from an artist's point of view than Felise; if less cultured and talented. Surely, if she tried, Barbara *could* make even Stephen Harrimay 'look at her', thought Christa.

Oh, what luck to have such power – that insidious fatal power that the beautiful women of history have in their time always been able to wield over great men. Christa clenched her

39

fingers and laughed because suddenly she wanted to cry. She felt so depressingly 'out of it' between two girls as lovely as Barby and Felise. To cover her feelings, she murmured:

"Now be good – I really think Mr. Harrimay and Felise are going to be married."

"There's many a slip . . . !" quoted Barbara. "Wait till I get my long varnished nails into your Felise!"

Now the girls giggled together. Then a nun came forward and said something in French, indicating that time was up and the patient must talk no more.

"See you later, darling," Barbara held out her hand to her friend. "And mind you tell the *Great Man*, I just live for his visit."

Christa walked out of the ward and down the stone steps of St. Georges into the golden summer's morning. Julia's car and chauffeur waited to take her back to the Boulevard Suchet. Felise had gone to her luncheon date at the Crillon. (With Stephen, she had been careful to tell Christa.)

Christa spent the rest of that day alone in the Rochés' apartment. A perfect luncheon was served to her. Feeling small and solitary in that wonderful dining-room, she sat at an oval-shaped, marble-topped table. It was laid with Brussels lace-and-linen mats, shining glass and beautiful silver. A Lalique bowl, in which rich, creamy camellias floated, served as a centre-piece.

The décor in this *salle* was dark blue and chalk-white; a midnight blue wallpaper encrusted with silver flowers – most striking, Christa thought – very modern. The heavy curtains were of white taffeta edged with navy blue frills. She wondered how much it must cost to clean them – *and* to run this exotic flat. *And* what Aunt Cath would have thought about it all!

But it had no particular appeal to Christa.

The Rochés' whole apartment to her had the impersonal touch of a small museum. One hardly dared touch a thing.

Christa ate a fish soufflé such as she had never eaten before, but refused the hock offered by Julia's dignified Swiss maid.

Then she reached a decision. She would be extravagant this afternoon and get her hair done *à la mode*. That was what they would call it in Paris, Christa thought. '*À la mode*.' In the fashion. She might even have a 'facial'. As for a dress – perhaps she had been unnecessarily proud to refuse Felise's offer of her 'cast-offs'. This suit would soon look a rag if she wore it all day, every day. What could she do?

The answer was forthcoming sooner than she expected.

She shyly asked Yvette – who spoke broken English – for the name of a hairdresser – one not too wildly expensive. The maid supplied it and Christa journeyed there on the Métro – her first experience of the French Underground. She found it confusing but quite an exciting experience. She was determined now to try and enjoy what was left of her ruined holiday. Personal appearance was obviously very important to people like the Rochés so she *must* smarten up.

When she emerged from the hairdresser's she looked, even in her own opinion, a different being. A clever young man had cut and shaped the thick fair hair, and set it so that it was much smoother, pulled back from her forehead and back-combed in bouffante fashion, over both ears. The assistant who gave her a 'facial' had seen to it that the young English girl left the shop looking *tout à fait Parisienne*. Delicate pink cheeks; darkened lashes, silver-green shadow that increased the size of her eyes, and a new shade of deep rose-rouge on the gentle fine-cut lips. Gone now was the schoolgirl. Even the cheap suit seemed to have taken on a new chic. The beauty-expert who thought the English *demoiselle très gentille*, had presented her with a tiny bottle of perfume. Christa then bought herself some cheap white gloves and a white straw 'Gigi' sailor hat from the Bon Marché. She felt quite proud of herself as she took the Métro home again. She was beginning to learn her way about. Would *Stephen* notice the change in her, she wondered. It was surprising how much she hoped that he would.

When she got back to the Roché apartment, she found Stephen there alone. It was five o'clock and Julia was still out.

Stephen, as usual smoking a cigar, was standing at one of the open windows, looking down at Paris. He turned as Christa came into the *salon*. For an instant he was astonished. He stared at Christa. At the smooth, newly-coiffured hair, under the white 'Gigi' hat, and at the self-conscious pink young face. He hardly recognized Christa. He had not imagined she could look so attractive or that her features were so basically good. But all that make-up, that conscious effort to be smart – *did he really like it?* Certainly it made her less of the dowdy 'schoolgirl', but the *Dorella* look had gone, too. (Faithless, golden-haired, golden-voiced, careless Dorella who used to let the Canadian sun shine on her bare head until it gleamed like the wheatfields around her. *She*, too, used to let that hair fall freely, childishly around her neck. But *she* had walked out of

41

his arms, out of his life, into the arms, into the life, of another man. Guileless to look at – yet full of guile. Better that Christa should not too closely resemble Dorella!)

Stephen made no comment upon Christa's changed appearance. In rather a brusque voice he said:

"I was waiting to see you on rather an important matter. Incidentally, how is your friend?"

"Better than I expected – almost normal again."

"Good. But you will remain in Paris for a few more days?"

"Yes – at least for four or five —" she began and her grey eyes were puzzled as they looked up at the man. He broke in:

"Then you could, perhaps, help me out of a fix."

"Help *you* out!" she repeated, astonished.

"Yes. One of our top secretaries – the one who deals with English and American correspondence – has gone sick. I need instant help in our Paris office which, as you know, is in this street. You are English and could cope with the shorthand, and you type quickly, I presume?"

"Why, yes, of course."

"Then would you consider taking the job until our Miss Maydew has recovered? You would receive payment in francs which would be of help in your present circumstances. If, of course, you do not wish to do this – you have only to say so – I shall understand. After all, this is your holiday."

Christa fingered her new white gloves and bag nervously. She felt her heart pounding. Surprise gave place to excitement and pleasure.

"But I'd love to work for you – for nothing!" she said breathlessly. "I already owe you so much."

"Nonsense. You'll be paid like any of our other employees if you care to take it on."

"I'd *love* it!" she repeated.

"Then tomorrow morning at nine o'clock, if you will come with me to the office."

"Yes, yes, I will be ready." Her voice was as excited as a child's.

He nodded and glanced at the ash on his cigar. It was a relief – Miss Maydew's illness had embarrassed him. When he was over here in Paris, the correspondence with English speaking countries, piled up. He heard Christa's soft quick voice:

"It's such a thrill – to be able to help your firm. Some sort of way, perhaps, of showing how grateful Barbara and I are for all you've done for us."

"That's all right, Christa," he said. "Take off your hat and I'll ring for tea. Julia should be back any moment."

When Julia Roché returned, she was so full of her own affairs (for she was not only a social woman, but co-director of one of the biggest perfume industries in France), she did not bother her head about the young English girl. It seemed to be 'a thing' with Stephen that he should befriend these girls and now he had offered Christa this job – let her get on with it.

Julia had spoken to her husband on the telephone this morning. Claude was tied up with affairs in Grasse. It was more than likely that she would have to fly down to him this week-end and then the girl would *have* to go. She could scarcely be left alone in this apartment with Stephen. So Julia smiled and congratulated Christa on being able to take over Miss Maydew's job, then retired to her room to rest. She was going to the theatre tonight with a party which included Felise. Incidentally Felise was furious because – uncertain as to whether Stephen would be in Paris tonight or not – the hostess had not booked a seat for him and now there was not one left in the house.

When Stephen realized this, he suddenly decided that he would fill in the evening by taking Christa Coombe out and showing her Paris by night. Why not? He would be at a loose end and she would be amused.

When he suggested it, she went so red, then so pale, that he felt quite embarrassed. Heavens! what an emotional young thing, he thought. But it might be interesting to show this lovely city by night to one who had never before set foot in France.

7

IN the car driving to the theatre with Julia, Felise fumed helplessly.

"If it wasn't that it would have looked so obvious I would have cancelled my seat and stayed with Stephen. Just *imagine* him spending the whole evening alone with that stupid dull little typist."

"My dear," Julia spoke slightly reprovingly, "you are being a *little* naughty. She is shy but not necessarily stupid. You can afford to be sorry for her."

"*Je suis jalouse*," Felise, glittering in her white evening dress, with Icelandic fox fur cape, and a collar of magnificent sapphires, quoted the famous French song. Whereupon Julia laughed outright.

"Darling Felise, don't be too absurd; you jealous of what you call a 'stupid little typist'! I'm quite sure Stephen is merely playing his favourite role of philanthropist. It would be all the same if the girl had a squint and was as ugly as sin."

But Christa Coombe was not as ugly as sin, and Felise knew it. And Stephen's sister had rather tactlessly told her that the young girl looked quite attractive tonight. Julia, in fact, possessed a kinder heart than Felise. She had made Christa accept one of her own almost new dresses – turquoise blue tie-silk, low-necked with long tight sleeves and draped skirt. Christa could not go round Paris at night in that awful grey suit of hers – certainly not if she was going out with Stephen. He would be embarrassed should they run into friends of his. The summer night was hot. Christa need only wear the dress and a scarf that belonged to it, and she would look presentable. It was one of Julia's many chic summer dresses, and looked charming with white shoes. Julia said now to Felise:

"Be advised, *chérie*, if you must feel jealous, do not show it – especially to Stephen. He has my nature. He would never like to feel himself at the end of an apron-string, even yours."

Felise sighed. Patience was not one of her virtues, and this waiting for Stephen to come up to scratch, seemed interminable.

Christa's evening out in Paris with Stephen was to her, one of the memorable nights of her life.

She had thought him reserved and cool. A man who looked at a girl as though she did not exist. But tonight he became another person – he was boyishly charming, and treated her as though he enjoyed her company. And when he first saw her in Julia's dress he gave her all the praise for which her modest soul had craved.

"You look very charming tonight. Congratulations."

Christa who had taken three times longer than usual to get ready and had hardly dared add or detract from the make-up the expert had applied, felt her pulses leap ecstatically.

"Oh, your sister was *too* kind to give me this gorgeous dress," she said. "But she is a little taller – I'm afraid the skirt is on the long side for me."

"No, it looks perfect," he smiled.

And, indeed, Julia's well-tailored turquoise blue dress fitted Christa's youthful figure like a glove, accentuating the slenderness of her tiny waist. The low neck-line left bare her touchingly immature neck. There were little hollows in her throat. Her bones looked extraordinarily fragile. She had the appearance of one who did not eat or rest enough, he reflected, suddenly intrigued by the young girl. Watching her more closely, as time went on, she seemed to him to be eaten up by an inner feverishness – some deep-rooted longing that she dared not betray to the rest of the world. He wondered what it was that she felt about life and how she endured the monotony of it; the constant privation and forced economy. Obviously she had a most unselfish disposition. If he had once thought her dull, he realized before this evening was over that it was not stupidity but her natural timidity, her sense of inferiority that made her tongue-tied. When she talked, it was not about herself, but largely of her friend, Barbara; Barbara's beauty and success.

During dinner, which they ate outside at one of those small chic restaurants under a striped awning in the Bois, it intrigued the man to try and make Christa discuss herself. She did so only with difficulty. She seemed unused to receiving attention. But when Stephen wanted he could be clever with women. He had always had a genius for inspiring confidence in the very young. Children and animals went to him without fear. Soon Christa lost her particular fears and told him freely about her childhood; the crushing blow that the double death of her parents had been to her, and afterwards, the gloom and misery of the years with an unsympathetic spinster aunt who had not wanted her. It shocked Stephen to think that in her most tender adolescent years, Christa had been the slave of a hard selfish woman who had made her cook and work in the house by day, and attend night classes in order to learn bookkeeping and shorthand, so that she could earn her living.

It did not seem possible to the man who had grown up in a family of wealth, and mixed with débutantes of his sister's social class, that little Christa Coombe had never been to a private dance, rarely gone out to a party of any kind and had never been spoiled or petted, nor known the real joy of living until her aunt died. After that, through her association with Barbara Lane, she had acquired a far nicer 'relative' in the friendly adopted 'Aunt Cath'. But even then, it seemed to Stephen that it was the beautiful Barbara who had most of the fun, and Christa who still made the sacrifices, and helped in the house.

Yet not one single complaint came from Christa's lips. She accepted her fate. She even counted herself lucky. She was never ill, although she looked delicate, she told Stephen. She had a good steady job and was thankful for it.

"I really am angry that your first journey abroad should have ended in disaster," Stephen observed as they reached the coffee-stage, and he ordered himself a Benedictine.

But Christa tonight had no thought for the train disaster. Big-eyed, nervously excited by the unaccustomed glamour of the surroundings in which Stephen had placed her, she sat entranced. What she would have to tell Aunt Cath and Barby! What a lovely restaurant this was – the little red shaded lamps on the tables; the flowers, the Hungarian music in the background; waiters rushing hither and thither, bearing tray-loads of dishes cooked by one of the most famous chefs in Paris. She kept looking at Stephen and listening to all the things he told her about Paris. What stupendous luck that Felise should have gone off with Julia, so that Stephen could take her out *alone*, she thought. In Julia's blue-silk dress, she blossomed and sparkled suddenly, and it quite startled the man to watch her increasing radiance.

He took her on to one of the big cinemas, but seeing that she could not understand one word and might grow bored, took her out midway through the film. He then asked her if she would like to go on to a night club.

"You might like to dance," he suggested out of pure kindness.

"Do *you* like dancing?" she asked seriously.

"I'm afraid I'm very bad at it," he said.

"Which means you don't like it," she said, shrewdly.

"But if *you* do, we'll dance."

"No," she shook her head and her eyes laughed, "I'd much rather see Paris; I mean could we drive around a bit."

That pleased him. He drove his sister's car for an hour, through the heart of Paris, and back along the banks of the Seine. He showed her the wonderful entrance to the Tuileries Gardens guarded by winged horses – Stephen's favourite statue, The 'Chevaux de Marly'. The Arc de Triomphe sweeping triumphantly up toward the starlit sky seemed to

Christa breathtakingly lovely. She adored the Rond Point des Champs-Elysées, gay with flowers and fountains. Then they drove back through the Bois again where the magnificent trees and flower-beds shimmered in the moonlight. There was so much to see, Christa could hardly take it all in. She found it utterly fascinating and told him so. They ended up in the Café de la Paix near the Opéra, sipped strong black coffee and watched the crowds drifting by. She was astonished to find that it was midnight already, but when he asked if she was tired, she shook her head.

"No, *no* – this has been the most marvellous treat and I do thank you so *very* much."

"It's been a great pleasure for me," said Stephen with sincerity.

On the way home he noticed that Christa's hair had blown across her face during their tour around Paris. The *Dorella look* had come back.

Stephen's good spirits vanished suddenly. He became conscious of a weariness that had its source in the mind and heart alone. It was not good for him to be forced to remember the one great love of his life and the anguish and frustration that had followed Dorella's betrayal of him along with the friend he had equally trusted.

He took Christa home and said good night with an abruptness that rather mystified her. She went to bed in a state of depression that equalled his own, because she fancied that she must suddenly have done or said something to irritate him. She stood at her windows, face blushed, yearning eyes gazing down at the great city. Her heart brimmed over suddenly with an emotion that was almost terrible in its burning intensity.

"Oh, I love him. *I love him!*" she breathed the words to the stars then covered her face with her hands and began to cry, because her love was utterly without hope of return.

That next day she began to work for Stephen. There was no time to be emotional.

She found the Paris office of Parfum Joyeux in a chaotic state. If not as big as Golling & Nash, everything in the new building was much more modern, luxurious – and rapid. The employees were mainly smart French females and sleek male clerks. Nobody bothered about Christa. But she applied herself to her job and worked feverishly to get through arrears of correspondence. So well did she do that Stephen was surprised.

Little Miss Coombe had neat methods and quite a business-like mind. He found that he hardly missed Miss Maydew.

He let Christa off during the afternoon to visit her friend. He knew the hours of the Hôpital St. Georges were restricted. He was kindness itself, she reflected, always so thoughtful. Again she was given an unexpected treat because he, personally, drove her to the hospital. He had promised to look in on her friend and he always kept his word.

En route, he bought a bunch of white roses and lilac for Barbara. A huge expensive bouquet wrapped in cellophane. Certainly he was not used to any form of economy.

Barbara was waiting for them as she had been waiting and hoping all day. Not so much for the visit of her friend, as for *The Man*. Barbara was much better – her thoughts were lucid again, her memory restored. She greeted her visitors languidly; her big eyes turned toward Stephen. The white bandage still encircled her temples. She looked like a classic statue. Stephen, who had barely noticed her on the boat and the train, was struck now by her extreme beauty. Certainly, she made little Christa look insignificant. He had never seen such a striking pair of eyes or such a graceful neck. He gave Barbara the bouquet, sat down beside her, and when she extended her hand, kissed it in French fashion.

"I am delighted you are better," he said. "Now you must get quite well then come and stay a night with us before you return to England."

"You've been absolutely wonderful to my friend and to us both, Mr. Harrimay!" Barbara exclaimed. "Oh, what *heavenly* flowers!" She buried her face in the roses and lilac, then with a significant look at her friend, added: "You wouldn't like to run out and buy me some cigarettes, would you, sweetie? I'm going to smoke even if it shocks the nuns, and I haven't got *one*."

"Please have these," said Stephen and emptied his case on to the bed.

Christa was about to sit down on the end of the bed when Barbara fixed her with another significant look.

"All the same I'd like some of my own, Christa, my pet."

Christa flushed. Her heart-beats quickened. She knew exactly what Barbara meant (she was so used to Barby!). She wanted to be left alone with Stephen and to practise what she called her 'wiles' on him. Certainly Stephen was not bothering about Christa now. He was lighting a cigarette for the invalid,

48

leaning close, marvelling at the luxuriousness of the eyelashes that fringed Barbara's brown lustrous eyes.

All the old sense of inferiority swept back into Christa's heart. Without a word she turned and walked out of the ward. Neither of them called her back. They seemed far too engrossed in talking to each other.

8

"CHRISTA says that you and your sister have been wonderful to her," said Barbara keeping her gaze on Stephen's face. Seen thus at close quarters she found him excitingly attractive. That face was aloof, proud, yet passionate.

He said:

"I think it's such a shame that your holiday should have ended this way. Christa tells me you have never been abroad before."

Barbara sighed.

"Yes – and it's been a devastating experience. I don't remember much about the actual accident – I just woke up to find myself in this bed. However, I'm getting on marvellously."

"There is still time for you to see Paris," Stephen said.

He liked not only looking at the pure classic mould of this girl's face, but listening to her voice. Barbara had one of those low-pitched husky voices which fell pleasantly on the ear. That hand he had just kissed – he had never seen a more perfect one. Long and slender with tapering fingers and exquisite nails. He had to keep reminding himself that she was a 'model girl' and that there were hundreds of such young women in her job – physically perfect. Queer, that on the boat and in the train she had seemed only one of a crowd. But lying in this narrow hospital bed, muffled up to the neck in a cotton garment three sizes too big for her, with bandaged head, she looked pathetic – and adorable. Not at all like Christa. No timidity in Barbara. She had a much more compelling personality. And she was so obviously delighted to see him, he could not help but feel flattered.

49

"I think it's wonderful of you coming to see me when you are so terribly busy," she said softly.

He made a non-committal reply. She added:

"You could so easily have let Christa go to a hotel and taken no more notice of us. Christa says your sister and friend have been terribly kind, too."

"You are English, and after a gastly accident like that, English people living in Paris should surely be hospitable," he smiled.

"Some wouldn't look at it that way."

Barbara laid her cheek against the flowers again, knowing full well that she made a very appealing picture.

"Oh, what a marvellous scent!" she whispered.

"I don't suppose they'll last," he said, "but I'll see that you get some more tomorrow."

"I'm to be allowed to leave in four days' time providing everything goes well. But by then half our holiday will be gone," she said sadly.

"Oh, dear – can't you get an extra week's leave – if your employers know what has happened – surely they'll extend your holiday?"

"They do know. Christa has written to my mother, and *she* will tell the Stores. But I don't suppose Golling & Nash will do anything for us – you know how heartless big concerns like that can be."

"But you'll need time in which to convalesce," said Stephen with a slight frown.

"We were supposed to be going to Dieppe at the end of next week," said Barbara, and now there was an effective break in her voice. "Oh, *dear*! I shan't have seen Paris and Christa won't get her bathing, either. She so loves to swim!"

"Dieppe is rather dull," he said, frowning. "Cancel your rooms and stay here and we'll see what we can do in Paris to make up to you for all you have suffered. I can get you theatre seats, and you can use our car and chauffeur to take you both sight-seeing – to Fontainebleau, to Versailles and so on."

Barbara's eyes brightened. She lay back on her pillow and glanced sideways at Stephen with her magnificent eyes. He returned the gaze. In a curious way he was not as moved by her, as he was by the shy little orphan, Christa Coombe. Added to which he had been genuinely shaken by her strange resemblance to Dorella. But he regarded Barbara in the way a professional lover of beauty and art might do. As a boy he used to interest himself in sculpturing. It was his hobby. He would like to remove Barbara's bandages, see the shape of her classic head, and model it in clay – perhaps later chisel it in marble.

She said:

"You make it all sound terribly tempting. I really must persuade Christa to stay on. She wanted to go straight to the sea, but I'd far rather spend the whole time in Paris.'

"What a nice child she is, your little friend," said Stephen, "and she makes the most excellent secretary. I think she is wasted in a typist's job at Golling & Nash."

That feline touch of jealousy which lies dormant in the average woman stirred in Barbara, even though it was her devoted friend whom he was praising. She gave a little yawn.

"Christa's a poppet – my mother and I have sort of adopted her, you know, because she has nobody else in the world. But I don't suppose she'll ever get very far. She's too reserved and diffident; just *won't* come out of her shell."

Stephen looked thoughtfully at the way Barbara's exquisite fingers manœuvred her cigarette. Seeing no ashtray, he cupped his hands and held them out to her, smiling.

"Better drop your ash in here – you can't let it fall on this spotless floor, or the nuns will tell you off!"

Barbara laughed and flicked the ash into the bowl made by Stephen's long sensitive hands. She said:

"Christa and I made up all kinds of stories about you on the boat. You would be amused to know what we said."

"I *am* amused," he said, "what *did* you say?"

"We decided that you were a diplomat; or at least a V.I.P. of some kind."

"Heaven forbid! I'm just an ordinary business man."

"You are certainly not ordinary."

"You're too kind," he murmured. "What else did you two imagine?"

"I daren't tell you."

"Now you've roused my curiosity. Please tell me."

"Christa's a bit of a romancer," laughed Barbara. "She makes up marvellous stories about the people we notice when we are out together. She said she thought you were running away from a wife."

Now Stephen laughed.

"Good heavens! I haven't *got* a wife."

Barbara's heart leapt. That was good news so far as she was

concerned. She had fallen totally under the spell of Stephen's good looks and quiet charm. She was even now dazzled by the fact that he must be very rich. She said:

"Oh, then, that girl Christa told me about – Miss Markell – is not – your – your —"

He cut in quickly:

"Miss Markell is a great friend, but I'm neither married nor engaged."

Barbara was afraid she had annoyed him and made a clever move to put herself in the right again.

"Do tell me all about Parfum Joyeux. I think it is the most *wonderful* scent in the world. Would there be the slightest chance of us going over your factory?"

"We have only a small factory in the North – not far from Saint-Cloud. Our chief one is in the South of France – in Grasse."

"I absolutely *adore* the perfume," exclaimed Barbara.

"I'll order a bottle of it to be sent to you," he said carelessly.

"Oh, thank you," said Barbara. "You're *so* kind," and added sadly, "Christa says our luggage may eventually be dug out of the wreckage but there won't be much left to claim or use again. It will all be ruined by water from the firemen's hoses, if nothing else."

"I shall see that you get compensation from the Railway Company. Meanwhile you must accept what help my sister and I can give. The loan from the British Consul is absurdly small and we must supplement it. We can't have you two in need."

"But Christa and I hate to borrow . . ." began Barbara in her silkiest voice.

"Under these conditions you must," and now Stephen took out a handsome crocodile wallet and extracted three or four of those big crisp French notes, each of which represented a hundred new Francs. When Barbara saw them, she made an idle effort to push them away, but Stephen slipped them under her pillow. He did not care if the money was never returned. It mean nothing to a man of his income. But such was his generous nature he could not bear to think that these two young girls who worked for their living, should have neither the money nor the opportunity to enjoy the few days left to them in Paris.

Then Christa came back. Immediately Stephen got up and offered her his chair. He must go, he said. His car and chauffeur would wait to take Christa back to the office. She was not to hurry. She must stay a little longer with her friend.

Now, as he said good-bye to Barbara, he saw tears in her eyes ... genuine tears because she was still weak and emotional; so he touched the lovely hand with his lips and said gently:

"Don't worry about anything, please. My sister and I will try to make it all up to you both."

After he had gone, Barbara turned the brilliant tear-filled eyes to her friend.

"Oh, isn't he *divine*!' she exclaimed. "Oh, Christa, he's a perfect dream and he was simply *sweet* to me. It just isn't *true*. How lucky we are to have come across him! He's sending me a bottle of Parfum Joyeux, and flowers every day, and did you *see* the way he kissed my hand?"

"Yes, I saw," said Christa, and laid a packet of cigarettes down on the bedtable.

She had had to walk quite a way to find a kiosk where the cigarettes could be bought. She was hot and tired and she felt when she got back to the ward that Stephen looked at her with complete indifference. Gone was her friendly attentive escort of last night. And she had certainly noticed the warmth with which he had said good-bye to beautiful Barby.

With all her heart Christa tried not to be jealous. She had never been so in the past – either of Barby or anyone else. She used to envy Barby occasionally, but begrudged her none of her success with men. And she had always accepted the fact that she, herself, was a bit of a nonentity. But now Barbara laid such stress on the fact that she had had a *wonderful* quarter of an hour with Stephen and that she was *sure* he admired her – it was too bitter a pill for Christa to swallow. She just could not compete with girls like Barby and Felise, she told herself hopelessly.

Barbara said:

"You've got to write to that hotel at Dieppe and cancel our room. We're *not* leaving Paris. Not on your life. With *The Man* – and *such a man* – to put us up and take us around Paris.'

"But Barby, we can't expect him to go on paying us all this attention. After all, we're nothing to him or Madame Roché."

Barbara narrowed her eyes and flicked a thumb-nail against the packet of cigarettes. Then she picked up one of the loose cigarettes Stephen had left on her bed and sniffed at it delicately.

"H'm . . . Turkish . . . I love Turkish cigarettes. Rich and rare – like him."

"Barby, we must be sensible and not take advantage," began Christa in a desperate little voice.

"Nonsense, sweetie, we're going to take all we can get," interrupted Barbara. "I shall, anyway, if you don't. If you *must* go to Dieppe you'll have to go alone."

"*Barby!*"

"Well, I mean it. A girl will never get anywhere if she doesn't seize her chances. I'm always telling you that. The great Stephen Harrimay took pains to tell me that he wasn't married – or even engaged to your Felise – What's-her-name."

"But, Barby, we're not in his world! He would never look at either of us in the ordinary way. It's just because of the train smash, and we oughtn't to take advantage of his generosity.'

"For all you know, he might look at *me*, any time, anywhere. I think he did just now," said Barbara, tossing her lovely head.

Christa fought against her inclination to argue further, but she looked positively horrified when Barbara drew the French banknotes from under her pillow and crackled them at her.

"Look at this, my love! Little Barby has done well. As soon as I'm allowed out of this dim spot, I intend to buy myself something nice to wear. Thank goodness with *my* figure I can look nice in cheap clothes, and if Mr. Stephen Harrimay wants to entertain us, *I'm* not turning him down."

"So you took money from him," said Christa, her cheeks scarlet.

"Just a loan, darling."

"And how will you pay it back?"

"When I win a football pool," said Barbara airily.

"You're impossible!"

"Look," said Barbara, "I'll slide into another coma if you don't stop lecturing. Do smile and be thankful that little Barby's brown eyes have done you a bit of good."

"Done *me* a bit of good," Christa echoed the words – sudden indignation blotting out her usual docile sweetness.

Barbara giggled.

"Then *your* big grey eyes have done *me* some good – I don't mind, so long as I see him again. Ooh!" she hugged herself with both arms. "What a *man*! I felt ready to die when he kissed my hand just now."

Suddenly Christa felt that she loathed this conversation.

She decided to ignore Barbara's acceptance of the money. She stood up.

"Well, I've got to get back to my job. I'll have to stay late now to finish all the letters."

"You are lucky – working for him," grumbled Barbara.

Suddenly, with unusual bitterness, Christa said:

"It's most unusual for you to envy *me* anything."

"I do believe you're cross with me," pouted Barbara, "and I've got a *horrid* headache."

At once Christa leaned down and kissed her friend – the friend to whom she owed so much. Yes – she owed both Barby and Aunt Cath years of friendship and hospitality.

"I'm not cross. You know I love you, Barby darling. Get better soon. Good-bye, I'll come tomorrow."

Barbara called after her:

"Tell the great Stephen that I'm absolutely *crazy* about him."

Christa pretended not to have heard that remark.

9

CHRISTA spent the next three days working hard in the offices of Parfum Joyeux. She only saw Stephen for an hour each morning when he rushed in to dictate his letters. Then he rushed out again. He seemed indescribably busy. In the late afternoon, sometimes, he came back to sign the letters.

At such times, he treated Christa with courtesy but quite formally – as he treated all his staff. He was too busy for any personal conversation.

Christa did not see him during the next three evenings spent at Madame Roché's apartment. Stephen had heavy social engagements both with, and apart from, his sister. One night he took Felise to dinner and the theatre. Christa knew that. Felise had come to the apartment for drinks, first. Nobody seemed to bother much about Christa now. The two women treated her politely but indifferently. She was excluded from most of the conversations, and was alone, after they went out. Quite understandable, Christa thought. She was left mainly to the ministrations of Yvette. Christa had everything that she wanted in the material sense, but she felt horribly alone. Julia Roché tried to be kind and even arranged one night for a distant cousin of Claude's who lived in Passy, to take Christa to the ballet. She had also insisted upon adding to Christa's store of clothes and had most generously 'thrown out' quite a number of suits and dresses, to say nothing of lingerie, which she told Christa to divide with her friend. Christa hated taking charity but felt she must accept these things and not appear ungrateful, because Barbara would be furious unless she did.

Christa no longer looked forward to her visits to the hospital. Barbara could talk of nothing but Stephen. The magnificent flowers that came daily with his card, from a florist in the Faubourg St. Honoré; the huge bottle of perfume that had been sent direct from the Parfum Joyeux offices, and which now stood on Barbara's bed-table. She went into raptures over the box of clothes that Christa bought her. She couldn't wait, she said, to get up and put on one of those marvellous summer 'ensembles'.

Stephen had been to see her again, she told Christa one afternoon, obviously with delight. He had told her he felt inspired by her to go back to his old hobby – sculpturing. He wanted to model her when she was out of the hospital.

"He admires me *terribly*," Barbara informed Christa full of conceit and excitement over her apparent success with Stephen.

Christa felt uneasy – over her own feelings – and Barbara's. It all seemed wrong. Neither one of them should be personally interested in Stephen. She did not want Barbara to be disappointed and she could not bear her own pain. She was far too deeply in love with Stephen Harrimay for her peace of mind.

"I'm sure he admires you," was her reply to Barbara. But she made another effort to persuade her to go ahead with their plans for Dieppe. The sea air would do her so much more good than staying in Paris, she said.

Barbara laughed this off. She even made Christa sit down and write the letter of cancellation to the hotel in Dieppe.

Christa said no more but she felt worried and confused. She could not blame Barbara for falling in love with Stephen. She was so much in love, herself. It was a terrible thing to Christa's way of thinking – that she and her adored Barby should both have fallen for this man. She was *afraid* for Barby, too. Christa was sure that Stephen meant to marry Felise Markell, and that his attentions to Barbara were of no great consequence. He was, she felt sure, acting just as a man would do toward a beautiful girl who appealed to the artist in him. But Barbara took everything he did or said with deadly seriousness and kept telling Christa that 'this was her big chance' – the chance they used to discuss and giggle over – of finding a rich, glamorous husband.

Christa stayed on in the Roché apartment feeling out of her depth and anxious to leave even if it meant seeing less of Stephen. Then came the week-end and two important things happened. Madame Roché had to fly suddenly to Nice, on business, and join her husband in Grasse. Before she left Paris she spoke to Christa. Stephen was present.

"I know you'll realize that you can't stay on here, my dear, but I've spoken to my cousin and she said you could go to her. If Miss Maydew remains away and my brother still needs you as a stand-in, you can get into Paris from Passy quite easily."

"But Barbara is coming out of hospital today," Christa said. "We can find a hotel, and really, my Aunt Cath, Barbara's mother – is writing such worried letters about Barbara's health, I somehow feel we ought to go back to London at once."

"That would be rather sad for Barbara who hasn't yet seen Paris," put in Stephen. "And I'm not at all anxious to part with my excellent secretary, either," he added.

This made Christa happy. But her face clouded.

"It's terribly nice of you. I – I don't quite know what to do."

Stephen was not looking at her now. He suddenly beckoned his sister to follow him from the *salon* in which they had been talking. Christa heard a murmur of voices out in the hall – then Julia said quite loudly and plainly:

"Oh, very well, do as you like, my dear, I don't really mind. I must go now or I'll miss the plane. I'll leave the whole matter to you."

Stephen returned to Christa. He gave her that warm friendly smile which so completely transformed his rather austere face.

"We've come to a very happy solution to your problems, I hope," he said. "Barbara is leaving the hospital. She can come here and be with you in the flat which will be empty while Julia is in the South of France. She is likely to be away for four or five days at least. I have a good many business dates and shan't be here very much myself but you two girls can enjoy

57

the flat and give that lazy staff of Julia's something to do. There isn't the slightest need for you to waste your francs on hotel bills or food outside."

Christa was speechless. She wanted to say: "*No*." She was quite sure that Madame Roché had not altogether approved this plan. Stephen was so generous and kind. But she also felt that she could not go on refusing his offers.

"I can't thank you enough," she said with a reluctance she tried not to show. "It's a perfectly wonderful plan, and I know Barbara will be thrilled."

"I'll arrange for the car to pick you up and you can bring her back here after tea," said Stephen.

Now he noticed the look of strain on Christa's face. She did not look well.

"My dear, are you feeling the heat and working too hard?" he asked. "It's pretty sultry in Paris at this time of year. I ought not to have asked you to do Miss Maydew's job. This is, after all, your holiday."

"Oh no, I *love* the office," said Christa passionately.

"You're extremely efficient," he said. "I've a good mind to offer you a permanent job."

Now the fair young head shot up. She looked at him with eyes no longer tired.

"Oh, that would be *marvellous!*"

"So you really like it at Parfum Joyeux," he said touched.

His correspondence had seldom been dealt with more efficiently. Miss Maydew and her predecessors seemed to make a lot of mistakes. Christa never. Once or twice when he had not been too busy, he had turned his attention to little Miss Coombe and decided that she was wasted in a huge concern like Golling & Nash where she was one of hundreds. Apart from her accuracy, she had a splendid memory. He had reached the definite conclusion that she would make a valuable employee in the firm.

"Look here," he said, "if you're not crazy about staying on with your present employers, would you like to work in our London branch? I could certainly improve on your present salary, and arrange it for you."

She was overcome. Her spirits soared. It was such a refreshing change for Christa to score a personal success.

"I'd simply adore it. I can't tell you how much," she exclaimed, her cheeks crimson.

Again he felt touched.

"We'll see what can be done," he said. "Let me know when Jacques comes with the car. I want to be dropped off in a street not far from the St. Georges. There's a shop there where they sell particularly good artists' materials. I'm going to get hold of some clay and snatch a moment or two to model Barbara's head while she is here. She has the most amazingly beautiful eyes – those heavy lids, *and* curved lips are classic. She's like a Greek goddess."

Down went Christa's spirits again. She said:

"I quite agree."

"I don't know why I didn't take up sculpturing as a profession," he went on, sighing. "I'm often sorry I didn't. The bronze of Miss Markell is my best work. You must see it. It is in her apartment."

"Yes," said Christa, almost inaudibly.

Now with the cold precision of the professional artist Stephen's gaze travelled critically over Christa's childish features.

"If there's time, I'll get you to sit for me, too."

She gave a nervous laugh.

"Good heavens – not *my* nondescript face, and this . . ." she indicated her hair, running her fingers through it. "Even the Paris hairdresser called it a 'mop'. I've got a double crown or something. It never stays tidy. Already, it's a mess again —" she broke off. Sheer nerves had made her say a lot of things that she did not really mean to say and which she was sure would not really interest him. She was unprepared for the strange haunted look that came over his face, as she fingered her thick fair hair. He seemed almost to glare at that untidy head. Then he said in a brusque voice:

"Do try to keep your hair tied back. It suits you better."

Then he walked out of the room. Christa stood still, a stricken look in her eyes. She was hurt and mystified, aware that he was suddenly annoyed with her and not understanding why.

She did not see him again until later that evening, but she spent half an hour or so trying to smooth her hair and do away with the back-combing which was now too bushy. She had never in her life had neat hair and she knew it. Even the hairdressers had only made her look temporarily tidy. But after one night it was all over the place again. Christa tugged at it, viciously, hurting her scalp, and glared at her reflection in the mirror. She even played with the idea of going back to the hairdresser recommended by Yvette and asking him to cut still more of that wild hair away – just to please *him*. Oh, what a fool she was, she thought bitterly. How silly could a girl become about a man – especially a man who was not in the smallest degree interested in her except as a machine-like secretary who had turned out to be better than his own personal assistant!

Her efforts resulted in the thick hair, damped down and brushed back, looking out of shape, and not as attractive as usual. Depressed, Christa drove to the hospital to fetch Barbara.

Later on, as the two girls entered the flat, Christa felt better and squeezed her friend's arm.

"It's terrific to have you here with me. I've missed you, Barby darling."

Barbara nodded. She was staring avidly around her, literally devouring the handsome appointments of the luxury home which belonged to Stephen's sister. Barbara had been driven in triumph from the hospital in Stephen's big car. The chauffeur had brought up her suitcase. She gave Yvette a superior smile and treated her as though she had been used all her life to the attentions of a smart French maid.

"It's amazing how weak I feel after the short time I have had in bed," she told Christa languidly. "I'll probably have to rest before dinner."

How easy she finds it to fit in with an environment like this, thought Christa enviously. She isn't as awkward or nervous as I am. She can carry off anything – anywhere – lucky Barby!

"Come into the *salon*. I'm sure you would like a drink. Tea or coffee," suggested Christa.

"I'd adore some coffee," said Barbara in the same languid voice.

The French maid's shrewd eyes sized up this new English arrival. Like everybody, she immediately fell victim to Mademoiselle Barbara's stunning good looks. Those toffee-brown eyes; that dark auburn hair; that divine figure. *Ooh, là là*! This must be the young lady Monsieur fancied. (Immediately Yvette's amorous French nature led her to suppose that Monsieur had more than an interest in the glamorous English girl who had been a victim of the terrible accident.) Nevertheless, Yvette turned up her nose a little as Barbara swept regally past her. She wasn't going to be patronized by anybody who wore second-hand clothes! And Yvette recognized Mademoiselle's dark blue silk two-piece with the scarlet braid on the short jacket. A 'throw-out' of Madame's. It was a suitcase of Madame's too, that Jacques had just handed her, containing, no doubt, further offerings from Madame. Yvette tossed her head and whisked off to the kitchen to prepare the coffee.

Christa led Barbara out on to the balcony where she could enjoy the glorious view of Paris on this tranquil summer's afternoon. The sun was still shining brightly, turning the Seine to liquid gold. Paris looked wonderful. Barbara regarded the view idly, then turned back to the *salon* which was much more to her liking. Everything excited her. The rich curtains and covers; the expensive ornaments and pictures; the fault-less *décor*. The extravagant luxuries that money could buy exhilarated Barbara. She forgot that she had ever been in an accident, or felt ill and weak. She drew a deep breath and turned her gleaming eyes upon Christa.

"Isn't this too wonderful? Have you ever seen anything like it except on films or in magazines? *just think* of our old lounge at home, Christa."

Up rose Christa's loyal blood in defence of Aunt Cath's little house.

"Well, it's different, but it is your home, and I've always envied you it."

"I'll say it's different!" laughed Barbara and sank on to the low velvet sofa, opened a Limoges box on the table beside her, and pulled out a cigarette. "Give me a light, darling."

Christa lit the cigarette for her friend.

"It is lovely. I knew you'd appreciate it."

"Out of this world. They must be absolutely rolling, these people."

"Of course. They are famous perfume manufacturers – just like Coty or Chanel or Houbigant."

"And Stephen – wonderful, wonderful Stephen!" sighed Barbara closing her eyes voluptuously. "He's out of this world, too. When do you think he'll come in?"

"I don't know," said Christa. She turned away and felt depression clamping down on her again. She heard Barbara rambling on in a dreamy sort of way: how she longed to see Stephen . . . how marvellous he'd been to her when he last visited her in the hospital . . . how she was going to sit for him so that he could make a sculpture of her . . . how this . . . how that . . . and always at the back of it all an underlying note of passion which Christa found almost frightening. What was the use of it – what was the *use*?

At last she turned to Barbara and spoke quite crossly.

"Oh, don't go on about Mr. Harrimay."

"Mr. Harrimay," echoed Barbara, jeering. "We *are* formal, aren't we?"

"Well, I'm working for him and he hasn't asked me to call him by his Christian name yet!" exclaimed Christa, her cheeks red.

"Oh, you are funny," laughed Barbara. "I don't think you've got any feelings. I don't believe you'll ever fall in love with anybody. You're so odd."

"I'm not odd!" said Christa indignantly.

"You are, otherwise you'd be like me – absolutely suffocated with excitement and mad about the man. Just think what's happened to us, Chris – coming to this fantastic flat as guests of the man who manufactures Parfum Joyeux. Someone our boss at Golling & Nash would have to receive in state, and crawl to, probably, seeing how well the stuff sells. And here we are in the family apartment, my dear, wearing gorgeous model dresses and on our own, now that Madame, the sister, has buzzed off. I don't see how you can be so calm."

"I'm not calm, really, not inside me," Christa began to stutter a little as she did when she was upset. "I just don't show my feelings like you do."

Barbara stretched herself out on the sofa like a lovely lazy cat.

"There's something so strong and fascinating about Stephen. Don't you *agree*?"

"Yes, I do but —" Christa stopped helplessly. How could she ever explain to Barbara or anyone how she, Christa, felt about life and people and especially this man, Stephen Harrimay. Of *course* she found him fascinating. She felt she would willingly serve him until the end of her days. But her approach to life and acceptance of fate were so different from Barby's. Possibly she was wrong and Barbara was right. It was better to place a high value on oneself and take it for granted that one could reach out and grasp the world if one wanted it sufficiently. Barbara was ambitious, self-confident, determined not to be crushed down by the avalanche of frustrations and difficulties fate pushed in her direction. She always used to be sure she was beautiful and attractive enough to find, eventually, a way out of the rut at Golling & Nash – *and* that she would marry for money. Christa held opposite views. She believed it best to be content with what one had – up to a point anyhow. Where marriage was concerned, she said, she *must* marry for love and love alone. Money would not come into it. Of course she could see that was possibly too romantic an outlook and that one should be more realistic, these days. But she wasn't made that way. And for Barbara to become seriously interested in a wealthy important man like Stephen Harrimay seemed to Christa utter madness.

She saw Barbara looking through her fabulous lashes, smiling in an enigmatic fashion.

"I know just what's passing through your mind, angel," she murmured. "You're always so *sensible*, and I'm not, am I? Well, cheer up, Chrissie. Don't look so gloomy and don't try to make me behave as sensibly as you do, because I can't and I won't. I've fallen in love with Stephen Harrimay and I'm going to do everything on God's earth to get him."

Christa gasped.

"*To get him?*"

"Why not? He's already told me I'm beautiful. He's interested in me and he's a bachelor. Add that up and see what it amounts to."

"You're really a bit mad," gasped Christa.

"But delightfully mad, you'll admit."

"Oh, Barbara darling, you stagger me. I can't ever argue with you. I always get the worst of it, but I just don't want you to get hurt, and I see danger ahead. I can't believe that because Mr. Harrimay has been so kind to us both, and his sister is letting us stay here and so on, that it means he's interested in you in a romantic sense. It's a bit too optimistic, isn't it?"

A low laugh from Barbara.

"You're a defeatist, my dear."

"No!" Christa titled her head now with a touch of pride. "I'm just more down to earth about things."

"Don't you think he's attracted by me?"

"I'm sure he is. You're marvellously beautiful, all men look twice at you and Stephen Harrimay is a sculptor. He looks at you professionally, too. But that doesn't say he's in love with you. I really do believe you think he'll end up by proposing."

Barbara lay back on the cushions. She puffed at her cigarette, twirling it in her long lovely fingers.

"Well," she said reflectively, "that isn't out of the bounds of possibility."

"Oh, really!" protested Christa.

"Wait and see," said Barbara.

Christa was quite glad that at this point Yvette came in with the coffee and some *petits-fours*. Barbara watched the maid put the tray down on the stool, noting the exquisitely chased-silver coffee-pot and cream jug; the Brussels lace cloth; the little fluted gold and white porcelain cups. She put on her languid voice again.

"Pour me out some black coffee, will you?"

Christa darted forward.

"I'm sure Yvette is busy. Let me pour out."

Yvette marched out, her lips tight. Mademoiselle Christa was *charmante*. The second Mademoiselle – no, far from it. Pour out her coffee indeed!

Christa was trying to divert Barbara's mind from Stephen. She discussed her health.

"How do you really feel? Is the head really better?"

"Practically normal," said Barbara and, pushing a rich wave of hair back from her forehead, showed her friend the thin red line of scar. "My doctor promised this will go quite white, and one day if I can afford it, I can have plastic surgery and it can be removed altogether."

"I'm thrilled for you, darling. But you just mustn't do too much all at once – till you're strong again."

Now for the first time Barbara turned her attention to Christa.

"You've been terribly sweet to me. Thanks for everything, Chris."

"I've done nothing. Besides – look what you and Aunt Cath have done to make my life different."

"I must say I rather envy you working for the Big Man himself," said Barbara, going back in her mind to the thought of Stephen. "How much do you see of him? What does he say to you? What do you really think of him?"

Christa sighed.

All these questions – Barbara really had it badly about Stephen. It was getting quite serious. Christa was forced to go on talking about him although she had little to tell Barbara other than that she was extremely happy working as secretary to him and that Stephen was always very considerate and that he had made this thrilling offer to keep her on and give her a job in the London Branch. (This piece of news she had already told Barbara.) Barbara referred to it now.

"I think it'll be a swell idea if you go on working for Parfum Joyeux. It means you'll be in continual contact with Stephen and you can act as a sort of go-between for us."

Much as Christa loved her friend, this seemed a little too much.

"I don't want to be a go-between for anybody, even you," she said coldly. "If Stephen Harrimay wants to see you – he'll do so, and not through me."

Barbara sat up and drank her coffee.

"I say! What's bitten *you*? You sound quite annoyed. Why, I half believe you're a bit jealous."

"Oh, Barbara, do stop it and let's make plans for the weekend!" exclaimed Christa, exasperated.

But Barbara had no plans that did not include Stephen Harrimay and, as she would insist on continuing to talk about their benefactor, Christa was reduced to silence. Silence and gloom. She did not really want to think about Stephen like this in a personal way. Barbara reduced her to such a state of mind that she even began to wonder if it was true that she was jealous – *jealous of beautiful Barby for the first time in her life*.

She was almost glad when Barbara produced a genuine headache and retired to her room to take an aspirin and lie down. If she went on in this crazy way about Stephen, Christa decided that she would be sorry they had ever taken advantage of his generosity. She tried to calm down, by writing a long letter to Aunt Cath, telling her how much better Barbara was and informing her that they were remaining here in Paris for the time being, but had cancelled Dieppe.

An hour later, Stephen came home.

10

STEPHEN had not intended to spend the evening with the two English girls who were his sister's uninvited guests. He did not exactly think of them in that light as he had made the arrangements for them to stay there but he was quite aware that he had put up a black mark over it with Julia. However acquiescent she might pretend to be, she obviously did not approve of his benevolence. He wasn't sure he altogether approved of it, himself. It was certainly carrying pity a little far. Once Barbara came out of hospital he could quite well have let both girls go and bothered about them no further.

What had led him to extend to them the hospitality of Julia's apartment? Again it was not only because he found Christa useful at the office. Was it essentially Barbara's exotic beauty that interested him? Yes – decidedly. Yet, it was not the *man* who craved to go on seeing her, but the *sculptor*. For a long time now, Stephen had been so busy that he could hardly give any time to his artistic hobby. But when he had first seen Barbara in the hospital with that white bandaged head that made her look like a veiled nun – his fingertips had ached to mould those wonderfully high cheek-bones, that pure classic line from brow to chin, in clay.

He had bought the materials he needed. He could get down to the job. He had the permanent use of a studio belonging to a friend of his – a distinguished French painter. Georges Delacroix owned one at the top of a building high on the hill in Montmartre. Stephen often used to go there before business became so exacting. His last model had been Felise, herself. Georges had been full of praise for that particular bust and lamented that Stephen had turned his talents to the family business.

"The world has lost a great sculptor," he had sighed not for the first time as the friends examined the completed bronze of the young pianist. But Stephen only laughed and made the usual reply to such a remark:

"I know I have talent, *mon cher* Georges, but I am also a materialist. My sister and her husband think it is my duty to carry on with my family business and increase the family fortune and I have agreed. Which proves that I am not an artist in the truest sense – the type to whom money is unimportant and for whom art comes first."

Nevertheless, the desire to model Barbara's face increased in strength each time Stephen saw her. He intended to ask her to sit for him tomorrow, perhaps in the afternoon after she had had a morning out with Christa. Stephen had a date tonight with Georges but at the last moment his friend telephoned the office to say that he had gone to bed with a sudden return of an old condition – a peptic-ulcer. So Stephen found himself at a loose end and decided to issue an invitation to take both girls out to dinner.

Yvette brought in the drinks and the three of them sat in the *salon* talking together when Stephen made this invitation. At once Christa caught the rapid warning look that Barbara flung her. She knew at once that Barby wanted her to make an excuse to absent herself. In Barbara's mind two was very much company and three a crowd. Especially tonight when there was a chance of her going out alone with the fascinating Stephen.

Christa turned her head away so that the others should not see the disappointment in her eyes. Her heart had leapt at the idea of another evening out with Stephen but she was no fool. She realized how Barbara felt. And after all, she, Christa, had had *her* dinner *à deux* with Stephen while Barbara was still in the hospital. . . . it was Barby's turn.

Christa heard Stephen's pleasant voice:

"What would you like – you two – dinner in the Bois? Or shall we drive out of town to a charming farmhouse I know where they have a fabulous grill? Or would you prefer to go and see a floor-show where you can be amused as well as fed? Not that I ever think the food is as good in those sort of restaurants."

"It all sounds terribly exciting," said Barbara on a high note of excitement.

Then Christa said quietly:

"If you will excuse me, I really don't want to go out . . . I've got a fiendish headache. I think it is the heat."

"Nonsense —" began Stephen.

"Oh. I know what Christa is like when she gets the *migraine*," broke in Barbara quickly. "She ought not to go out. That is if *you* don't mind putting up with me alone, Stephen."

He had asked them both to drop the 'Mr. Harrimay'. He

was not a man who liked formality although Christa kept to it strictly and rigidly in office hours for which he was grateful.

He looked thoughtfully at the two girls. The sheer physical delight of Barbara's appearance, as usual, electrified him. Again, not as the man but the artist, he traced the curve of that voluptuous mouth and the heavy-lidded eyes. In ancient Greece she might well have been a goddess. She was stunning tonight, he thought, in one of her newly acquired dresses – blue and silver brocade, Chinese style with a little upstanding collar and short slit skirt. Certainly she was the sculptor's, the poet's, dream. It was almost an effort for him to turn away from her and glance at Christa.

Barbara made poor Christa look colourless. Yet – the deep-thinking man in Stephen – the man interested in human nature, philosophy, even metaphysics which had been one of his most absorbing interests when he was at Oxford – was more mentally intrigued by Christa than her friend. There was a haunting quality in her pallor, her thinness, the eyes that were as grey and strangely sad as a mountain pool. What did they hold, those eyes, he wondered. What feelings, what passions were concealed behind that gentle nervous façade? That there was an amazing strength and purposefulness in Christa he had already learnt since she worked for him. She was the feminine type that suggested fragility, even meekness. But there was nothing either meek or fragile about her. He was convinced that in moment of danger, of physical or mental pain, Christa could be as strong as steel. That, in itself, captured his imagination. She was so much the antithesis of her girl-friend whose exciting beauty was there, written for all the world to see, betraying with it her passionate desire for life. But one didn't know what Christa wanted or indeed if she wanted anything.

She suggested a kind of passive resistance to any attempt to probe deeply into her heart. She almost gave the impression that she would be afraid of love – of passion. In themselves such things were challenging.

Stephen could imagine that a cruel or heartless man might try to make love to a girl like Christa just in order to test her reactions. There might well be a hidden fire waiting to be dis-covered and if and when it flamed she might experience a deeper passion than any Barbara was capable of. These reflec-tions flitted through Stephen's mind, but only in a vague sense. He was really concerned with satisfying his artistic desire to make a good sculpture of Barbara. At the same time he did not want particularly to spend this evening alone with her. He was not anxious for a flirtation and he was well aware that it was what she wanted. He was also astute enough to believe that Christa's headache was a myth. He decided to be blunt.

"I am sure you are just showing how tactful you are because you think that I don't want a party of three, Christa," he said lightly, "but such isn't the case, I should feel most proud to take out two such attractive young women one on each arm."

Christa's hopes rose again. Might she . . . dared she accept without upsetting Barbara?

Her colour rose. Stephen saw it. How different the young girl looked, he thought, when she woke up like that. But what was the matter with her tonight. She didn't look as nice as usual. That smarmed-down hair with no shape to it – it was grim! It had been flattened to an almost ludicrous extent. Why on earth? Then Stephen grimaced and remembered. He had ticked the poor little thing off for having unruly hair – the Dorella-look which so absurdly troubled him. She had gone to the trouble of trying to do what he wanted, even though it spoiled her looks. He felt suddenly remorseful for his own stupid behaviour. He felt very sympathetic toward her.

"Well – isn't it so?' he persisted. 'Won't you forget the headache and come out with us?"

By this time, however, Christa had received another of Barbara's flashing glances, this time a beseeching one. Christa put aside her own wishes. The headache must remain, she thought ruefully.

Quite firmly she declined Stephen's invitation.

Stephen and Barbara went out alone.

Barbara left the apartment with the great Stephen Harrimay – or as Christa would have put it – swept out of it regally, thrilled, and triumphant.

Christa watched them get into Stephen's car and faced an evening alone. Not that she minded being alone. Not that she begrudged her beloved Barby the wonderful time she would have (for Christa knew what an interesting companion Stephen could make). But she would not have been human if she had not longed to be with them. Lucky Barbara, to be able this evening to listen to Stephen talk; dine with him, enjoy the food and wine that he chose; enjoy Paris with *him*. He was such a marvellous escort and such an unusual one. All the girls in the office were crazy about him. Christa could hear the remarks made at times by the young French typists at Parfum Joyeux.

"*Comme il est beau!*"

"*Il est brave*, Monsieur Harrimay, *charmant!*"

Yes he was all those things, Christa agreed. But to her he was as inaccessible as the stars. Barbara's attitude frightened her. It seemed such madness for her to think that she could ever mean anything more in his life than just a lovely girl who had been injured in an accident and whom he had befriended.

Christa spent a restless evening, not quite knowing what to do. Finally she went to bed – there to lie awake and think about Stephen. Think about those two alone together in wonderful, exciting Paris.

Christa could not sleep. Finally she sat up in bed with a French dictionary and a French novel – which she found in the apartment, and attempted some translation. She felt that it would be good for her to learn to speak and read a little French, even though she might never have to use it in the London office.

Every now and then she would raise her head and stare at nothing, remembering Stephen, feeling uplifted by the knowledge that she would still be working for him once she got back to England. Or, at least, working for *his* firm. It would be marvellous, instead of that old dreary slavish routine at Golling & Nash. But what would Barbara do if she had to go on working for G. & N. alone? If only Stephen would find *her* a job in his firm, too.

Christa was actually asleep when at 2 a.m. Barbara let herself in to the apartment. She woke up with a start as the bedroom door opened. Barbara switched on the light and swept in with no consideration for her friend.

"Oh, hello —" began Christa drowsily, then paused. She saw Barbara's face. No longer radiant. Her eyes were stormy and her lips an angry line. She peeled off her gloves and flung them angrily on to the twin-bed beside Christa's.

"Well, that's *that!*" she said in a sullen voice.

Christa rubbed her eyes.

"Haven't you enjoyed your evening?" she began again. This time Barbara interrupted in a furious voice.

"No, I have not."

"But why?"

Barbara sat down on the end of the bed, unbuttoning her tunic.

"I just haven't – that's all."

"But I don't see how you could have helped it – out in Paris with him," said Christa incredulously.

"He isn't human," said Barbara. "He's just a cold machine!"

"Barbara!" protested Christa with a hard laugh. "*Really!*"

Barbara swung round on her, her magnificent eyes flashing. "Oh, I can't expect you to understand. You're a cold fish, too!"

Christa was wide awake now and rather upset. She was used to Barbara making scenes. Even Aunt Cath admitted that her darling daughter was at times rather spoiled and temperamental.

"Barby darling," said Christa gently, "why do you say a thing like that? You know perfectly well I'm not a cold fish."

"Well, you conceal your feelings so well, nobody would think you had any. I suppose I don't hide mine. I showed what I felt when I was with *him* tonight, and it didn't work. It seemed to have the opposite effect."

Christa coloured. Now she understood.

Before she could comment, Barbara began a lengthy story to which Christa listened with growing concern. Barbara admitted that Stephen had done everything to give her a wonderful evening. Oh yes . . . they had dined in the same beautiful little restaurant in the Bois de Boulogne to which he had taken Christa. A superb meal . . . and he had been charming. Afterwards he had hinted that she might like to see one of the Paris floor-shows so they had gone on to the newest and most popular of the night-clubs where they had seen one or two first-rate cabaret artistes. Champagne had flowed and they had danced.

But he had been so stiff, so polite – so *correct*. He hadn't once unbent, Barbara complained bitterly; he had even held her while they danced as though she might break. And at least a foot away from him, too! He had talked all the time and she had had to listen, but she wasn't interested in his knowledgeable conversation about Paris or people. She had been *bored*. Bored and disappointed.

"He paid me one or two compliments about my appearance and my dancing but you would have thought he was just not flesh and blood." Barbara went on, her cheeks flaming, her eyes smouldering with resentment. "And when I suggested he should come up here for a drink and say good night, he refused. He didn't even kiss my hand. The only thing he did do was to ask me to sit for him at the studio at three o'clock tomorrow. But I tell you *he isn't human*."

Christa's feelings were mixed. This was very tricky, she thought. She knew quite well what lay in Barbara's mind. Barbara had wanted Stephen to go mad about her and end the evening with a passionate embrace and a promise of more to come. She had probably been much too forthcoming, abandoning her usual languid artificial pose for the intense warmth of a girl deeply attracted by the man she was with.

Christa didn't know Stephen Harrimay very well but she understood him better than Barbara could ever do. She remembered her own evening out with him. He had asked *her* to dance but been glad when she refused. He didn't like dancing. He preferred to show her Paris by night, and she had wanted to see it with him. While he talked she had hung on his every word. *She* hadn't found him a bore. Far from it. And the last thing on earth she would have expected was for him to enter into any kind of intimate relationship; be it only a kiss or a touch.

She looked sadly at her friend.

"Oh, Barby darling, why didn't you enjoy what you could this evening and not ask too much. Oh Barby, I told you, darling, not to expect Stephen Harrimay to fall in love with you."

Barbara sprang to her feet.

"You're wrong. He will yet. I swear I'll *make* him."

"Barby, you're mad – you can't *make* a man fall for you."

"I can. I have made other men go crazy about me – you know I have. Look at that doctor who attended me last year – he refused to go on treating me because he said he felt he'd fall in love with me if he did."

"Oh I know, I know how you attract most men. And Stephen thinks you're beautiful. He's asked you to sit for him, hasn't he? But you expect too much."

To Christa's utter surprise, Barbara now burst into tears. Christa had seldom seen her cry. She was normally so cool and self-possessed.

"I'm madly in love with him. I can't bear it. I'm just crazy about him," wept Barbara.

Christa alarmed, got out of bed, sat beside her friend and put an arm around her.

"Oh, darling, please don't be so upset. I can't bear it. It's so *silly*! You've only known him such a short time. He

72

lives in a different world from ours. You must be realistic about it."

"I don't care how short a time I've known him. He's everything in the world I want. For me it was love at first sight."

"You must give him time —" began Christa, although in her heart she was not at all sure this was the right thing to say. Neither could she with any sincerity feel that she wanted Stephen to return Barbara's love. She was not really the type of girl to make Stephen Harrimay happy and vice versa although he had the money and position she wanted.

Barbara pushed her away.

"You don't understand. You'd never fall madly in love at first sight with anybody. You're cold, and so is he."

Now Christa stood up. Her warm affectionate desire to comfort her friend faded.

"I am *not* cold and I don't think you have any right to say that Stephen is. I think this is all rather absurd."

Barbara was amazed. Christa had never before spoken to her so unsympathetically.

"You're all right. You've got a job in his London office. You'll on go seeing him. It's all very well for you to feel so pleased with life. Perhaps you fancy yourself as being more his type than I am. You've always got your head in a book and like to discuss things that bore me."

"Now you're being absolutely ridiculous, Barby. You know perfectly well I don't consider myself Stephen Harrimay's *type*. I don't think either of us comes into his orbit. But you do more than I ever could, because you're so marvellous to look at and he says so."

Barbara changed her tune. She caught Christa's hand and lifted a face wet with tears, beautiful and pathetic enough to melt any heart.

"I'm sorry, Chris, I'm a pig. You're always so sweet to me. It's just that I was so disappointed over this evening. I think you're right. I expect too much. Tomorrow at the studio I'll be different – act more 'aloof'. I'll rouse his curiosity. Oh, I'll make him really interested in me before I've finished; you'll see. Chrissie, darling, give me your blessing and say that you understand even if you're incapable of feeling the way I do."

Christa tried to give her friend that 'blessing' but the words stuck in her throat. She did wish Barbara would not keep accusing her of being without any feeling just because she, Christa, was by nature more reticent. Heavens, she thought,

73

what would Barby say if she knew that Stephen affected her just as deeply as Barbara herself was affected. Only she hadn't Barby's vanity or self-confidence. It would never have entered her head to imagine that she attracted Stephen.

In the end, of course, Christa had to reassure Barbara. Then she lay for a further half hour listening to Barby make her plan of campaign for a future 'attack' on Stephen's feelings.

When Christa finally fell asleep she felt in the depths of depression.

It was a depression in no way lessened by the fact that her temporary job with Parfum Joyeux came to an abrupt end that next evening. Miss Maydew returned to work. Stephen himself told Christa this when she took the letters in for him to sign at half-past four that afternoon.

He handed her a small slip of paper which she saw to her surprise and confusion was a handsome cheque.

"Oh – no —" she began, pink in the cheeks.

But he interrupted:

"Yes *of course*. You came nobly to my assistance. Please take this. But Miss Maydew is coming back in the morning, so you will be able to have that rest you came for. But believe me I shall miss your excellent work. You are a far better secretary than Miss Maydew. She's a nice creature but she fusses. That's her chief fault. You never do. You have a quiet personality and it has a tranquillizing effect on me, I assure you."

Christa laughed but bit her lips. It was quite impossible of course for her to tell him how she would miss the job here with him. She said, shyly:

"But you did mean what you said – about – about me working for you in London?"

"Not often for me, personally. But for my London manager, yes. Tam Davis is the name. By the way I had a word with him on the phone about you. He says there are plenty of would-be secretaries in town but not many either efficient or reliable and he is only too delighted to take you over. His own P.A. is leaving to get married. They all do in time," Stephen added with a laugh.

"Well, I shan't," said Christa before she could restrain herself.

Stephen, who was standing by the big plate-glass window of the modern office which Parfum Joyeux had only recently built, threw her an amused glance.

"Oh, I expect you will also – in time," he said.

74

"I doubt it," she said. "Anyhow I promise I'll do my best for Mr. Davis."

"You'll like him. He's a cheerful soul – a Scot, as the name 'Tam' might suggest, although not a very recognizable one. His people moved from Edinburgh to London when he was still a small boy and he has no Scottish accent. He took over the management of our London Branch about five years ago. He's nearly thirty and still a bachelor. Very popular with the opposite sex – rather a good amateur pianist, in fact. Not Felise Markell's kind, but all jazz and hot stuff. He recently composed a Twist number that was played on TV and had a fair success. He's the exact opposite of myself – out with the girls and often dances madly till all hours. Sometimes . . ." Stephen laughed, "I wonder Tam doesn't get married – in self defence. He's so frequently in a jam with some beautiful creature."

Christa had only half listened to this eulogy about the man for whom she was going to work in London. What she did hear about Mr. Davis held no great interest for her. She was concentrating upon Stephen. She thought of Barbara and the outing of last night that seemed to be such a fiasco from Barbara's point of view. Christa was aware that Stephen had just come from the studio to sign these letters. He was not as smartly dressed as usual but wearing casual slacks and shirt with a light jacket over his shoulders. He looked the artist – not the business man. His personality fascinated Christa. She asked, shyly:

"How did the sitting go?"

He sat down at his desk.

"Oh, fine," he said lightly, "Barbara makes a wonderful model. She never moves. Not like Felise – Miss Markell – who couldn't sit still for more than two minutes while I modelled her."

"How long will it take you to finish the head you are doing of Barbara?"

"I don't suppose I will have time to do much more before you girls leave Paris, but I can take it over to London with me and perhaps finish it there."

Christa found herself bursting with curiosity to know how that session with Barbara had really gone off, and if Barby had behaved more sensibly this time. But she said nothing. Again she thanked Stephen for the cheque, and started to walk out of the office. He spoke to her as she reached the door.

"Have fun tonight, you two. The car is at your disposal.

I shan't be in for dinner. Miss Markell is giving a dinner-party for a young Jugoslav violinist who has just escaped from behind the Iron Curtain, and to whom she is playing patron. He's giving a private concert for some of Felise's friends at her house tonight. No doubt I'll see you and Barbara tomorrow sometime. How much longer is there left of your holiday?"

"Barely a week," said Christa, "but of course we shall be leaving Madame Roché's apartment long before she gets back. I don't feel we should take advantage of her hospitality – or yours – much longer."

Stephen looked up at her with a pleasant smile.

"No need to hurry. My sister won't be back from Cannes till Thursday."

"We shall leave before then," insisted Christa.

"Well, we don't have to say good-bye this moment," said Stephen and smiled again. "When you do get to London, you'll report to Mr. Davis, won't you? You will, of course, be handing in your notice to Golling & Nash."

"Yes," said Christa, "I intend to write to Mr. Percy Nash, who deals with personnel, before I leave Paris."

She tried to feel compensated by this thought for handing the Paris job back to Miss Maydew. Every day since she had been here, hard work though it was, she had enjoyed to the full working for Stephen – seeing him so often. Now it was over, and somehow she felt that everything was over; that in a curious kind of way he was 'signing off' – almost as though he had lost interest in her or Barbara.

Unknown to her, Stephen was busily observing quite closely the changing expression on Christa's small pale face. And, as always, the peculiar sadness of her large grey eyes struck at his heart. She didn't appear to be unhappy yet she looked it. He was a perceptive and sensitive man and quickly perceived and felt the sorrows of others. He was quite positive that Christa Coombe was a lonely person; curiously out of her depth, and out of tune with this rat-race that they called *Life*. She was so withdrawn – so unfathomable at times – it made her interesting to Stephen even though her timidity could have an irritating effect. On occasions it made him almost want to take her by the shoulders, shake her and say: "*Don't look like that. Don't be so easily hurt, or so generous and unselfish. These are wonderful qualities but life is hard and you've got to fight if you want to make a success – if you don't want to go under . . .*"

Yes, he would have liked to have said something of that sort. It was quite annoying the way Christa unconsciously made him wish to protect her – look after her, *lecture her!* And as for that wonderful silver-fair hair – now so flattened, so scrupulously brushed back and held in place by a wide bandeau – he detested the new method of doing it. He said:

"Why *do* you wear that band? It doesn't suit you."

She gasped and went scarlet.

"But you told me you preferred my hair tied back. You *told* me . . ."

He remembered yet again what he had told her, and why. He was angry with himself for allowing her personal appearance to affect him in the slightest. He snapped at her:

"Okay – you don't have to take any notice of all I say. It's damned cheek of me to make personal remarks about your hair. I'm far too blunt. Only I wish you'd go back to doing your hair as you used to – it looked charming that night I took you out."

"I'd just come from the hairdresser then. It was tidy —" she began, her heart beating very fast, her lashes flickering. She looked, he thought, like a startled nymph. One didn't dare say anything to this girl. He muttered:

"You take everything and everybody far too seriously."

Now she went absolutely white.

"I'm terribly sorry."

If he had an answer ready for that, she didn't hear it because she ran out of the room and closed the door behind her.

Stephen blotted a letter he had just signed, then pulled a packet of cigarettes from his pocket. He scowled as he flicked on his lighter. What a to-do about nothing. What the hell did it matter to him, anyway – how Christa Coombe did her hair? Why the hell did he have to get himself involved with her and her emotions? One couldn't deal with such ultra-sensitiveness. He wished he had never had anything more to do with Christa after the train accident – in some quite alarming and incomprehensible way she had infiltrated herself into his thoughts – his life! No wonder Julia and Felise both thought him 'round the bend'. What the devil was he doing – troubling himself about a little nonentity of a London secretary? As for her girl-friend – Barbara was a menace. He wasn't going to say anything to Christa but he had regretted bitterly ever taking Barbara out – or starting this bust of her. She was as beautiful as an angel, with nothing angelic about her. He found her

77

rather a bore – she talked too much and about nothing. She was egotistical and greedy. And he wouldn't be a man if he wasn't aware that she was making a bee-line for him. He didn't want to be drawn into an affair of any kind with a girl like Barbara. Yet that warm, glowing, sensuous beauty of hers was not altogether to be denied. She was devilishly attractive to a man, if only in the physical sense.

He had only partially enjoyed his two hours in the studio with her. She had been less overpowering than last night. He had found her stimulating to model. The artist in him had revelled in the flawless lines of her face and long lovely throat. Yet once away from Barbara, he did not think of her. It was her less beautiful friend, Christa, whom he remembered when she wasn't with him. Christa, who interested him in quite another and more poignant way.

Then he told himself to stop thinking about both these girls. He decided to enjoy his evening at Felise's concert – to be nicer to her than usual. Felise was an old friend and almost as beautiful as Barbara and *much* more talented and charming. Now Felise was a girl he *could* marry.

But as usual the very word 'marry' chilled Stephen. No, marriage was not for him. There was never going to be another Dorella in his life.

He received several important telephone calls before leaving the office; one from Cannes, from Julia to say that things were going well at the factory and that she would definitely be staying down there until the Friday of this week.

"How are your protegées faring?" she asked lightly.

"Oh, all right," was his abrupt answer. "They'll have left by the time you get home."

"Well I'm rather glad to hear that," came her blunt if laughing reply.

Somehow the laugh annoyed him. And busy though he was, he kept remembering the way Christa had looked because he had been so horrid about her hair. He supposed he ought to say a kind word to the poor kid before she departed.

But when he went into the room usually occupied by Miss Maydew and another more junior secretary, he was told that Miss Coombe had already gone.

He continued to think about Christa with a certain amount of compunction. He called in at his sister's apartment on his way back to Georges Dalacroix's studio where he was sleeping for a night or two. He had time to spare before going to

Felise. He would have a drink with the girls. But he found that Christa and Barbara had gone. They were eating out Yvette told him. And, Yvette added with some pleasure, the two *demoiselles* had informed her that they would be leaving for good *après demain*. The heat in Paris was too much for them, they said. They had decided, after all, to spend the rest of their holiday in Dieppe.

Stephen was surprised – and also intrigued. What had brought about this *volte-face* he wondered? When he had last seen Barbara – she had been so full of Paris and the thrill of staying here. It must be little Christa who had organized this sudden departure. He *hoped* grimacing that it was not because he had offended her about her silly hair.

He felt ridiculously worried for the rest of the evening.

11

THREE months later – a golden September day – one of those warm misty beautiful mornings when London looks its best – Christa knocked on the office door marked MR. T. W. DAVIS.

"Come in," said the breezy pleasant voice with which she had grown familiar. She never heard it or entered this office without feeling that she was lucky (rather more than that) to have got this job. It was as different, as she often told Aunt Cath and Barbara, from working at Golling & Nash as it could possibly be. In the big departmental store she had felt like one of the cogs in a giant wheel that kept turning relentlessly. And the machine was like a Robot, without feeling, not recognizing the joys and sufferings of those little cogs.

Here at Parfum Joyeux, Miss Coombe was a *person*, not merely to be worked, but considered. They were all nice to her from the 'Boss' downwards. Christa as Mr. Davis's secretary-in-chief had, herself, become a person of some importance. She had never before felt the least important. She used to take a back seat and, perhaps because of her close friendship with Barbara, had accustomed herself to being in the background whilst Barby attracted all the attention.

Now she was *the* Miss Coombe who looked after the Boss's office and papers, made his appointments, reminded him to keep them, carried out his orders and helped to soothe frustrated or difficult clients when supplies of the popular perfume were short, because deliveries were held up.

It was an exciting business and, somehow, full of that glamour which had hitherto been lacking in Christa's life. Even the atmosphere of the building as she soon found out, seemed to be impregnated with sweet odours as though little drops of Parfum Joyeux were constantly being spilled, and scented the air deliciously.

These were handsome offices with large plate-glass windows overlooking Hanover Square. The place had a similiarity to the Parfum Joyeux headquarters in Paris, which made it seem nostalgic to Christa and continually brought the thought of Stephen Harrimay into her mind. Here was the same *décor*; bright 'shocking-pink' carpets, dove-grey curtains, white Venetian blinds, white leather chairs, crystal chandeliers, and wonderful flowers in all the showrooms. Glass shelves holding those endless bottles; thousands of boxes of Parfum Joyeux in all sizes; always in the same grey and gilt boxes stamped with the 'shocking-pink' flower which was the trademark.

It was equally lush in Tam Davis's private office. Above his big flat Swedish wood desk there hung an enormous colour photograph of the firm's stall in a Paris exhibition of the past, when Parfum Joyeux had first leapt into popularity. Across the other side of the room was a large framed photograph of Stephen Harrimay standing beside a certain French *Duchesse* who had opened a new shop for him in Cannes.

Whenever Christa came into Mr. Davis's room, her eyes immediately travelled to that photograph. It was as though she could not stop looking at the lean tall figure, the strong arresting face with the well-known attractive smile. She was hopelessly in love with *The Man* – the being to whom she owed her whole change of fortune and, later, her precipitous crash into the dizzy world of love. A passionate love which sometimes was almost too strong for Christa to endure. It terrified her.

She had seen little of Stephen since her return to London. Once in July, not at all during August and twice already this month. He was staying now in his London flat and working with Tam.

They were on a new scheme. Christa, who took all the letters, knew everything about it. Stephen and the Rochés were planning to open yet another branch in Edinburgh. The last time Stephen had come over from Paris, Christa had had to book a sleeper for him on the night train to Scotland.

She saw a lot of him when he was actually here but always on business—never outside. But he had, only yesterday, found time to talk to her on a more personal note. She had just finished taking dictation. Tam was out at the time.

"How are you getting on, Christa?" he had asked her. And when she had told him that she was tremendously happy here and ever grateful to him for giving her this chance, he said in his gentle way:

"I'm so glad, my dear. I must say you look well – not quite so thin."

'*My dear!*'

Those words were lightly uttered, without much meaning, within the dry framework of common use. Yet they brought the blood flaming to her cheeks. Stephen pushed back his chair and with a slightly amused smile added:

"By the way, the hair is looking very pretty. Different style from Paris. Yes?"

That had brought another scorching blush to Christa's cheeks. She laughed nervously and said that she was glad he approved and that it was kind of him to be interested (and all that sort of thing). But inwardly she had felt recompensed for all the unhappy moments he had given her on the same subject which she had never quite understood. Her hair in Paris used to seem such a thorn in his flesh. She had decided that Stephen did not like a wild windswept appearance, and equally disapproved if she flattened and smarmed the curls down too drastically. So she took a middle course these days. Her present salary allowed her to afford a good hairdresser. She had had her hair shaped and set at Antoine. It was sleek but smart, curving into both cheeks, worn high up at the back, with a tiny black velvet bow in front.

She had begun to buy better clothes – with an attempt to emulate Madame Roché's simple elegance. In the office she wore severe grey or dark brown suits. No jewellery except for gold ear-rings. Even Barbara had complimented her on the way she was turned out nowadays and Aunt Cath said nice things such as "I always knew my little Christa had it in her to become a glamour-girl."

That, of course, just made Christa laugh but at least she felt that through knowing Stephen Harrimay and his sister and coming to work here at Parfum Joyeux she had risen above the level of the nondescript and rather hopeless young girl who had gone over to Paris with her friend on that fateful holiday

She walked into Mr. Davis's office.

He was on the telephone. As soon as he put down the receiver he had something to tell Mrs. Brand, who managed the advertising side. He spoke to her through the intercom.

Christa stood quietly waiting, pad and pencil in hand. As usual she had to tear her gaze away from Stephen's photograph. She had been wondering all day if he meant to come into the office. When she turned her gaze to her employer, it was with a smile. Tam Davis always made one feel happy. He was such a jolly, genial sort of man. Very big and rather on the plump side which made him look older than his twenty-nine years. He had the sort of dimples and baby face that seem to go with men of overweight, and not much hair which added to the infantile appearance. But he had an attractive mouth and laughing eyes and a rich delightful voice. He was a man whom people instinctively liked. Children and animals adored him. And behind his genial façade he was astute and business-like. A tireless worker on behalf of Parfum Joyeux. Stephen had once told Christa that Tam had increased the output and profits by fifty per cent during the short time he had taken over.

Christa also knew quite a bit about Tam's private life, because he was as much of an extrovert as Stephen was the reverse.

"Christa," he would say as the lunch-hour approached, "go to the cupboard and pour me out a coke with a lump of ice in it – there's a poppet. No – no gin; nothing stronger in office hours. That's my line. Have a coke with me, and tell me all about yourself."

She would drink the coke but wouldn't tell him anything. Eventually he started to confide in her. She knew all about his love-life. It was as amusing as Tam himself. He was not, he admitted, a 'stayer' in the emotional arena. He would fall into it, then scramble out with equal rapidity. Pretty girls fascinated him and he was always getting into scrapes. Christa found herself often having to answer the telephone with many a tactful explanation as to *why* Mr. Davis was out; or away. And at times she had been called upon to give Mr. Davis her personal advice upon ridding himself of an over-enthusiastic dance partner.

"I don't understand myself," he sighed to Christa on one occasion. "Nothing seems to last. At first – all champagne and kisses and mad Madisons. Then, a few weeks later – a hangover. I get so easily bored, Christa. What would you do in my shoes?"

"Just be a little more cautious, Mr. Davis. You do rather rush into things. Look at all those flowers you sent from Constance Spry to that girl you took out last Saturday. Chocolates on the Monday, too. By Tuesday she'd thought she had got you."

A chuckle from Tam.

"I'm ashamed of myself but that's me. They shouldn't take me seriously. You don't, do you?"

"Well – I wouldn't take it at all seriously if you sent me flowers and chocolates," she laughed.

He gave her a long thoughtful look.

"I believe you mean that, you funny little thing. Nothing seems to move you. That's what makes you such a good secretary, I suppose – you're as solid and inscrutable as a little sphinx."

He often called her the sphinx.

It was fun working with Mr. Davis – of that there was no doubt. But today Christa entered upon another phase in her relationship with her genial employer. At his usual 'coke hour', as he called it, he asked her what she was doing for lunch.

"Nothing. I am quite willing to stay in and work if there is an emergency."

Tam Davis smoothed back his thinning hair, and eyed his secretary through lashes that were as luxuriant as his hair was the reverse.

"Don't you think of anything but work?"

She coloured. Christa's habit of blushing never failed to move Tam to a kind of tenderness which he described to himself as paternal but which he knew well was fast becoming the contrary. After three months of close association with her in this office, he was 'getting a thing about her'. She had begun to intrigue him and haunt his thoughts after he went home. Why, he didn't know. She was pretty without being stunning – like that auburn-haired friend of hers whom he had seen once or twice when she had called to collect Christa. Barbara was a 'wow'. But there were so many 'wows' in Tam's life and he was fast becoming tired of them. They were so much of a muchness. Beauty seemed too often encased in the rather unpalatable wrappings of disdain, chilly hauteur, or complete inanity. At times something even approaching nymphomania. He was fully aware that most of them had an eye to the main chance. Big bottles of perfume direct from the factory, dinners, theatre tickets, or birthday and Christmas presents. Tam, when he was immersed in one of his 'affairs' could be very generous. But this secretary of his was different. Christa so far had only been connected with his business life. As a rule in the office he was much too busy to think of her as anything but an assistant. But lately he had started to watch her more closely – and with deepening interest. She was beginning to get under his skin. She was so cool, so reticent, so absolutely dedicated to her work.

He had asked her once if she had a boy-friend and she had given one of those bright blushes, and shaken her head. He had felt surprised. He was aware that she was alone in the world except for her adoptive aunt and friend, Barbara. And that she lived in a 'bed-sit' in Nightingale Road, Wood Green.

Tam felt it was a waste that a sweet intelligent little thing like Christa should have no real home of her own, and no fun, but he had never heard her grumble. She seemed quite content to give all her spare time and affection to the Lanes.

Tam, who knew a thing or two about women, wasn't at all sure 'beautiful Barby' was too good for Christa, whom she pushed into the background.

Tam was intrigued by the story of Stephen's first meeting with the two girls. Barbara was probably the lure. Stephen had told Tam he had been crazy to model her gorgeous head. But according to Christa, the work had never been completed. Stephen had little time to spend on sculpture when he was over in London.

Tam did not imagine his Director was really very interested in either of the girls.

Like others who knew Stephen and his sister, Tam imagined Stephen would eventually marry Felise Markell. And why not? She was a lovely talented girl and obviously in love with him.

"How about having a spot of lunch with me today for a change?" Tam suddenly asked Christa.

She was startled and a little embarrassed.

"Oh, Mr. Davis!" she began.

"Of course you will," he went on lightly, pushed some

84

papers into the drawer, locked it and put the key into his pocket. "Say in half an hour – at the Empress. That, as you know, is my favourite haunt. You just walk into Bond Street, then through to the alley-way in Berkeley Street, and you're there."

He gave her no chance to refuse. But she was rather worried about clothes.

Three or four months ago she would have felt herself to be inadequately dressed; not at all equipped to eat in a smart West End restaurant with a man like Mr. Davis. She would have suffered from agonizing shyness. But she was more self-possessed these days, more able to cope with the big smart man about town; Tam, with his Austin-Healey car, his smart suits (never without a flower in his buttonhole), his clubs, his race meetings, his squash and the tie, which Christa had learned was Harrovian. He was so much 'a gentleman', Tam Davis. He had a big job, and – so it was rumoured in the office – was a nephew of Sir Robert Davis, Bart., and would inherit his money and estates. Sir Robert was an elderly widower without a son.

The other girls in the office all adored 'Mr. Tam'. They were fascinated by the big, buoyant jolly young man, and Christa, from her quiet background, watched and noted how each girl fondly thought herself the one and only recipient of the quick flirtatious glance or flattering word.

"*You're looking a sight for sore eyes this morning, Miss West . . .*"

"*You've done a brilliant job, Miss Baker*" (*etc., etc.*).

As Christa walked into the Empress, she felt flattered because she had been asked to lunch by the Boss, but uneasy. She had no illusions and she had not the slightest intention of being numbered among Mr. Davis's conquests. Besides she did not want to have to leave Parfum Joyeux. A thousand times no – when it was connected with *Him*, *His* concern. There was always a chance of seeing *Him* here. No – she could never bear to disassociate herself from Stephen.

Tam was a few minutes late, for which he apologized when he came dashing in. He ordered a sherry for her and a gin for himself; soon she began to relax. He recounted the reason for his lateness. A girl, of course.

"You remember that little red-head whose mother kept writing and telling me what a cad I was – I ran into her just as I parked the car at a meter in the square. Damned lucky getting one. London traffic is infernal. Anyhow, Penelope pinned me and I couldn't get away."

Christa smiled at him over the rim of her glass. Tam was wiping that big pink baby face of his with a large silk handkerchief. He was always complaining of the heat.

"What a wonderful title for a book!" she murmured – "*Penelope Pinned Me*."

Tam gave his rich chuckle.

A waiter handed them two enormous menus.

"Shall we order?" suggested Tam, "Then go to our table after drinks."

As a rule Christa ate a simple meal in the small café frequented by most of the office staff. This was different. The Empress was full of famous people. The menu was superb. This meant smoked salmon and Chicken Maryland, fresh peaches in brandy and iced hock. Tam insisted. Tam couldn't have been more attentive. Toward the end of the lunch he helped her off with the short jacket she was wearing. His arm rested against her neck for an instant and she felt him gently pulling her closer. His voice took on a caressing note.

"This is marvellous, Christa," he said. "We ought to have done this long ago. Being with you is as refreshing as dipping one's finger into a sparkling brook. You are an adorable person, my dear little secretary – you really are."

She edged gingerly away from the big man.

"Mr. Davis —" she began.

"Can't I be 'Tam' while we are out together?"

The brilliant colour that so fascinated him, flooded her face. She had the most beautiful fair hair he had ever seen and that tiny black velvet bow was most enticing. Not that she seemed to realize it – she wasn't the type of girl to entice any man consciously.

He continued on a serious note:

"Well, can't we dispense with office formalities?"

"I don't think it would be wise."

"Who wants to be wise?"

"You do – very often. And especially in the morning after you have been unwise."

He threw back his head and laughed, at the same time pulling a cigar from his pocket.

"How sensible you are."

"Not in the least. But —"

86

"No doubt the heart has its reasons," he broke in lightly. Tell me your reasons for wanting to stay on the Mr. Davis-Miss Coombe level when we are alone."

"I don't think it matters because I don't think we are likely to be out on our own very often," she said drily.

He pierced the end of his cigar, lit it, puffed at it, then looked sideways at her through the fragrant smoke.

"So you haven't enjoyed lunching with me?"

"Of course I have. It's been wonderful. I think it's the most beautiful restaurant I have ever been in," she said earnestly looking around the handsome crowded room with its attractive gallery.

"The place is attractive to you but I'm not?"

"Mr. Davis – you're joking."

"I repeat what I said. You've enjoyed the lunch but not being alone with me?"

Christa turned and looked up at Tam with those large grey eyes which gave so little away, he thought; so fascinatingly little.

"If you must know – I *have* enjoyed being with you," she said. "You're a wonderful host. Marvellous."

"'Wonderful' – 'marvellous'. Are those empty words or do you mean them, my little Sphinx?"

She laughed at this name.

"Of course."

"Shall I tell you something, Christa?"

"What?"

"I want to hear you call me 'Tam' and not Mr. Davis."

"Tam," she repeated obediently, laughing again.

Now his fingers groped for her hand and folded over it. She was startled to see him looking at her quite seriously – without the usual grin that made the round boyish face look like a laughing cherub's.

"My giddy aunt, Christa," he said in a low solemn voice. "Something quite frightening and unusual has happened."

Her fingers moved nervously in his.

"What?"

An instant silence. Christa's heart beat faster, with nerves rather than emotion. *This* she hadn't expected. Temporarily it dumbfounded her. A waiter poured out some coffee for them. After he had gone, Tam spoke again:

"I want you to take me seriously, Christa. I'm not just trying to flirt with you or to have what you call one of my 'wows'.

You're not the wow-girl type. You're a strange, solemn and to me quite enchanting character. I never really know what you are thinking. I certainly don't know what you are feeling. There have been moments when I've even wondered if you have feelings. You've seemed just a damned efficient automaton. Then I watch that heavenly colour come into your cheeks and the way you suddenly look like a startled fawn – and I realize that you are full of feeling. Extremely sensitive, in fact. Christa, do you know you have the most beautiful grey eyes in the world?"

She gasped.

"Mr. Davis —!"

"Tam," he corrected her.

"Tam, then. You can't – you mustn't say things like that."

"And why not?"

"Because you mustn't."

Her fingers were struggling in his like an imprisoned bird.

"It's going to be most awkward," she went on.

"What is?"

"Oh you know exactly what I mean," she retorted quite angrily, "It won't do for us to get on to this sort of footing. I shall only have to leave the office if we do."

He continued to imprison her hand. He went on questioning her relentlessly.

"What sort of footing do you refer to?"

She began to stammer.

"You're impossible! You *know* what I mean. You're just a frightful flirt, and I don't want to be flirted with."

"I know I'm a frightful flirt and I am quite certain you don't want to be flirted with," he said in a strangely quiet voice, "but I happen to have no desire to flirt with you, Christa. When I told you just now that I had fallen in love with my secretary – I meant it."

"I don't believe that."

She had gone quite pale. He saw it. How right he was, he thought, to believe that Christa Coombe had depths of feeling that no man had ever yet plumbed. He felt suddenly very tender and full of the desire to be gentle and kind to her. He was also considerably stirred by the nearness of her slender young body and the trembling of her small yet surprisingly strong young hand. That was what attracted him – the fascinating mixture of strength and delicacy in this girl, both physical and mental. In her work she never seemed to put a wrong foot forward or forget anything. She showed a dogged devotion to duty. But for a long time now he had found himself anxious to get behind the mask she put on for the world. He was sure this façade was a kind of self-defence.

He said:

"Christa, I'm not just fooling. I know the list of girls I have been out with is a yard long, and you are well aware of it. You've had to help me out of several difficulties, which I appreciate. You've probably got a bad impression of me. But right inside me, darling, I'm a serious chap. I've always intended to settle down and get married, only up till now I've been too busy. I haven't honestly had time to do more than fool around. But I have at long last made my choice. And I hope you'll take me seriously, as I want you to. I love you and I am asking you to marry me."

Christa was stunned. She had thought 'The Boss' was a 'terror' with the girls but by no means a cad. Too kind to want to hurt anybody. Some of the 'wows' he got tangled up with were far less kind – *and* all out for themselves. But that he should take *her*, Christa, seriously and actually want to *marry* her . . . that staggered her. Despite all her protests and arguments he went on saying it. He kept her there in the Empress trying to make her accept him. It was long after she should have been back in the office from lunch.

Christa could well believe that Tam would settle down and make a good husband. His sort usually did. Instead of being a hard-worked secretary without a home of her own, she could live in a big flat in Eaton Square, enjoy Tam's sophisticated life with him. Amongst other things he said:

"I suggest we get married by special licence – straight away if you'll have me – fly over to Paris for the first week of our honeymoon then go on to Majorca. I'd like to take you to my favourite hotel in Palma. It's glorious at this time of the year. The bathing is out of this world!"

She remained silent. Tam offered her so much materially. And she liked and respected him too. He kept telling her he loved her and that she was the only girl to whom he had ever proposed marriage, and when she asked why, and said that she couldn't understand his wanting to marry such an insignificant little person as herself, he tried to tell her that she wasn't as insignificant as she made out, and that she happened to appeal to everything in him. Then of course, up came the name of Stephen.

'S. H.', as Tam called the Director . . . "S. H. told me when he first mentioned your name that you were an unusual sort of girl. He was dead right. I can't actually think why he didn't keep you in Paris for himself."

That was the precise instant when the world which had been spinning around Christa all the time Tam kept up his emotional bombardment, came to a standstill. It was as though all that was locked away in the depths of her heart suddenly surfaced at the very mention of *that name*. Now there fell upon her a crushing sadness. She sat still, letting Tam ramble on. He offered her the earth – *his* earth – and begged her to 'think things over'.

"I expect I've scared you. You look scared as hell, poor poppet," he said tenderly. "I'm sorry, I ought to have led up to this far more tactfully. I haven't been very clever. It is the one time when I haven't – maybe because I am truly in love with you and afraid of losing you. Please, Christa darling, don't turn me down out of hand. Think it over quietly and tell me tomorrow. Or if you like, come out with me again tonight for dinner. We could talk some more and get to know each other a bit better."

She stared blindly at the people around them. She felt as though her entire being had been pierced through by the arrow of remembrance. The remembrance of Paris and Stephen and what he had grown to mean to her and how every fresh meeting with him since she returned to London had sharpened her hopeless desire and thrust her farther into the darkness of despair. For to love Stephen meant utter misery for her. She barely existed for him; she knew that. For him she never would exist except as a girl to whom he had just been kind and who was now a member of his London branch.

"Christa – what have you got to say to me?"

She looked up into the beaming blue eyes with their ridiculously long curly lashes, and realized in a way why girls fell for Tam. He was extraordinarily lovable. Yet she could not marry him. As a friend he was wonderful. But as a husband he had no appeal for her.

She tried to tell him this, stuttering a little.

"I'm t-terribly honoured – it's f-frightfully good of you to want to marry me – I mean – oh, please don't think me ungrateful – I just don't want to marry you, Tam. But I respect and like you as a friend so much. You're marvellous really —"

She broke off. He saw her underlip quivering and knew that

she was near to tears. He knew too, that the most extraordinary thing had happened to him – Tam Davis. The playboy-cum-business man who had never before been serious about a woman, had just been turned down by the one and only girl to whom he had ever proposed marriage. He felt stricken, yet somehow his sense of humour prevailed and with it his sense of kindliness towards this rather timid and enchanting young girl who had wound herself around his heart without meaning to; without trying. His fingers pressed hers in a warm reassuring way.

"Darling little thing, don't look so tragic and please don't worry about me. I can 'take it', although it is a hefty blow. I somehow hoped you might care for me a bit or, at least, come out with me tonight and talk about it again."

"No – not tonight, and please, Tam, let's go on being good friends," she said earnestly. "Oh Tam, I don't want to have to leave Parfum Joyeux!"

He released her hand, leaned back and took a deep breath of his cigar.

"My sweet little Sphinx, I haven't the slightest intention of allowing you to leave Parfum Joyeux. S.H. was absolutely right when he said you made the perfect secretary. You may not want to marry me, but don't take my invaluable P.A. away from me *please*."

Her small face looked crimson and troubled. She chewed nervously at her lips.

"Oughtn't I to leave?"

"No. You're going to forget I ever proposed to you and we'll remain jolly good friends. Eh what?"

His eyes were smiling at her in such a friendly happy fashion that it was a bit difficult for Christa to know whether he was truly upset or just taking rejection in his stride. Nobody could know what went on in anybody else's mind and heart.

Her hands were still shaking. Tam's proposal had come as a shock. Now the big moment was over and Tam was talking airily about future changes in the firm.

He was going up to Edinburgh with S.H. next week, he said. Mrs. Brand, the most senior employee of the London office after Tam, would be in charge. Tam was sure that Christa could cope with the correspondence, and he'd be on the end of the phone if she needed him – staying at the Caledonian Hotel. Had she ever been to Edinburgh? Tam liked Edinburgh. He was a Scot by birth, but he had been brought up in England. He put her completely at her ease. She, herself, was laughing and talking again by the time he had signed the bill and they left the Empress. But she felt rather as though she had been run over by a steam roller. It had left her a bit flattened.

It was only later in the middle of the afternoon's work that she had time to lift her gaze from her desk, think about Tam's proposal and realize all that she had refused. She began to feel depressed. Not because she regretted making the refusal but because of the bleak outlook. She might possibly never marry, she reflected. It wouldn't be much fun to live and die an old spinster in some room, alone with a cat, or a dog, and an old-age-pension! It would have been so marvellous to have an attractive husband and lots of children and a home of her own. She could have had all this with Tam. But she just knew it was impossible for her to marry without love. More especially because Stephen Harrimay had set a standard so high, and become so godlike in her estimation, that no other man could come up to him.

The buzzer went, summoning her to Mr. Davis's room. When she entered she found that the Director, himself, had come in and was sitting on one side of Tam's desk. The sight of the tall rather graceful figure, and the dark leonine head, made her cheeks go pink. Her whole body seemed to quiver.

Stephen gave her a charming smile.

"Hello. How are you?"

"Very well, thank you, Mr. Harrimay . . ." Her voice was quite cool and formal, like her use of his surname. Then she caught Tam's eye and she was relieved to see the old roguish twinkle in them. At least she had not lost his friendship, she thought gratefully.

Stephen said:

"Mr. Davis and I have been talking over a few business items. It looks to me as though the A.G.M. of the firm will take place in Paris at the end of October -- the 30th in fact. There is also to be a conference of perfume-manufacturers in Cannes on the 31st."

Christa stood listening attentively, watching Stephen. He went on:

"Now there's also to be a reshuffle of personnel, Christa. Much as we shall miss Tam Davis in London, we directors think it is a good thing if he goes up to Scotland and stays there while the Edinburgh factory gets going. This possibly means that he will be there for six months."

"Och ay!" put in Tam with a rich rolling Scots accent. His baby face took on a comical look of tragedy. "I'm being booted out of my nice warm office in Hanover Square and sent into the cold cold blast of Princes Street."

Christa clasped her hands behind her back suddenly, digging the nails into her palms.

Oh, God, she thought, they're going to ask me to go up to Edinburgh with Tam where I shall never never see *him*. Oh, how awful!

It was positively the worst moment of her life. She couldn't say 'no' if she were really a loyal employee of Parfum Joyeux, and if it was Stephen's wish that she should be transferred.

Stephen continued:

"Yes, it's quite a reshuffle for us all. Monsieur and Madame Roché will tackle the Paris branch and I'm going to make my headquarters here in town. If you like to stay with me as my personal secretary, do, of course, Christa. But I could, on the other hand, send you up to Edinburgh with Mr. Davis."

Silence. In an agony of embarrassment Christa stood looking at the two men. Then she thought that Tam did the nicest thing in his life; she knew that he might want her to go to Edinburgh with him. But he also seemed to realize that it would be awkward for *her* in the circumstances; in a strange city where she would have no friends and be so entirely dependent upon him. He said:

"I think it would be better for Christa to stay on here with you, S.H., as she knows the London ropes so well now. I'll find some tough freckled Scots lassie wi' a bonny ta-r-r-rtan to gladden my eye and look after me. Not that she'll be as bonny as our Miss Coombe, bless her little heart!"

Christa felt enormously grateful. She wanted to run across the room and throw her arms round Tam's neck and kiss him right there in front of Stephen. Her heart sang. She felt deliriously absurdly happy and excited. This was *too* marvellous. Stephen was coming here permanently and *she* was to become his P.A. It would be just like that wonderful week in Paris over again.

She tried to regain her composure but found it hard. It was a starry-eyed Christa who said:

"Of course I would rather live in London near my adopted aunt and cousin, Barbara."

That was only half the truth. Much as she loved Aunt Cath and Barby, it was really that she wanted to stay near *him*.

Stephen gave her a slightly dubious look, she thought, and asked:

"And how is the beautiful Barbara?"

"More beautiful than ever," said Christa generously. "And she was only saying the other night that she hoped you would be able to finish that head one day."

"Well, I can now that I'm going to be in London permanently. Are you on the phone at Wood Green? Give me the number. I'll ring Barbara one day."

Christa wrote the number down and handed it to Stephen. She felt elated because he had even remembered the place where she lived. Completely unconscious as to how she felt about him, Stephen then commented upon her air of good health. The child looked radiant, he thought.

"Working for our firm seems to suit you." he said lightly.

"Oh, it does, it does!" said Christa.

Tam Davis, swallowing his own bitter pill of disappointment, gave one of his rich chuckles.

"You'd never think how hard I work the poor girl, either. Kept going till all hours."

"She'll be complaining to her Union," Stephen was still talking on a light note. Then he added: "Now, back to work, Tam. That will be all, Christa. We've put you in the picture. The switch over won't be for another fortnight anyhow, when Mr. Davis moves up to Scotland. Otherwise your work will be unaltered. Oh, with one little addition – you started with a salary of twelve guineas a week. I know you have been overworked and that you've responded very nobly to the many emergencies, and done very well. When you start with me, your salary will be raised another three guineas. All right?"

"Oh yes, thank you *very* much, Mr. Harrimay!" she exclaimed.

She walked out of the room as though treading on air. As the door closed on the slim neat figure, Stephen said:

"Extraordinarily nice girl, that. She was utterly wasted as a typist at Golling & Nash. She brings quite a bit of intelligent thought into her job which is a lot more valuable than good shorthand or typewriting. Besides which, as they said in Paris, when she took old Maydew's place, she never gets rattled. She goes calmly on. And she's got an astonishing memory. She caught on to Maydew's work in twenty-four hours."

"You've said it all," agreed Tam. Then suddenly the big cheerful young man blurted out what he really felt about Miss Coombe.

"I don't mind telling you, S.H., it's just as well I'm taking the high road and she's staying on the low. I've been fool enough to fall in love with her."

Stephen gave his London Manager a startled look.

"Good gracious me, Tam."

"Yes. Don't ask me why. She isn't at all dazzling. It's just something one can't define about her. Yes, that's it – an indefinable quality and of course those big grey eyes *get* me."

"'Send you', my dear fellow, I believe is the modern way of putting it," said Stephen humorously but added on a more serious note: "I'm sorry if things haven't gone well for you."

"So am I. But it's the luck of the game. She didn't pull any punches. She just told me outright that she couldn't consider marrying me."

"I'm surprised, I must say. I'd have thought she'd have jumped at it."

"You flatter me. But I dare say I appear a fat old so-and-so to that young thing. It always surprises me that she's so mature in her job. At other times she strikes me as being a complete child."

Stephen tried to reorientate his thoughts entirely from business to Christa. Surprised though he was by what Tam had told him, he had to admit that little Christa Coombe had haunted his own thoughts – if not in quite the way she filled Tam's. But he had often thought about her. Remembered only too well her strange elusive charm *and* the nostalgic beauty of that Nordic hair. Strangely enough Dorella was fading completely into the limbo of forgotten things. Her image had been superimposed upon Christa – and with it, the memory of a boy's hopeless passion had vanished.

Queer thing, fate. And it must have been sheer fate that led him on to the train from Dieppe to Paris, and involved him in that accident which brought those two girls into his life.

He said, on a note of curiosity:

"Is there another chap somewhere on the horizon for her, do you suppose?"

"I've sometimes thought it though she has never told me so. But she's very close. I call her the Sphinx."

"H'mm H'mm," said Stephen – and wondered.

Christa caught her usual bus back to Wood Green that

95

night, her mind in a positive whirl. She, who had once felt herself to be a little nobody right in the background of things had this day received a proposal of marriage from the Boss. Her salary had been raised (which she badly needed). And she was going to be Stephen Harrimay's secretary.

She couldn't wait to tell Aunt Cath and Barbara.

12

"You must be round the bend!" said Barbara.

Christa looked unhappily at her friend. She could see that Barby was in one of her worst moods. She had been on her feet all day modelling new hats and showing them in the new penthouse restaurant. She was tired. She was bitterly jealous because Christa had told her that she was to become *his* secretary when he took over the London office. She obviously felt it was crazy of Christa to have turned Tam Davis down.

Up and down the lounge, Barbara walked, with her pantherine tread. She always looked wonderful, Christa thought – even like this in the old pair of slacks and cotton shirt into which she had changed when she got home. She had just set her hair and tied it up in a chiffon scarf. She had also creamed her face. Yet in spite of the greasy skin and no make-up, she looked classically lovely. Christa felt no envy – only that inevitable inferiority complex when she caught sight of her reflection in the mirror over the mantelpiece and thought her own face so insignificant after Barbara's.

Mrs. Lane sat in her usual arm-chair sewing a button on one of Barbara's jackets. She had already prepared tonight's supper. It would be ready in half an hour.

Catherine Lane was tall and thin like her daughter but with none of Barby's brilliant beauty. She had thin, poor hair, turning grey now, and hazel eyes. It was from Barby's father that *her* looks had come. He had been one of the most handsome men Catherine Lane had ever known; with the dark auburn hair and brown eyes of his Cornish mother. Barbara's fiery temperament came from her father too – yes, from poor

Oliver, Catherine Lane thought, recalling her dead husband. And now she suspended needle in air and watched Barbara working herself up into one of her 'states'. Oliver, too, had been permanently discontented – fed up with his own life; disappointed because he had never made good, but lived and died an underling in the Civil Service.

He had loved her in his way, but it was Catherine who had done all the real loving, and who had the warm heart. She would have followed her husband blindly over the edge of a cliff, if he'd asked her. To him, she had been just the woman he married and of whom he had soon grown tired, and who cooked for him well, slaved for him in fact, and saved for him. At times he had hardly bothered about her. But their pretty little girl he had adored and spoiled.

Now Barbara at times did not seem to bother much about her mother. It was from Christa that Catherine Lane received the warm love and sympathy that she missed in her own home. Her dear adopted niece! How fond she was of the child, and how delighted she had felt because lately Christa seemed to have blossomed into a much happier and more confident person than she used to be. And nobody had been better pleased than Catherine Lane when fate had stepped in that summer holiday and directed Christa's life into new and more successful channels. But it seemed a tragedy that Barby should have fallen so much in love with this wretched Mr. Harrimay. He obviously had little use for her.

Like Christa, Mrs. Lane had once or twice tried to quench the fire of this hopeless passion and make Barby realize that she did not come into the orbit of Stephen Harrimay's thoughts But the girl seemed possessed – and she had the sort of tenacity and blind obstinacy that makes human beings fight madly and stupidly for the unobtainable. She did not accept the fact that Stephen Harrimay would have none of her. She kept declaring that he was only waiting his time, and that he would soon send for her, and complete the model of her head. She even believed quite sincerely that eventually he would fall victim to her beauty.

Her good looks were rather fatal, the mother thought sadly. They seemed to get her some place – yet nowhere, really. She attracted the wrong sort of men. She was always being rung up and taken out, then she would come home, having turned her nose up at whichever young man had fallen seriously for her. She was so hopelessly ambitious. That was the trouble. Stephen Harrimay was the incarnation of all she had ever desired – and she would not be diverted from him.

At first she had sulked when Christa started to work for Parfum Joyeux, then seemed to get over it and was glad of the contact with Stephen. She was always asking Christa *when* she had seen him, and *if* he had asked after her, Barby, and so on.

But this evening she was at her worst.

Why had Christa been so idiotic as to turn Tam's proposal down?

"You've never had a proposal before. You were offered a big position, money, and a marvellous time – I hear they are very gay in Edinburgh – and you'd travel, too. Then you chuck it all away. Oh, what a little fool you are, Chris; and a selfish one, too."

Christa looked at the other girl, stunned.

"Selfish?" she echoed. "But how?"

"Well, look what it would have done for Mummy and me," exclaimed Barbara, lighting a cigarette and flinging the match into the empty grate with an angry flick of her wrist, "if you'd become Mrs. Davis and had money. You could have done a lot for us – asked me to stay – and what's more, through Tam Davis, got me a better job. And I'd have had far more chance of meeting *him* whenever I stayed with you."

Catherine shook her head at her daughter. The mother had a sense of humour left, if little else, and now she laughed.

"Hold on, Barby darling – you're going a bit far. I really don't see why poor Christa should marry some man just in order to give *us* a good time and make *your* way easier."

"You don't understand me. You never have!" cried Barbara turning on her mother.

It was at times like this that Christa, with complete selflessness and out of genuine love for these two, acted very successfully as peacemaker.

"Oh, but *I* understand you, Barby!" she said, "and I know Aunt Cath does, only she is trying to be kind to me. Believe me, I understand that it would be a jolly good thing for everybody if I married Mr. Davis, only I'm just not built that way. I'd do anything in the world for you and Aunt Cathy, Barby, but I couldn't marry a man I didn't love."

"And I," put in Mrs. Lane, "no matter how cross you are for my saying so, think it dreadful of you, Barby, to suggest that Chris should sacrifice herself for us. It's really very naughty of you. What would you say if she married Mr. Davis and gave you a marvellous time, and helped you to see lots of Mr. Harrimay, and then you saw her being miserable!"

Barbara cooled down. Her passionate outbursts were generally short-lived. While they consumed her, she seemed to lose all control and reason. But in her heart she knew that she was wrong, and she was remorseful for making these two people who loved her and were always good to her, so miserable. In an altered voice, she said:

"Oh, I dare say I'm the one who is round the bend – not Christa. Life seems to send me cuckoo these days. I'm sorry. Obviously I don't expect Chris to marry a man she doesn't care for, for *my* sake. I was just being fatuous."

Christa put her arm round her friend's shoulder.

"Anybody would go round the bend after a long day at Golling & Nash – don't I know it! I realize it all the more nowadays that I am so well placed with Parfum Joyeux, and it's such a pity, because I really do like Tam but I —"

She pulled herself up with a jerk, her cheeks flaming. She had been about to add *"but I happen to be in love with Stephen . . ."* That was the last thing she could ever tell Barbara in the circumstances.

Mrs. Lane put away her sewing.

"Let's eat," she said brightly. "I've got a lovely piece of haddock for you, girls, and I've done it in milk. I'll poach some eggs to go with it."

Barbara drew a long sigh as she looked after her mother's retreating form.

"Poor Mummy! To her, the highlight of the day is having found a nice piece of haddock. That's what kills me – I'm so terrified *I* shall fall into the same ghastly rut."

"But you won't!" Christa soothed her. "One day somebody wonderful will come along and take you out of all this —"

"Pity Tam Davis didn't propose to *me*," said Barbara with a brief laugh.

Christa stared.

"But would you have accepted, even though you are in love with another man?"

"No, I wouldn't," said Barbara, climbing down. "I only said that. It's Stephen I want. Only Stephen."

Christa moved to the window. She looked out at the darkening street. It was a fine September night with a hint, perhaps, of the chill autumn evenings ahead. She shivered and moved back into the cosy, well-lit lounge. She was so fond of this room which had been like home to her for so long. It was shabby but the pale curtains and yellow Wilton carpet were in good taste. They had been bought when Barbara's father was alive and there had been more money to spend. Barbara had the taste. Out of her own money, she had bought some of the attractive lampshades and ornaments. The television was hired – Christa helped every week towards it. And lately they had all three joined forces and redecorated the walls in this attractive contemporary paper with its pattern of green tropical leaves. Rather exotic (to please Barby's eye more than Aunt Cath's) but Christa liked it.

Every evening she came straight here, washed and changed into slacks and ate her high tea with the family. She had to turn out later and go three doors down the road to sleep. There just wasn't a bed for her in Mrs. Lane's home. But the arrangement had worked out well and Christa always felt one of the family. It upset her because Barbara was so unhappy. She did not want her to hitch her wagon to the wrong star. Stephen could never never really come into her life. It was a worry to Christa when Barbara began to bombard her with questions about him. How did he look? What did he say about *her*? Was he interested in finishing that head?

Christa sighed and answered with as much detail as she could although it was not agreeable to her. Oh dear, she thought, what a hopeless position – she, herself, being so much in love with the same man. The only good thing was that Barbara didn't seem to guess.

With some reluctance, she quoted Stephen's actual words about her friend.

"*And how is the beautiful Barbara?*"

Barbara swung round, her eyes shining.

"Did he really say that?"

"Yes."

"Then he *hasn't* forgotten me, and he really *does* admire me!"

"Of course," repeated Christa a trifle sulkily.

"What did you say?"

"That you were more beautiful than ever."

"You *swear* you said that?"

Christa began to feel cross.

"Yes, I did. Oh, do let up, Barby!"

"Why? I'm only asking you what he said about me. What's biting *you*?"

Afraid that Barby might begin to suspect the truth, Christa controlled herself.

"Nothing. I'm – just tired. What with all this affair of Tam and the proposal and – and everything – I'm worn out."

"Did he mention seeing me again?" persisted Barbara.

"Stephen?"

"Yes, yes," said Barbara impatiently.

"M'm," nodded Christa. "He said that now he was going to be in London permanently, he might phone you and suggest a time for you to sit for him, so that he could finish the head."

"Oh! How *terrific*!"

Barbara was on her feet now, and after throwing her cigarette-end into the grate, lifted her arms above her head and stretched voluptuously.

"I know I've not been completely wrong. He *is* interested in me. Oh, Chrissie, thank you for telling me."

Christa could not bring herself to reply. The whole thing was getting on her nerves. But Barbara seemed happy and relaxed again.

She apologized for her display of temper; she kissed Christa; she chatted excitedly about the expected telephone-call; where she would be asked to go for the sitting – what a darling Christa was for telling him that she looked more beautiful than ever; on and on until Christa began to feel she could bear no more. She went upstairs.

In Barbara's bedroom she switched on a light and sat brushing her hair. Staring into the mirror she felt as though she looked at a ghost – she looked so tired and pale, with enormous eyes. This dual passion which she and Barbara shared, each in their different way and so differently expressed, was dreadful, she thought. Quite dreadful. She wished to God that it had all never happened. It was fast becoming a nightmare. Barbara's constant coaxing or bullying and trying to make her pave the way for Stephen to meet her was really intolerable. And it destroyed all the joy Christa had felt earlier this afternoon when she had been asked by Stephen to stay on with him in London as his personal secretary.

Worse was to come for Christa later that evening, for that call from Stephen came through for Barbara after they had finished eating.

Christa was then in the kitchen with Aunt Cath, doing the washing-up. Barbara was in the lounge, ironing. She was in such a good mood she had offered to iron a shirt-blouse for

Christa, which Aunt Cath had this morning taken out of the washing machine.

The telephone bell rang. Somehow Christa had a feeling about that call. Then she heard Barbara's rich exciting voice:

"Hullo, Stephen – wonderful to hear from you."

Christa stopped drying the dish in her hand. She had to listen now. *She had to.* She did not know what Stephen was saying but she could guess. He was making an appointment with Barbara. She heard Barbara say:

"Yes, I'd adore it of course. I can't wait to see the head finished . . . What's that? Meet you on Sunday? Yes, I think I can. Yes, I'm *sure* it'll be all right. Wait a minute, and I'll get a pencil and write down the address." And then . . . "Oh yes, your flat in St. James's Street and Christa knows the address. Yes, of course . . . I'll ask her . . ."

Christa closed and unclosed her eyes. The vibrant passion in Barbara's voice appalled her. She didn't *want* Barbara to feel like this. She wished Stephen had not made contact again but of course he was an egotist like any other man (like most artists!). He wasn't concerned with Barbara's feelings. He just wanted to complete his work. Besides he couldn't possibly know how madly Barbara had fallen in love with him.

Christa shut the kitchen door almost violently, refusing to listen to any more. Then Barbara burst into the kitchen, looking glorious, Christa thought. Radiant with excitement and pleasure. How could any man, even Stephen, fail to be attracted by all this glamorous perfection? And supposing he *did* eventually fall in love with Barbara?

"I'd have to be pleased," Christa told herself, "I'd have to say I was *glad*."

She went on with the drying-up, doggedly, while Barbara told her that she was to sit for Stephen on Sunday morning at his flat.

"I'd hoped I'd be alone with him, but he tells me one of his sculptor friends in London will be dropping in for coffee. He wants to see Stephen's latest work. He's some Scandinavian named Jorgensen, or something. Stephen thinks *he* might like to do a bust of me, too. He works in marble and is well known in Denmark."

"There you are," said Christa, "all these men want to model you."

Barbara gave a conceited laugh.

"It'll be amusing but I do hope I'll get a little time alone with Stephen."

Mrs. Lane looked at her daughter and removed the cigarette from her lips.

"All this business of wanting to be *alone* with Mr. Harrimay – what does it add up to, dear? What do you really expect?"

Barbara shrugged her shoulders.

"Anything might happen, my dear Mummy. You're so innocent."

"Really, Barby —" said Mrs. Lane, "I can't understand why you young girls always think the previous generation know nothing. I assure you, I may be fifty, but I've had my own experiences – I was never beautiful, but I had a good figure and I was not the prude you make out."

Barbara burst out laughing.

"Come and tell us your experiences, Mum, and when I get back from St. James's Street on Sunday, I'll tell you mine."

Christa walked out of the kitchen.

13

DURING the few weeks that followed, Christa came to the definite conclusion that there was something in that old saying that life is inclined to give you something with one hand and take away something else with the other.

She was not really permitted thoroughly to enjoy her renewed status as Stephen Harrimay's secretary. There were too many extraneous frustrations and annoyances to blunt the edge of her enjoyment. Even the good-bye with Tam was not easy. He left London for Edinburgh almost at once but insisted on taking Christa out for dinner the night before he left. He was as usual amusing and friendly but there was no real pleasure for her either in the excellent dinner or the outing. He took her to The Society to eat and dance. He was a good dancer, was Tam, but she afterwards wished she had not gone out with him at all because he seemed more than ever in love with her. At times he showed his deep depression because of her lack of response and she fancied that a sad wind chilled the warmth of the evening and destroyed the friendliness of the atmosphere. She learnt the unpalatable lesson that there is rarely hope of friendship between a man and a woman once one or the other has admitted being in love. Finally Tam told her that he would always adore her, and that any time she wanted to change her mind she could 'nip up to Edinburgh'. But she had the feeling that after he was gone they would never again meet on the old care-free pleasant footing.

To crown all, just before midnight Stephen Harrimay came into the restaurant with Felise Markell. This was by no means the sort of place that Stephen usually chose for dinner but Felise liked dancing and it was she who had chosen The Society, after she had been with Stephen to a private musical *soirée*.

It was the first time that Christa had seen Felise after she left Paris. Much water had flowed under the bridge since then. Felise might be the same person but Christa definitely was not. The two girls greeted each other in that watchful way of two women who have no use for each other but they exchanged 'hellos' with apparent warmth.

"How *nice* to see you again . . ." from Felise, in her honey-sweet voice.

"How are you, Miss Markell?" from Christa, politely.

And from Stephen:

"Well, well – *here's* an unexpected meeting! Tam, you old so-and-so, I didn't expect to find you here hitting it up with my secretary! I expect you've made her dance every dance, knowing your terpsichorean passion. She'll be falling asleep over her shorthand-pad in the morning."

"Not I," said Christa, "I'm fresh as a daisy."

"She looks rather like Bobbie Burns's daisy, comes to that," said Tam with a show of cheerfulness in front of his chief. (He had met Felise Markell before in Paris and knew that it was an accepted fact that there might one day be a 'thing' between Stephen and this girl.) Tam continued:

"'*Wee, modest, crimson-tipped flower*' rather describes Christa, as a matter of fact."

Christa grimaced.

"I don't mind being called 'crimson', but I can't stand that old Victorian word 'modest'. It makes one sound like someone out of a Victorian ark."

"Well, you look very charming," said Stephen.

Felise put her tongue in her cheek. She was glad that the head waiter was beckoning them now to their table. Felise had only arrived in London this morning. She had been looking forward to going out with Stephen again. Of course she had heard from Julia that he was quitting the Paris branch and remaining in London. This hardly pleased Felise. But it had been a satisfying coincidence from her point of view that she should have just been given the chance of a series of piano recitals on B.B.C. television. It meant that she, too, would be in London for a while, and she intended to make good use of her time. She would see a lot of Stephen.

She was not really jealous of a young girl like Christa – a 'typist' as Felise called her – who was in her eye, a nonentity; however she had felt a little *bouleversée* after hearing that Christa was now a permanent employee of Parfum Joyeux London, and working directly for Stephen.

While the two girls stayed at Julia's flat after their accident last June, Felise had suspected that Stephen, the sculptor, was interested in Barbara, as a model. But later on Felise wondered whether it wasn't Christa whom she should fear – a *little*, anyhow.

The young girl was looking attractive tonight. She had improved out of all recognition since the early summer. That severe sleeveless dress of black pleated chiffon, high at the front and low at the back, was drawn in at the tiny waist by a wide velvet belt. It made her hair and skin look dazzlingly fair. Her thick truant hair was smoothed back with a black velvet bandeau.

She wore no jewellery except a gold cross and chain which somehow gave her a curiously virginal and dramatic look of which she was certainly unconscious.

Where on earth did she buy that beautifully tailored dress, Felise wondered, and it was only after she got home that she suddenly burst out laughing, remembering that she had seen the black pleated chiffon many times before – on Madame Roché. Julia had charitably passed on so many of her 'cast-offs' to those two girls. To Felise it was really rather funny. But that night at The Society the little London typist certainly looked as though she had walked straight out of an *haute couture salon*.

Stephen was in a good mood. Business was going well and he was even looking forward to taking over the London branch As for Felise, he had as usual enjoyed the company of the young French pianist at an excellent concert. He was always aware of her feminine attraction as well as her musical talent, yet strangely enough she did not move him deeply nor ever had done. It was quite a pity, he thought.

What was it that really attracted a man? Certainly not mere looks. No – it was that indefinable *something* called 'charm' . . . that strange alchemy that binds inexplicable spells over men and women, forges unbreakable links – *and* causes half the trouble in the world.

Just such a spell had enslaved Stephen when he fell in love with Dorella. Now his heart seemed touched by the sight of Christa's hair and radiant fairness tonight; enhanced by the exquisite simplicity of the dress that revealed the slender lines of her *petite* figure. She was definitely stimulating to his senses. But he was out with Felise, he reminded himself, and Christa was with Tam. Besides which, Christa was his secretary and it wouldn't be a good thing for him to start 'getting ideas' about her. He never would, of course. He was far too busy to allow himself to become interested in any woman for more than a few minutes.

He bade Tam and Christa 'good night' and moved on to his table with Felise. Soon after that Christa and Tam left The Society.

Tam drove her home in the Austin-Healey, chatting as usual in his genial way. But she was inarticulate as she sat beside him; lost in her thoughts of Stephen – horrified because she found herself bitterly envying Felise Markell who would now be dancing in Stephen's arms. She was a lovely and wonderful pianist and an old girl-friend and *not* his employee (like herself).

How mixed up life could become! How utterly tantalizing, thought Christa.

That next day Tam left for Edinburgh.

Life went on in its hectic fashion at Parfum Joyeux. Christa grew used to hearing that buzzer that used to summon her to Tam's office but finding Stephen now at Tam's desk. Used to the thrill of it and the wild way in which her heart leapt whenever she answered the call and entered the room, knowing that he watched her walk across the floor, and occasionally looked up to smile at her as he dictated his letters. Used to exchanging the usual formalities with him; to discussing business, to taking his orders. Used to making his appointments for him – or breaking them. Yet never really accustomed, because her heart never agreed to slow down; yet she *knew* it was foolish and useless to allow the tempo to quicken-in such a way. In *his* eyes she was a machine like her typewriter, and must remain so.

She must be grateful for the privilege of being able to serve him, and content that life was so enriched by the mere shadow of his presence. So she expected nothing more – asked for nothing. It was a pleasant surprise when Stephen paused in his hectic hurried life to come down for a moment from the pedestal of 'The Boss' and ask her how she was, and what she was thinking.

"I often wonder what lies behind that calm brow and those big solemn eyes," he said on one occasion; and when she stammered and answered "*Nothing*," he laughed and looked at her again with a mixture of curiosity and amusement in his handsome eyes.

"Get away with you! All that cool unconcern and strangely youthful façade hide considerable intelligence and understanding, my dear. You're an exceptional secretary and you know it. You wouldn't be where you are if you weren't."

She felt quite sick with happiness at his praise.

"Thank you very much. I'm glad you approve of me."

"But I work you to death? Sometimes you're an hour late going home."

"I assure you I don't mind," she said fervently.

"No – that's what's so nice about you. You seem to have the good of the firm at heart – not only to be interested in the pay-packet."

"That is absolutely true," she said.

Her eyes were shining. She spoke with enthusiasm. But his mention of her being late home had reminded her rather unpleasantly of the trouble at Wood Green.

Barby, of course.

The gay Barbara had entirely vanished again, leaving sulks, tears and even bitterness. A bitterness toward her, Christa, which was undeserved and very hurtful.

It all started after Barbara returned from that sitting for the completion of Stephen's work.

When she came in Christa was busy doing her good deed of the week, which was to cook the Sunday dinner in order to give Aunt Cath a break. She liked to go to church in peace. Barbara, white and furious, flung her bag on to the table and launched into an attack upon the unfortunate Christa.

"You seem to have sneaked your way thoroughly into Stephen's favours and left me out of it. I just don't come in anywhere. He was as cool as an icicle. He asked me to sit down and then went on with the work, and even while he looked at me it was without any personal feeling. It was bad enough to have his friend, Jorgensen, there most of the time. They talked madly about sculptures and all their own affairs and behaved as though I was just a model, and an *un*paid one at that! I was offered a glass of sherry at the end of it. Then they called a taxi for me."

She broke off, her eyes stormy and full of tears. Christa who had just been basting the joint, put it back in the oven and stood up, wiping her hands on a tea towel, her heart sinking.

"I really don't know why you should go on at me," she said rather more coldly than she usually spoke to Barbara. She could stand just so much from her cherished friend and no more. One thing which Christa could never put up with was injustice. "I'm sorry if you haven't enjoyed the session but I don't see why you blame me. In any case 'The Boss' did not ask you to go just for a social get-together and I think if he had offered you money it would have been insulting. I just don't understand you."

Then Barbara burst into tears, which really alarmed Christa. Barby wasn't the type to cry easily. She broke into a fresh tirade.

She understood Christa, she almost shouted. She was a little hypocrite. Pretending to be so meek and mild but ever since she became an employee at Perfum Joyeux she had been angling for Stephen Harrimay's attention. Did *she* think she was going to break through that wonderful armour of his – get behind that cool steel of reticence he put up? – Did *she* think just because she was his P.A. and had turned down Tam Davis that she was a *femme fatale* who could get any man? If so, she was mistaken, and it was mean, *mean* of her not to have tried more to further Barbara's interests. Christa had done absolutely nothing. When Stephen took Barbara down in the lift to the flat entrance, he had mentioned Christa, and said how efficient and helpful she was to him (here Barbara's voice took on a sneer); had told her that he was sometimes worried because Christa appeared so pale and fragile, and he thought he overworked her (more sneers) and that he was going to take her down to the South of France next month because he would want his own secretary with him at this conference.

"You – *you* to go to Cannes with Stephen!" finished Barbara sobbing hysterically. "Not a thought for me!"

Christa stayed still – speechless. She was quite appalled by such an outburst yet although she resented Barbara's unkindness she could still find it in her heart to be generous and even sympathetic with her. Poor old Barby, she *had* got it badly. Christa, who herself loved Stephen so much could understand the force – the quite frightening force – of feeling and the accompanying frustration that must inevitably follow lack of requitement.

But Christa, apart from this, had just received an unexpected piece of good news that she had not known before. She was going to be asked to fly with her employer down to the South of France in October. That was news indeed, and she wouldn't have been human if it hadn't boosted her morale and brought her intense secret joy. But the joy was short-lived, because she could never bear the unhappiness of others and she was so desperately sorry for Barby. It seemed so terrible that a girl who was so beautiful should be making such a hash of her life. She just didn't seem able to act reasonably. A lot of it of course was the fault of the father now dead. Aunt Cath had often told Christa how hopelessly Oliver Lane used to spoil his pretty little daughter. Everything had been for the child. He fed her vanity without thought for the psychological consequence. When Barbara was five he had insisted on his wife entering the child for a beauty contest which she won easily. After that she had been photographed and flattered in public, and been taught that nothing mattered except her beauty, until she grew up believing that she was irresisitble.

But that had not been the case. She frightened men off – even the men who fell for her at first sight. She was much too eager – not for real love, but for admiration; Christa knew that. It had become a vice with Barbara. Perhaps it was why she had always been friendly with Christa – because in the beginning Christa used to flatter her, too, and kept in the background.

But now because Christa was coming into the foreground,

Barby was upset. Especially because of her crazy notion that she could, if encouraged, lure Stephen Harrimay into her toils.

"Oh, Barby —" began Christa coming towards the other girl with outstretched hands, meaning to kiss and comfort her and once again smother her own desires. But Barbara edged away – then with glittering eyes and flushed cheeks, dramatically declared that this was the *end*, and that if Christa didn't help her get Stephen, she would commit suicide.

Christa stepped back, her heart beating violently.

"Barby, how can you *say* such a thing? It's wicked for anybody to threaten to take their own lives and you know you wouldn't do it. You're only putting on an act."

"I'm not. I tell you I shall kill myself if I can't get Stephen. *You*'re all right. You've got everything. You're always with him and you're going to be more and more with him. It's damnable and I can't stand it."

"But Barby, you behave as though he had once led you to believe that he had fallen for you. I warned you in Paris that wasn't true."

Barbara glared.

"Maybe you think he has fallen for *you*!"

Christa froze, put down her tea towel and walked towards the kitchen door. She was trembling.

"You really are round the bend, Barby," she said.

At that moment Mrs. Lane came back from church in a nice peaceful Christian spirit, and found herself pitchforked into this unattractive scene between her daughter and her adopted niece. Deeply distressed, she started to try and deal with Barbara but soon realized that she had no control whatsoever over her beautiful wayward daughter, and never had had any. Barbara was sitting at the kitchen table, head on her arms, crying bitterly. Once again Christa climbed off her high horse and forgot her own injured feelings. She whispered to Auth Cath to leave them alone, then set to work to try and talk sense to Barbara.

"You really are a muggins, darling. Do try and be more rational and pull yourself together. How could you ever suggest that I thought Stephen Harrimay would ever look at *me*! Much less so than at you. I keep telling you he isn't interested in girls at all. He's wedded to the job and I'm just his paid secretary. He never notices *me* as a person."

Barbara was much too busy with her own feelings to notice the sadness in Christa's eyes. Christa went on:

"Darling Barby, please don't be so unhappy and don't ever *ever* talk about suicide again. You were only saying that for effect, weren't you? You couldn't possibly have meant it."

This was the stage at which Barbara simmered down and crawled rather abjectly out of the dark emotional ditch into which she had fallen. After a few moments she went up to her room, bathed her face, made up and came down looking as beautiful as ever except for her swollen eyelids. She was as Christa always remembered her after a scene – full of remorse and quite reasonable again.

"I didn't mean to be so nasty to you, honey. You are such a darling to me and I don't deserve it. And of course I know I am a fool about Stephen and I'm sure you have no designs on him. I suppose I was mad to think I could ever really attract him. It was just that his indifference toward me today drove me insane."

Christa was enormously relieved. She made a cup of tea and sat beside Barby while she drank it. Barbara, looking wan and sad, said:

"All I ask is that when you fly down to Nice with *him* for this Cannes conference, you'll put in a word for me."

"But how can I?" asked Christa, avoiding Barbara's dark hungry gaze.

Barbara made all kinds of suggestions; Christa could extol her virtues, she said, and tell him how many men fell for her, Barbara, and wanted to marry her; what a wonderful wife she would make for a man of means for whom she could entertain and look glorious. She even ended on a note of humour.

"You could say that it was a pity Tam Davis hadn't proposed to me instead of to you, because you've always been too romantic and wouldn't mind bread and cheese in a back flat, but that *I* was born to be the wife of a man of means, and so on."

To all this, Christa listened in silence. She didn't like it and she didn't think that Barbara was putting herself in a very good light. It all made her feel rather sick anyhow, knowing how she personally felt about Stephen. But Barbara had become affectionate and coaxing, and went on begging her to do all she could to bring about another meeting with Stephen.

To try to make him aware, at least, that Barbara found him so attractive. A few tactful clever hints would be enough, she said.

Unwillingly, Christa promised to do her best.

Then Aunt Cath came down for lunch and the unhappy scene was over. Barbara always seemed able to forget her outbursts and carry on as though nothing had happened, leaving everyone else exhausted. During lunch she was quite gay and making her mother and her friend laugh at her amusing stories about Stephen's Danish friend, who was rather an attractive man. Immensely tall and fair, Henrik by name.

"He wants to 'sculpt' me too. He has asked me to give him a sitting and suggested lunch one day. He studied art in Paris with Stephen when they were boys . . ."

Now the conversation was all about Henrik but when Christa mentioned the hope that Barbara would take advantage of this and go out with the handsome Dane, Barbara twisted her lips and threw Christa a meaning glance.

"Maybe I will, maybe not. But I still want you to do what I asked you: you understand, when you go to France, Chris."

Christa sighed.

"Yes, of course."

Mrs. Lane walked to the sink, lit her usual cigarette and shook her head as she turned on the tap.

"My goodness," she muttered to herself, "Barbara really can be trying and Christa's a little angel to her – to both of us, God bless her!"

14

During the week that followed, Christa had little time to think about Barbara's tantrums because she had her own difficulties to contend with at the office. Excellent though Tam Davis used to be at his job, Stephen found it necessary to make several changes after the 'take-over'.

Christa, working in close association with her new 'Boss', found also new facts of his character to note and admire. In

Paris he had swept in and out of the office like a whirlwind. In London he was not out so much.

The sudden threat of a strike at the Grasse factory necessitated constant telephone communication between Stephen and Paris. He was also busy working on a new advertising campaign which included Adela Brand, who managed that side. She was efficient but rather a dominant character – Stephen found her unattractive.

It was Christa who seemed to understand his requirements and cope with him when he was rushed. He had a lightning mind and expected others to be as quick-witted as himself. Christa never lost her nerve even when she had to face a sudden avalanche of work.

The junior typists held her in some respect. But Mrs. Brand could be as turbulent and awkward at times as Barbara. There was a complication of business which implicated Christa. A mistake in the orders of big supplies on the photographic side of Adela's department.

Mrs. Brand herself had drawn up the original scheme for the distribution of new leaflets advertising the perfume for London wholesalers. Stephen approved the layout and the prices. Christa has done the letters and later typed the draft for the contract. After it was too late to withdraw, it was found that five hundred pounds had been misspent because one particular order had been duplicated. In the end it was proved to be Adela Brand's fault but at first she lost her temper and accused Christa of an error in the actual copying. She tried to throw the blame upon the entire typists'-pool. This resulted in Christa, despite her dislike of such things, being forced to go to Stephen and justify herself. Stephen cleared her of blame. Mrs. Brand resigned. Christa had never really liked her and was relieved by her departure. The woman who took her place, Olga Jacobs – Jewish, dark, attractive and first-class at the job – had come to Parfum Joyeux from another big perfume manufacturer's where Adela was now working. Adela with some malice had, apparently, warned her against Mr Harrimay's private secretary.

Christa found herself being treated with a touch of cool disapproval by Adela's replacement. One morning she met Olga Jacobs, in the central hall when she arrived to work. She saw Olga glance at her wrist-watch.

"Ten o'clock, Miss Coombe? Did you oversleep?"

Christa turned red.

"No, I didn't, Mrs. Jacobs. I had to do a job for Mr. Harrimay on the way here."

"Oh really?" drawled Olga with a freezing smile.

It was nothing – but one of many pinpricks. Just another jealous woman.

Christa for the first time in her life found herself in a position that other women envied – but it had its drawbacks as well as privileges. Even one of the typists, Pat Westerham, who was a nice eighteen-year old with whom Christa had shared several cups of tea and a cigarette, said something one day to open Christa's eyes as to how the younger members of the staff regarded her. Pat had started to tell Christa that she wanted to go out for the day with a boy-friend who was on leave from the army, and that she must invent a dental appointment in order to get away, when suddenly she stopped talking and grimaced.

"Well, go on," smiled Christa.

"Not me! You'll tell the Boss and I'll lose my job. I forgot who I was speaking to."

Christa flushed.

"I wouldn't *dream* of repeating your confidences, Pat."

"Well, I'm not risking it. You can forget about my dentistry," Pat giggled.

Afterwards Christa came upon her whispering to one of the other typists, Jill West, as Christa walked in with some work for them they stopped talking abruptly. She was made to feel as if she were a spy. They didn't dare be too friendly with her because she was the Boss's P.A.

That sort of thing was unimportant but gave Christa a few headaches. It soon became plain to her that one couldn't be confidential secretary to a Big Man and find life all plain sailing.

The constant nagging from Barbara that she should try to arrange a meeting for her with Stephen went on relentlessly. Christa was never allowed to forget it and in itself it was nerve-racking. It spoiled things for Christa.

But life had its compensations. One afternoon in October Stephen relaxed at the end of the day's work and talked to Christa not as employer to secretary, but as friend to friend.

He wanted to know how she spent her spare time and what sort of interests she had outside the office. He seemed to become suddenly aware that she was looking off-colour.

"You really ought to take a holiday. You didn't get a proper one in Paris, you know."

"I did. I had a wonderful holiday and I don't want another one."

Stephen poured himself out a drink and offered Christa one. She refused. While he drank his and smoked one of his cherished cigars, he looked thoughtfully at his secretary. She was an amazing little person, he decided not for the first time – it seemed that she had the most amazing resources of energy and vitality to draw upon, yet her waist was tiny and her face so delicately drawn, she looked as though she might break in two if roughly handled. He had never seen such small fine bones. He had discovered a treasure when he took her on in old Maydew's place that day in Paris, he kept telling himself.

He said:

"My sister, Madame Roché, was asking after you on the phone the other day."

"How exceedingly kind of her," said Christa with a bright blush.

"Sit down, sit down. Don't stand there," he said. "I want to talk to you about our few days in Cannes. We're off in ten days' time, you know."

She had by now received official intimation of this trip but his confirmation this evening brought her a feeling of tremendous happiness. She had been so afraid that the arrangement might never come off.

"I am looking forward to it," she said. "It will be wonderful."

He looked at her with that sudden sweet smile of his. She smiled back, inwardly glowing. She adored him. She hated it when he looked absolutely spent as he did this evening. He was not as robust a man as Tam Davis who could work all day and play all night and not show it. Stephen Harrimay was highly strung – artist as well as business man. Who should know better than Christa who had worked with him through so many crises? There was always some fresh difficulty to be coped with in Big Business these days. Sometimes Christa wondered why Stephen bothered to work so hard since money was not his main objective in life. She knew that he sometimes wondered the same thing, because he had said so. But she presumed that it was largely for his sister who was heart and soul in this family business, along with her French husband.

"Of course you have never been to the Côte d'Azur, have you?" he asked Christa now.

"No."

He sighed:

"How wonderful to be so young and never to have seen the Côte d'Azur. The very thought of that makes me feel rather blasé. I shall quite enjoy seeing it through your uninitiated eyes, my dear child."

She burst out laughing.

"You make it sound as though you were old enough to be my father."

He laughed with her.

"No, I'm not that but you are extraordinarily young for your age – yet not in your work," he added hastily, "and that is why my sister remembers you and your efficiency. She says she hasn't employed a good English stenographer over there since you left."

"I can't believe that."

"You'd be surprised. It isn't that they can't type or take shorthand at fantastic speed, or that they aren't fully trained; it's just that *je ne sais quoi* that is required of a P.A. and which many miss. But you never get rattled and you never obtrude. Priceless assets!"

Something within her was singing . . . singing . . . and her pulses were beating fast to the rhythm of his praise. But she said quietly:

"Thank you. I don't feel I really deserve all that."

He thought:

"She's really a sweet creature – very sweet indeed." Aloud he said: "We're due in Paris on the 30th October. We fly down to Nice the next morning. There is going to be such a lot of paper-work due to the switchover here plus the new place in Scotland – I'll need a secretary with me all the time. Sure you want to come?"

She found it difficult not to show just how much she wanted it. She answered a little breathlessly:

"Of course. It will be a tremendous experience for me."

He got up from his chair and walked to the stand to fetch his coat.

"Just jot down this reminder – to ring up my friend Colonel Nye who runs the Cadogan Travel Company and who does most of our firm's Continental booking. Ask him to reserve us two seats on the 10 a.m. plane to Paris, and then on the morning *Caravelle* from Paris to Nice the following day."

Inwardly wildly excited, but still outwardly calm, Christa nodded.

"Yes."

"We shall be going down on the Thursday and I think we'll come back on the Monday morning. My sister wants me to stay over the week-end. It will be a chance for you to see the place and get some rest and sunshine. We're having quite good weather at the moment but the forecast is none too good here, so I reckon we're due for a timely fog in London."

"Yes," she repeated, watching him intently because he was no longer looking at her, but busy putting on the silk scarf which he always wore. She knew that scarf. She knew so many things about him. She loved him with all the power of her being, and without hope of return.

"The Paris office have booked our rooms at the Majestic in Cannes," he added. "I prefer it there to the Carlton where most of the chaps at the conference will be staying."

She was writing down everything he said. The next time she lifted her gaze to him he was standing in front of her hat and gloves in hand, looking pensive.

"Going straight home, Christa?"

"Yes, I nearly always do."

"Don't you ever have any fun? Is it all domestic chores for you, and television?"

"Not always. Sometimes Barbara and I go to a cinema or, if it's fine, take a walk in the Park."

He shook his head as though uncomprehending of her life and her world. He thought of his sister with every moment filled with the social round in Paris. Of Felise, who was now plunged into the world of television, entertaining and being entertained by her musician friends or producers. Lately he hadn't really seen much of Felise – he had been so tied up. Now suddenly he found himself wishing that he could relax right away from everybody he knew, with this soothing endearing girl, Christa – the person who was always here when he wanted her and who always seemed to do the right thing at the right moment.

In a slightly amused way he threw a glance at that wonderful hair which used to be a bone of contention. The Dorella-look no longer worried or distressed him. The memory of Dorella was fast fading. In a queer way, Christa Coombe had laid the ghost of the past. The thick fair hair was no longer Dorella's but *Christa's*, and hers alone.

"Do you remember," he said suddenly, "in Paris on that June night, how we stood on the Pont Royal and saw the stars dipping into the water, and the lights twinkling along the river-banks! How beautiful it was!"

"I remember it all," she whispered.

But, as though embarrassed by his revival of that memory, Stephen bade her an abrupt good night and walked out of the office.

She stood a moment with her notebook in her hand. She was tense and troubled. The shorthand notes were obscured. She felt quite blind – her thoughts were so chaotic. Yet she was in a state of blissful happiness because he had so much as recalled that evening's entertainment when he had shown her Paris.

Christa travelled home that October night in the usual discomfort – queued for her bus – and felt tired and rather damp in the drizzle which was just beginning to fall. But she was still in a daze – a world of her own, dominated by the thrilling memories of Stephen and of the exciting journey she was going to make.

It was only a short time before those ten days ended and the big moment came for Christa to leave London with Stephen.

Only ten days – but it seemed like ten years and she, who generally slept well, had wakeful restless nights and had been right off her food. Mrs. Lane observed it.

"What is the matter with you, Chris?" she kept asking. "You're not yourself."

Christa had tried to laugh this off but inwardly said:

"No, I'm not. I'm a girl in a dream – a wonderful dream and I'm terrified I may wake up."

She supposed that it was natural, when something absolutely marvellous is going to happen, you live in secret terror that it may never take place; that something will happen at the last moment to cancel it. Tension had mounted for her in office hours, too. Every time Stephen had pressed the buzzer for her, her heart would take a downward plunge and her hands grow cold when she walked into his room. Oh, she couldn't *bear* it if he were to say "*It's all off.*"

But Stephen didn't say it. And soon there came a dizzy hour for Christa when she packed her bag under Aunt Cath's surveillance.

Dear Aunt Cath! She had washed and pressed everything that Chris might need, and even Barby had been extra sweet and bought her a new silk scarf from Golling & Nash to wear on the plane. Barby knew all the answers to problems on 'chic'. It was more 'chic' to wear a scarf, she said, when you travelled by air, than a hat. But there would be Paris, first, so she must take *one*. Which? A breathless conference between Aunt Cath, Barby and herself. Finally Chris decided on the white felt beret which she had bought at a sale before she left Gollings, and which suited her piquante face. And to travel she would wear her grey suit with a white jersey and gilt necklace and ear-rings and her tweed coat.

Then when Christa was ready for the journey, Aunt Cath unconsciously made the most tactless of remarks and mentioned that it was quite like "seeing her off on a honeymoon". Just a joke. Christa went crimson. Barby looked down her nose and muttered coldly that "it wasn't funny".

Then Christa kissed them both good-bye, alternating between the wildest joy and unhappiness. At the office Stephen's car picked her up with 'The Boss' and drove them to London Airport.

"Honeymoon," Christa kept thinking with a wry smile. "What a hope! Poor old Aunt Cath! As for Barby, she looked as though she could kill me."

Poor Barby – eaten up with jealousy!

How completely her life had changed, Christa thought as she drove in that luxurious car toward Hammersmith and the Great West Road. What a dazzling change from the summer of this year when she and Barby had left England by the cheapest possible route to Dieppe.

Stephen hardly spoke to her. He was reading the headlines of a morning paper which he had so far been too busy to look at. He had only thrown her a cursory glance when they first met, reminded her to bring her notes and adding with a dry laugh: "But I don't need to remind *you*!"

15

ALL the way to the Airport, Christa kept stealing little swift timid glances at the stern handsome profile of the man who meant so much in her life. She forgot herself so far as to luxuriate in the fantasy that this *was* her 'going away' after the wedding. *Oh, dear life, what a mad, mad thought and how crazy can you get, Christa Coombe?* she asked herself. But just *think* if Aunt Cath's words had made sense; think what it would be like to be the newly-made wife of such a man! Of course he wouldn't be reading a paper, he would be holding her hand and telling her how much he loved her.

Stephen raised his head, put down the newspaper and looked out at the traffic.

"Good thing this new flyover. Saves a lot of time."

She almost laughed aloud. It was such a descent from the romantic clouds to reality.

Then they were at the Airport. There was a rush for the customs, the passport bureau, and the final walk down the long glass-covered way and out to the tarmac.

As an air-hostess smiled and showed her to her seat beside Stephen on the plane, Christa went on thinking her secret warm thoughts.

"What's the harm in me living in a world of my own. *He* will never know about it!"

But (she pulled a face) this was no honeymoon. No holding of hands, no exchange of thrilling glances.

She only sipped the champagne that Stephen offered, and looked out of the window. Now they were off. And she experienced the thrill of rising thousands of feet into the air within a few seconds, the jet engine pulsating, winging them up through the clouds toward the electric blue sky and brilliant sunshine that waited for them above the 'ceiling' of cloud.

Stephen now stopped working out business problems and glanced with some amusement at the young girl's pink, excited face.

"Pretty marvellous, isn't it? Every time I go up I salute this side of mechanical progress. The world would be a damned good place if we could only eliminate the destructive element."

"I've never flown before," she ventured to remark.

"Amazing girl," he said shaking his head. "You've done so little and yet are so quick to grasp important points of business."

He started to talk to her about herself and her background and, inevitably, the subject edged round to Barbara.

"That friend of yours is fantastically good looking. I rather think, and so does Jorgensen, my Danish friend, that the bust I've done of her is one of my absolute best."

For Barbara's sake, Christa fastened eagerly on this unusual praise of her friend by Stephen.

She discussed Barbara's physical perfections. Then she forced herself to be a little more personal – it really was a difficulty for her because all her instincts were against it.

"Barby's a wonderful person altogether."

"I know you think so, Christa. You're a very loyal friend and I hope she appreciates it."

"Oh, she does," said Christa fervently.

"I don't know that I'd call her very '*sympathique*', if you know what I mean by the word."

"Yes, I think I do."

"She tries too hard, if you know what I mean by *that*," added Stephen bluntly.

Christa flushed. She knew exactly what he meant. With all her heart now she wanted to stop talking about Barby, but even during the few moments before she left home this morning Barby had implored her afresh to try and influence him in her direction. "*Make him realize how really marvellous I am.*"

Christa exonerated Barbara by saying that she may be a little spoiled because all men fell so much in love with her.

Stephen gave a tolerant smile.

"Not this one!"

Christa moistened her lips with the tip of her tongue. Oh dear! She wasn't doing very well for Barby. Once again she forced herself to continue praising her friend and said into the bargain:

"She admires you tremendously, you know."

"Oh does she!" said Stephen in none too encouraging a voice and turned and looked out of the window.

The steward was bringing round the champagne bottle to top up his glass.

Stephen felt a trifle irritated by Christa's continual and too fulsome praise of Barbara. He wasn't interested in the girl except as a model and he never could quite understand why such a nice person as Christa could be so attached to that young woman who, in his opinion, was egotistical and over-sexed. On the whole Stephen was not in a mood for any girl this morning. He was sick of females. He had had a difficult evening with Felise last night.

Not for the first time she had kissed him good night rather too affectionately and expected an equally warm response.

"Oh Stephen, I never see enough of you," she had said as she put her arms round his neck.

This was outside the door of her flat. He had just given her dinner at The Caprice.

"I'm sorry, my dear, but I am really very busy these days," he had answered. Then kissed her lightly on the cheek, put on his hat and started to walk toward the lift.

She had called his name. He turned back to see her looking strained, her large eyes full of tears.

"Sometimes I think you deliberately avoid me," she said angrily.

Feeling distressed and awkward because he was really a a great admirer of hers, he had tried to argue against her accusation without committing himself. But Felise lost her usual well-bred control and attacked him. He had kept her hanging around long enough, she said. Everybody in Paris, including Julia, had expected them to marry long ago. When Stephen assured her gently that he had *never* mentioned the word 'marriage' but enjoyed their friendship, which he hoped would continue, she said that he had changed completely "since those two wretched English girls came into his life after the accident".

"I don't know whether it is your precious secretary or that rather crude beauty, you have been sculpturing, who you prefer, but I think you're just making a fool of yourself, Stephen. They're both mad about you and there's something I don't trust about that little secretary with her big eyes and '*Yes, sir*', '*No, sir*', attitude. Whenever I have seen her in your office I have noticed her giving you hungry sidelong glances. You men never know what hits you until it is too late. You're going to find yourself in a most awkward position. Julia agrees with me. She thinks you've been far too nice to those girls."

Those were only some of the things that Felise had flung at Stephen.

They parted on a slightly chilly note. But when he got home Stephen received a telephone call and a profuse apology from Felise.

"I can only excuse myself on the grounds that I am over-working – I've been practising day and night for my first TV show tomorrow, as you know. Promise you'll forgive me."

He promised. But he afterwards decided to see less of Felise. If she was really in love with him like this it would not be fair to her for him to give her any further encouragement. He just did not care for her that way. He wondered if he ever would meet a girl to whom he could give everything.

Later that night he remembered what Felise had said about his secretary. Those words: "*I've noticed her giving you hungry sidelong glances* . . ." made him feel definitely uncomfortable.

What absolute rubbish! Little Christa wasn't like that at all. Barbara, yes; but not this younger girl with her strangely light grey eyes and timid manner.

He turned his head to Christa now as he sat beside her in the Paris plane. For a moment he had experienced an extra-ordinary sensation of peril as though he stood on the very brink of something dangerous. The danger lay of course in the truth – the truth of what Felise had said and which at the time he had thought merely catty and stupid. And the truth was revealed when he caught Christa's sidelong glance and read that hunger – frank, unashamed and inexpressibly sad. It had an almost paralytic effect upon him, not only because it was unexpected but something to be reckoned with. It put him on his guard. It raised all kinds of difficulties and problems that had never so much as entered his head before. It just couldn't be true, he thought, that his careful cautious efficient little secretary 'had ideas' about him. Ideas that were not at all connected with their employer-secretary relationship. He didn't know what to say or do. Besides, he was baffled by all this. Why would she have plugged Barbara to him, for instance? What was the game?

She began:

"You'd l-like B-Barbara if you knew her better . . ."

Then Stephen lost his temper.

"Oh, for heaven's sake, stop throwing your girl-friend at my head. I don't want her. Would you please open my brief-case and find that letter from the Dutch importers who say

123

that last case we sent of hand-lotion was damaged. I'm going to meet Van Doncken at the Conference and I want to be refreshed with the facts."

She literally shrank away and groped for the attaché case which he had put at his feet. She had to lean across him. He suddenly saw the nape of her neck; it looked extraordinarily youthful and appealing; slender, with the fair silky hair clustering around it; it was like a child's neck. Yet there had been nothing childish about the expression he had just surprised in her eyes. "*Hungry*" Felise had called it. God, yes! It had been too full of feeling.

Stephen, himself, was threatened by an emotional reaction, the exact opposite of all it should have been. *He didn't mind Christa being in love with him*. The idea didn't fill him with repugnance as it had done when Barbara had chased him, or with regrets, such as he had felt over Felise Markell. It actually intrigued him to think that this reserved little creature who was such a mixture of strength and weakness should be capable of giving him such a look. And he was so taken aback by his own perceptive state where Christa was concerned that it made him close up like a clam. He grew taut and rather cruel. He snapped at her:

"Do hurry, Christa."

She sat up, breathing quickly, and produced the letter he required. He could see how white she was and that her fingers trembled. She looked stricken. It was too absurd, he thought. But probably she was frightened of him and her shaking hands had nothing to do with her personal feelings for *him*, as a man.

He set his teeth and thought:

"*Oh to hell with these women* . . . the less I have to do with them the better. I ought never to have brought my secretary with me. It was sheer laziness – just because she had everything at her finger-tips, and I thought it would lighten my load."

But was it only that? Wasn't it because he had thought Christa's company would be pleasant and soothing and that it would be so nice for the girl to have the benefit of the sun down in the South of France?

Until they touched down at Le Bourget he kept the conversation on a strictly business level and was unwarrantedly brusque with her.

By the time they had reached Paris and the offices of Parfum Joyeux, Christa was in the depths of despair. She didn't know that she had betrayed herself to Stephen but she imagined she had offended him by pursuing the subject of Barbara. She did not know what to do. Barbara had put her in an impossible position. Christa was torn between her affection and pity for her friend and her own common sense. She had realized it might be tactless of her to plead Barbara's cause quite so flagrantly.

Wretchedly she told herself that now she had spoiled the whole of the time she was to spend with her employer. It was as though he had frozen up on her. He took little notice of her from now onward. Once they started work in the Paris office, he had small chance to speak to her on anything but business, anyhow. Madame Roché was there to receive her brother, along with Claude her husband, and all the directors disappeared into Claude's own room.

Julia had greeted the young English girl in quite a kindly fashion and remarked upon how much better she looked than in the summer. She added a few words about the London branch, and the good work Christa had been doing, then sent Christa off to Miss Maydew's office.

There, Christa had to try and be cheerful and talk to the garrulous Miss Maydew, and also to chat with some of her former English-speaking friends in the office. But deep down inside she was tragically unhappy. Stephen was angry. The heavens had fallen in for Christa. Nothing could be right any more. She couldn't even look forward to continuing the journey to Cannes.

Alone with her brother, Julia said:

"You look fine, *mon cher*."

"I am, thank you, dear Julia."

"All well in London?"

"Excellent, considering the usual difficulties of today and the effect of the Common Market *impasse*. Tam Davis is going to do well in Edinburgh and I am counting a lot on this conference. We ought at least to be able to stabilize the rising cost of making our perfume, generally speaking."

Julia proceeded to tell him a few things about the Grasse factory, then asked after Felise.

"Still determined to be a bachelor while poor little Felise eats her heart out?" she teased him.

He snapped at his sister:

"*Pour l'amour de Dieu*, my dear, don't push Felise at me any more."

Julia raised her elegant brows. She had never seen her brother so rattled.

"Sorry, sweetie, I didn't mean to annoy you. By the way, little Miss Coombe has developed into quite an attractive child. Of course I remember that hair – it's a marvellous colour. She must have become indispensable for you to have brought her over like this. I could have taken Maydew down to Cannes with us."

"Maydew drives me mad. She never stops talking in that refeened voice of hers."

Julia laughed.

"Oh, well, I'm sure Miss Coombe will be an asset – for both of us."

Stephen remained silent. Once again the existence of Christa and her strangely elusive personality were being thrown at him rather more often and more powerfully than he liked. And once again it was his own unorthodox response to the mere mention of her that flung him off his equilibrium. What the devil is the matter, he asked himself. As if the colour of that damned girl's hair is of any importance! And why the devil *had* he brought her over to France anyhow. Was Julia going to misconstrue his every action?

He only saw Christa alone once before they all left the office. There had been a general meeting of the Paris staff during which Christa had sat on one side of Stephen taking notes. Miss Maydew was working with Claude and Julia.

Later, Christa brought Stephen a couple of letters to sign. He wanted them flown at once to London. She was just about to leave the room again when he called her back.

"Oh, Christa! That will be all for today. Don't wait."

She turned but did not look directly at him. Uneasily he saw how pale and unhappy she seemed. He could not stop to analyse either her attitude or his own, but on a kinder note, he added:

"Everything okay, Christa?"

"Yes, thank you," she answered in a low voice.

"You're staying the night with Maydew, aren't you?"

"Yes."

"I've asked her to take you out to dinner somewhere and send the bill to us here. Sorry I can't do more but I'm dining with my sister."

Christa flushed hotly and threw back her head.

"I – we didn't expect you to do any more for us. I'll be

perfectly all right with Miss Maydew and I'm quite sure we can stand the cost of our own meal."

He felt furious. She was being difficult. He was equally annoyed with himself because he supposed it was his own harshness that had upset Christa.

He almost growled the words:

"Very well – good night. See you on the *Caravelle* tomorrow morning."

She turned and left the room.

For the second time that day, Stephen muttered "*To hell with women.*"

But during that entire evening in Paris with his sister and brother-in-law it was about his fair-haired grey-eyed secretary whom he continued to think with uneasiness.

For Christa it was a completely wasted and miserable night. She felt that she had been flung from the pinnacle of happiness on which she had started the journey, into an abyss of despondency. She had upset Stephen. He was still cross with her. She could not be comforted even by the fact that he had used her Christian name in the office, and expressed some interest in what she was doing this evening. She began to feel the whole position was untenable and decided that if she were to go on feeling like this about her employer, she had better hand in her notice. All these months she had been suffering from the pangs of a hopeless love but had retained a sense of humour and been able to laugh at herself because of the utter impossibility of ever having such love returned. Now, things had become so bad she could no longer bear the pain. She couldn't even laugh at herself any longer. So it was the end. Certainly she would never mention Barbara's name to him again. She even began to feel a vague resentment against Barbara for being the initial cause of the trouble. Everything had been wonderful until Christa had tried to interest Stephen in Barby.

Christa kept up some pretence of enjoying the evening with Miss Maydew who insisted on taking her to an expensive restaurant at Mr. Harrimay's expense, and afterwards to an American film with French captions. Christa ate little and saw nothing of the film. In the darkness of the cinema the tears kept trickling slowly down her cheeks, and she kept wiping them away whenever Miss Maydew's attentions were fastened upon the film.

The lights of Paris were as brilliant and beautiful as ever

in the dark chill of the autumn night. But Paris had lost its glamour for Christa. There was no more brilliance for her, nothing of the dizzy joy she had felt the last time she had been here; when HE had been her companion.

She almost ran away that night and never reached Cannes at all. It was only the more practical and sane side of her that argued against being so silly.

So in the morning she found herself in the *Caravelle* with Stephen and the Rochés flying down to the Riviera.

It was a marvellous flight, and a magnificent aircraft. Stephen was quite good-tempered this morning. He smiled and chatted to Christa when they first met, but he sat beside his sister. It was Claude Roché who shared the double seat with the secretary behind the other two. Monsieur Roché was a nice man, deeply attached to his elegant, clever English wife. He had no real interest in Miss Coombe, but like most men, he found those big grey eyes of hers rather fascinating. And something about that secretive little smile that played sadly at times about her fine cut lips, was reminscent of *La Gioconda*. He told her so and was rewarded by one of her crimson blushes. He thought:

"Old Stephen has taste. *La Petite* has quite a touch of *allure*."

But Christa took no interest in Monsieur or the journey that should have been so wonderful.

When eventually they fastened on their safety-belts and circled over Nice, those big eyes of hers were full of unshed tears. Her first glimpse of the astonishingly blue Mediterranean and the handsome town with its white wedding-cake municipal buildings, casinos and flower-filled gardens, was blotted out. Her pleasure had been ruined. She could do nothing but stare abjectly at the back of Stephen's head.

16

In Cannes, the golden Mediterranean day had ended. Business for Christa, too, was finished. She had been told to take the evening off and do as she wanted. She had been introduced to one or two friendly French secretaries from the Grasse perfume factory, but what with the language difficulty and her state of mind, she had declined any invitations. She decided to spend her evening alone.

Now she stood on the balcony of her bedroom at the Majestic looking over the palm trees and the courtyard, across the Croisette to the sea. All day it had been that same brilliant blue, like the faultless sky. A wonder and amazement to Christa. She had seen nothing like it before. Miserable though she was, she nevertheless felt a faint thrill of pleasure in the beauty of the exotic coast, the colourful flowers and trees, the attractive shops. And it was so warm. Like midsummer in England, she reflected. Only now did she need a cardigan, because once the sun set, the temperature cooled down.

She watched a white motor-boat dashing through the water towards the harbour, churning up iridescent foamy spray. Through the blue dusk lights began to glitter along the coast and from all the big hotels and cafés. They twinkled from the yachts in the famous harbour – mooring for millionaires from all over the world.

What a day it had been! First, the general meeting and conference in the board room of Parfum Joyeux up at Grasse. That wonderful ride up the mountain road. Thrilling, the sight of Les Alpes Maritimes. When she was a teenager, Christa used to be fascinated by the thought of France, look longingly at posters, and devour coloured brochures from Tourists' Centres. And here she was at last. Her bedroom, in one of Cannes' more exclusive hotels, was more luxurious than any she had ever occupied.

She had been on stony ground with Stephen all day – near him, yes; taking down notes, giving him the documents or letters he needed; using her utmost efficiency to serve him. But she was, she felt, only a tiny cog in the big wheel that turned the commercial routine of Parfum Joyeux. All day to him she was just "Miss Coombe". She received barely a smile or a personal word or glance.

She had expected this week-end to be a great thrill instead of which it had proved sterile and bitter. She had never felt more lonely. Never more conscious of utter failure. In doing her best for Barbara she had failed *him*. And she loved him so much that she wanted to die.

"*Serve you right for letting your attention fasten on such a man who is miles and miles out of your reach*," she kept telling herself. "*You are no better than Barby, only a shade less hysterical. And you ought to know better.*"

She had lunched in Grasse with other employees in the beautiful modern factory. She had been presented, like the other girls, with a small bottle of the famous perfume. She had experienced the thrill of lunching out of doors in the sunshine at a long table – delicious scampi, grilled veal, cheese-soufflé, washed down by the *vin du pays*. It should all have been great fun, and she as Mr Harrimay's personal assistant, should have been able to hold her head high and feel delighted with herself. Instead of which – only this crushing sense of misery – almost despair.

Stephen only said one kind word to her – just as his car had dropped them at the Majestic, half an hour ago.

"Hope you've made a suitable date for tonight, and will enjoy yourself. Pop into the Casino. I'll treat you to the *salle de jeux* and you can watch the idiots who lose all their money, and the few lucky ones who make a packet," he had said, smiling.

She had answered: "*Thank you very much.*"

"I've got this party out with my sister," he added almost apologetically, "otherwise I'd be more sociable."

Christa took no comfort from that. She felt that he had turned the light of his countenance from her; that she was less than the dust to him. She had blotted her copy-book so completely by pushing Barbara down his throat. She had turned herself into a crashing bore.

But how could she know that his semi-apology had arisen from a very real remorse in Stephen because he had been so irritable with her all day and must leave her completely alone tonight. Obviously his place was with Julia and Claude. Henri Dinard, managing director of the Grasse factory, was giving them dinner. They were going to drive along the sea front to La Napoule to one of the most famous fish restaurants on the coast.

Bouillabaisse was the speciality. Stephen was rather partial to this dish, but for some inexplicable reason he wished he could avoid the dinner and show Christa the beauty of the Côte d'Azur – as he had shown her Paris. Her joy, her sensitive response to everything – had been so refreshing. He had never forgotten it. He would like to experience that pleasure again. He would like to make *her* look a little happier. Silly, ultra-sensitive little thing! Her big grey eyes were so mournful. They filled him with absurd tenderness. He did not know whether he wanted to pick her up in his arms and kiss her or shake her like a doll. But Christa was no doll. She was 'all there'. She hadn't made one mistake during the conference. Henri Dinard, who had spoken first in French, then in English for the British records, had congratulated him on his secretary.

Dinard had been with Parfum Joyeux for ten years – before Stephen first joined the company after leaving University. Henri was a good friend and privileged to make the sort of remark that he had uttered after the conference broke up.

"*Tiens! Tiens!*" he had said (they always spoke French together). "The little English *demoiselle*, your *secrétaire*, has charm and *une manière competente*. And she looks like a *petite Tanagra* figure. *Ravissante!*"

Stephen had smiled and answered in the manner of men:

"*La bonne chance; hein?*"

A flippant exchange of words but Stephen remembered. *Competent and charming*. Dear little Christa – yes! If only she wouldn't keep making constant efforts to plead the cause of her dear friend Barbara.

Seven o'clock found Christa walking through the well-lighted streets alone; bare-headed, hands in the pockets of her coat. She turned off the Croisette into the Rue d'Antibes, where the shops were still open. So unlike England, she thought. Nothing like Golling & Nash here, closing dead on time, business at a standstill, to please the Unions! All the gay little shops in Cannes were willing to go on serving and selling.

This was a one-way street. Hundreds of cars seemed to roll down toward the Casino-end of the town. Crowds jostled Christa on the pavement. She kept hearing snatches of conversation in English, American, Italian, every kind of language. Cannes was a great resort for the tourist. It was also a great change of scene for Christa. It still seemed so deliciously warm compared with an autumn night in London.

But every time she saw some girl strolling arm-in-arm with a boy-friend, looking happy and contented, she felt as though her very heart would screw up with pain. To be happily in love – to be *loved* – must be so marvellous. It would never happen to her, now, never. The image of Stephen blotted out all other visions and nothing she could do obscured his face from her.

A healthy hunger and thirst seized Christa later on, and she stopped at a little restaurant and found a solitary table. Urged by an English-speaking waiter, she ordered a plate of spaghetti with one of those delicious French rolls and butter. But somehow as soon as she began to eat she felt a constriction in her throat and a loss of appetite again.

She was utterly wretched – even homesick. Everybody else here seemed to be with *someone*. She wished that she had never come down to Cannes with Stephen. She wished she were back in Wood Green with Aunt Cath and Barby. She was scared that she would burst into tears, and decided to try and fininish the spaghetti quickly and go.

A young, good-looking French boy, glancing at a *Paris-Soir*, was watching her across the room. She was suddenly conscious of his over-ardent glance. She looked away, her delicate lips closing tightly. Nothing daunted, the French boy slipped into the empty seat opposite her.

"*Bon soir, M'mselle. Vous permettez?*" he began.

She looked up at him. He had mischievous eyes and strong white teeth which he showed in a wide smile. In a way she would have liked to have talked to him – to anyone – but she had an idea that an amorous Frenchman would not be the right recepient for confidences from her tonight. So with burning cheeks, she muttered:

"*Non, merci.*"

He shrugged and rose, bowing gracefully.

"*Je m'excuse.*"

After he had returned to his own table she felt sorry she had snubbed him. It was perhaps rather stupid of her. She forced herself to eat the spaghetti and asked for the bill. Laboriously she counted out the necessary francs, then left.

The French boy looked after her, rolling his eyes heavenwards.

"Bon Dieu! Une petite frigidaire! Ces Anglaises!"

Once in her bedroom at the Majestic, Christa dissolved into the tears that had been threatening all evening.

The warm, delightful room with its rich wedgwood-blue satin curtains and carpet and attractive furniture, was blotted out by the torrent of tears that poured down her cheeks. She flung herself face downward on the bed and cried until she could cry no more. Then she undressed, walked into the bathroom and tried to extract forlorn comfort from the luxury of the steaming hot water and having a bathroom of her own. She slipped into one of those white towelling dressing-gowns which always hang on the back of a French bathroom door, dried herself, then put on the pale blue nightgown which she had bought at Marks & Spencers – such a pretty one with lace yoke and blue ribbons. After brushing her thick fair hair she slid between the sheets of the springy, comfortable bed and turned off the light.

She began to cry again. When finally she dozed, it was uneasily. The bedroom was noisy after the peace and quiet of Wood Green. Here in the South of France at ten o'clock, life was only just beginning. She remembered now that Stephen had told her to go to the Casino; nothing ever really started there until ten.

Was she a fool not to take advantage of his offers and enjoy her few nights down there? Was she a hopeless fool to allow herself to fall so desperately in love with her employer? Oh, if only she could have been like Barbara, who would have allowed that handsome young Frenchman to have talked to her and taken her out. Possibly he meant no harm. Anyhow, lots of girls allowed themselves to be 'picked up'. She knew Barbara had done so because she had told Christa about it. *"I'm just not like that,"* Christa always thought. *"I just can't take up with anyone."*

After her first sleep, Christa found it difficult to compose herself and sleep again. She kept dozing off and waking up. Finally she switched on the light, and with a deep sigh, got up, put on her dressing-gown and sat at the writing table. She opened the blotter and pulled out a sheet of notepaper. She found her own Biro. The electric clock on the wall showed that it was one o'clock in the morning. What an hour to write a letter, she laughed to herself mournfully. But she was going to write one. To Stephen.

She had quite made up her mind. This state of affairs could

not be allowed to go on. She refused to sink her pride one inch lower. Not for another day would she behave like a crazy love-sick schoolgirl. Tomorrow when she saw Stephen she would appear coolly indifferent *and* enjoy herself. But first of all she was going to hand in her notice.

Of course it was a terribly difficult thing to do. It was like cutting off her nose to spite her face. She would never find another such wonderful job or another man like Stephen to work for. But she could not continue to be personal secretary to a man who was able to reduce her to such a pitiable state. It was not his fault. It had just happened. As for Barbara – Christa was finished trying to help Barbara, too. No more acting as a go-between. From now onward she would be bitter, cynical and hard.

So the new 'bitter, cynical and hard' Christa composed her letter of resignation. Not one but several were written, then torn up and consigned to the wastepaper basket. Her head ached with crying so hard when she read the final letter:

Dear Mr. Harrimay,
    First of all I want to thank you for all you have ever done for me ever since our first meeting, and for the wonderful chance you gave me to work at Parfum Joyeux (in the other letters she had put 'work for *you*' but she had decided to be less personal). *I have thoroughly enjoyed it and benefited by the experience, but regret that because of circumstances beyond my control* (that was true in more senses than one, she thought), *I am afraid I must leave Parfum Joyeux. I will of course wait until you replace me which I am sure will not be difficult, and meanwhile will continue to do my best for the firm. Again my thanks.*
                Yours sincerely,

"*His sincerely!*" That made her laugh as she read the words aloud and it was not a very happy laugh. Oh, Stephen, *Stephen!* Wonderful, maddening Stephen. So utterly, hopelessly out of her reach. If only she could have written what she really felt, poured her whole heart out on this paper and signed it as she would have liked to have done: "*Yours, yours, absolutely yours in every way; mind, heart, soul, all of me, yours . . .*"

But in this kind of thinking madness lay. It was time she took herself to task and behaved sensibly. As soon as she got back to London she would start looking for another job, and no doubt the time she had spent with Parfum Joyeux would in itself constitute a good reference.

She grew calmer. She folded the letter, put it in an envelope and addressed it to Stephen. She decided to slide it under his door. She knew which it was – three away from hers on the corner just before the lift.

When she stood outside Stephen's suite she saw to her surprise that the entrance door was wide open. A light burned in the little hall, but the bedroom, the door of which was also open, was in darkness. It looked as though he were still out, but that the last valet or *femme de chambre* to enter had gone off in a hurry without shutting the main door.

Christa slipped quickly into the hall and through to the bedroom. She laid the note on the pillows on one of the twin beds. Stephen, to whom money was of little account, always booked a double room. He had told her so. He liked the space.

Her spirits were very low. What she was doing was so very final. It seemed now that this was the end of all association with *Him*.

Then suddenly her heart seemed to stop beating and a wild throb of shame and embarrassment shook her whole body. For she could only reach the bedroom door before Stephen appeared. He met her face to face. It was a considerable shock. She had not heard him coming down the thickly carpeted corridor.

He wore a dark grey suit with a red carnation in the button-hole. The flower looked a bit wilted. He, himself, had a tired air. His handsome eyes were full of astonishment and his voice was equally surprised.

"Good *gracious* me, what are *you* doing here?"

For an instant Christa was too tongue-tied to answer. She did not know how to cope with such a situation. She began to stutter, but stopped. Stephen spoke again.

"Well, since you've decided to pay me this early morning visit, why not come back into the room and tell me what this is all about."

"No – I – I —" she began to stammer again, but realized her hopeless inadequacy and shook her head.

Stephen narrowed his gaze. He was certainly amazed to find Christa in his suite. A glance at his wrist-watch showed him that it was close on two o'clock.

He had had an exhausting day and the night had been much lengthier than he had wanted. The dinner at the restaurant La Mère de Terre was excellent as always and the *bouillabaisse* full of shell-fish laced with garlic and the chef's special seasoning, had come up to expectations.

Julia was as delightful as always – a most efficient, poised human being, his sister. Claude was equally efficient, with the exquisite manners and contrived charm of the typical Frenchman. Henri and Marcelle Dinard were both fat, jolly, mad about their food and good company. And to make up the sixth there had been a rather attractive widow who worked in the Grasse office and was a cousin of Marcelle. Yes – very attractive, Chantal Lemaire, Stephen decided – a red-head with large blue eyes, and a tall slim figure. Stephen had met her many times before in the business and felt a natural masculine admiration for her.

During dinner tonight she had proved herself an entertaining companion, and the artist in him had once or twice been stirred by the exceptional beauty of her hands which were very white with long pointed fingers.

"I must model those hands," he had said during the dinner.

Her eager reception of his offer and a certain look in her eyes had then warned him off. No, he wasn't going to become involved with Chantal. Widows could be dangerous. All women had so far proved dangerous to Stephen, and strangely enough he had started to think about his young English secretary again. It was positively damnable the way that young girl infiltrated herself into his consciousness, he reflected. There must be something very strange about Christa. She was not really as physically alluring as any of these others – Felise, Barbara, Chantal. Yet he went on thinking about her and reproaching himself because he had been so irritable with her today.

To find her like this in the early hours of the morning, apparently waiting to see him in his bedroom, was a vast astonishment. He could not be blind to the fact that she looked extraordinarily attractive, obviously in her nightgown, and wearing a cornflower-blue candlewick dressing-gown which set off her extreme fairness. After Chantal's heavy Parisian make-up, Stephen thought Christa's face touchingly young and pure. She had a marvellous skin. The 'Dorella-look' had come back with a vengeance. The fair thick waves of hair were tumbled about her slender neck giving her a strange look of abandonment which, combined with her childish air of innocence, was extraordinarily attractive to Stephen.

"I – I've just written you a l-letter," she began to stammer.

"Written me a letter?" he repeated. "What on earth about? Surely you haven't spent your first night in Cannes writing letters, my dear."

To cover her confusion she adopted an air of injured pride – tossed her head.

"No – certainly not. I've been out to dinner. I wrote the letter when I came back. I meant to – to slip it under your door, saw it open and that you were not in, so I put it on your bed."

He shut the door of his suite and was standing now with his back leaning against it. He had the stump of a cigar between his fingers and puffed at it for a moment, staring down at her with a puzzled sort of expression, combined with benevolent amusement.

"You always look so scared of me," he said. "Why?"

"I'm not at all scared. But I suppose you think it odd finding me in your suite like this."

"You have a perfect right to write me notes if you want to. But what was it that couldn't wait till morning or rather I should say *later* this morning."

Her heart beat painfully fast. She frowned and her lashes fluttered nervously.

"I – you'll see when you read it."

"You make me curious. Let's open the letter, shall we?"

"No. Good night. I must go," she began wildly.

But suddenly he reached out a hand, tooks hers and drew her back into the room, switching on the lamp by one of the twin beds.

This was an even more sumptuous suite than Christa's; the décor was charming in the soft light; the jalousies had been closed for the night; dark violet taffeta curtains were draped handsomely across the windows. There were books, papers and magazines on the table between the beds. On one, the valet had laid out Mr. Harrimay's pyjamas – brown silk piped with white, made here in Cannes. There was also a brown satin dressing-gown on the end of the bed.

"Don't run away for a moment," said Stephen. "Let's examine this letter together. I cannot think what you have said to me. I'm intrigued. It isn't about the job, is it? We've all been saying what a good secretary you are but it would be slightly overstepping the mark for you to remind me of my appointments and commitments at 2 a.m. . . ." he laughed.

She stood there in an agony of embarrassment and wished he would let her go. His strong fine fingers around her wrist caused her an agonizing thrill of excitement. She was quite sure he was going to be annoyed with her again when he read her letter. She was furious with herself for having been caught out this way. She began to tremble when he sat on the edge of the bed, took up her letter and opened it. While he read it, he laid the cigar-end down slowly on an ashtray beside him. Soon she saw his lean, clever face tauten and the tolerant smile vanish. Now he was angry again, she thought miserably.

He looked up at her:

"This I *didn't* expect! Might I ask for a further explanation. What are the circumstances that you say are 'out of your control'?"

"It's my – my private affair," she stammered.

"So private that you can't tell your employer why you are handing in your resignation?"

"Yes," she said between her teeth.

He crumpled her letter up in his hand.

"I'm afraid I don't understand, Christa. You seemed so happy – in fact you've told me many times that you were enjoying your job."

She nodded, the nervous colour coming and going in her cheeks.

"I – I really don't want to discuss it."

He stood up and came slowly toward her.

"We *are* on the high horse, aren't we? What's biting you? Aren't you enjoying the South of France? But that can't be why you want to leave Parfum Joyeux. Suppose you try and explain."

She felt trapped but she would have torn her tongue out rather than speak the truth. She said:

"It's . . . it's . . . oh, I keep telling you, it's a personal reason."

"So you really want to quit Parfum Joyeux?"

"Oh, God," she thought, "why must he be so persistent? If only he knew the misery he is causing me."

"Yes," she said despairingly. "I must."

Silence. She locked her hands convulsively behind her back feeling the palms damp with nerves.

He only half saw her face through the falling shadow of

that beautiful bright hair. And now suddenly he knew that the last thing he wanted was to go back to London and find a new P.A. – let Christa go right out of his life. Good God, he knew there were other secretaries – it was just a question of waiting and finding one – but he had grown used to Christa and she did have that exceptional talent for being discreet, tactful and responsible. Only during that flight to Paris had she upset him. He wondered suddenly if her decision to leave was because of his attitude toward her since then. Quite gently now he said:

"I think I understand, Christa. You've taken umbrage because I snapped at you, not once but several times today. I admit I was annoyed when you plugged your friend Barbara. I can't think why, mind you."

"Oh, it's not just that – you don't understand – I *can't* explain," she cried disjointedly.

"Perhaps I do. Perhaps I don't. But if you enjoy working for me I don't see why you should choose this time and place to resign from the job. Quite frankly, Christa, you suit me and I don't want to lose you."

That was some comfort to her – a lot, in fact. Marvellous to have this wonderful man bothering to try and make her change her mind. She looked up at him gratefully.

"Thank you. Thank you so much – but I still want to leave."

"Dammit," he said angrily, "but *why*? Why do you want to put me to all the nuisance of training someone new to all my ways? You've only just begun to have the business at your finger-tips and you say you've even been trying to teach yourself French. Well if you want to know, I had decided to have you privately taught, because I thought it would be useful if you became bi-lingual."

She felt torn but determined not to give in.

"I'm afraid I must go . . . please, Mr. Harrimay . . ."

"Mr. Harrimay . . ." he broke in moving his head from side to side irritably. "I thought we were friends out of office hours. You used to call me 'Stephen'."

Christa began to feel quite faint.

"I may have done . . . I don't know . . . I . . . I must really say good night . . ."

But he had not the slightest intention of letting matters rest there. He did not understood the reason why Christa's resignation from the job had given such a nasty jolt to his *amour propre*. But it opened his eyes to the fact that he did not want to part with her. He could see her shaking from head to foot. Dammit, how emotional she was! How much too sensitive, yet unlike these other women – Barbara, even Felise. Christa had never made demands upon him, or gestures toward him, nor so much as intimated that she looked upon him not only as an employer but a man who might look back at her. There was, and always had been, something exceptionally virginal about Christa. Unusual for this day and age, he told himself cynically, when the average girl knew very well what she was about and brought 'sex' into almost every form of association.

"Don't stand there shaking like an aspen leaf, you silly little noodle," he broke out furiously.

She looked terrified and turned to go. But he stopped her. He was angry with himself rather than with her. Stephen, the man, the artist, the *lover*, was wide awake now – and all the emotional side which he had once betrayed to Dorella – rushed over him like a torrent for the first time in years.

Christa's delicate trembling figure, that small face, absolutely white with misery. that look of fear in those huge eyes, captured his imagination completely. Stephen, the self-possessed man of the world, lost his head.

"Dammit," he said again, caught her round the waist, swept her into his arms and kissed her mouth through the golden veil of her hair. Hair that was fragrant and silky under his lips. And her lips were sweet and delicate, and extraordinarily seductive although he knew that it was neither in her nature or her intention to seduce.

The warmth of that kiss intensified. His whole being had begun to clamour for her. He wanted this delicate white and gold nymph of a girl. He wanted to shake her into warmth and response and to make her take back her decision to leave him. Above all he wanted to banish that look of terror from her face.

She was so small that his arms seemed to envelop her entirely.

What lay in Christa's mind and heart as she felt the passion of Stephen's lips upon hers was indescribable. For a moment it was as though all her senses were paralysed and then, as though the hot sun itself touched the core of her being, she thawed. Like the petals of a flower her lips opened to his. It was the first kiss of passion she had ever given – or received. But she gave these kisses to him with all the hunger of her young heart. Instinctively her arms were around him. Breathlessly she went on kissing and being kissed, until the wonder and delight and glory of it all seemed to destroy her. She gave a little moaning sigh, slackened her hold on him and shook her head violently from side to side.

"Oh, no, no! NO!"

He was more controlled but almost as vanquished by that moment of revelation between them. Christa, whom his sister had called a nonentity, and who considered herself so unimportant in this world, had suddenly, dangerously, become attractive to him as *a woman* —

"Let me go," she begged him, pushing at him with helpless hands. At once he did as she wished. Taking a handkerchief from his breast pocket he ran it across his lips. He was surprised to find himself shaking. And it took a lot to move Stephen that far. He said:

"My God, that's torn things, hasn't it?"

She put both hands up to her cheeks and shook her head without speaking.

"Christa," he said, "come and sit down on the edge of the bed and let us talk."

"No, no, I can't."

He gave a short laugh.

"Not very proper in my bedroom, I suppose. Two o'clock in the morning and all that."

"Oh, don't make fun of me," she broke out looking up at him with sudden spirit, her face flaming. "You do nothing but make fun of me and you had no right to kiss me like that."

Suddenly Stephen gave her an impudent boyish smile.

"And you had no right to kiss *me* like that, either."

"Oh, how can you!" she protested.

His expression changed.

"I thought it pretty marvellous," he added in a low tone.

Uncomprehendingly her large eyes stared at him. She had stopped trembling, but her whole body was on fire. She put up a hand and pushed the untidy waves of hair back from her forehead.

"Please let me go back to my own room now."

"I wouldn't stop you for anything if you really want to go."

"You know I must," she said indignantly.

"All right. If you think it will be more *comme il faut*, get dressed and we'll go down to the lounge and continue our discussion. This hotel doesn't pack up until much later I assure you. Many of the guests will probably still be over in the *salles de jeux*."

"Why do you want to talk to me any more?"

"Don't you want to talk to me?"

"You keep confusing me!" she complained, drawing her dressing-gown tightly around her.

"Look, Christa," he said, "I'm a bit confused myself. Did you expect me to be anything else after those kisses. Didn't they mean anything to you?"

In a stupefied way she shook her head.

"Of course. But it can't have meant much to you."

"Why do you think I kissed you like that? Was it just an ordinary casual embrace, do you suppose? A sort of 'I want to keep you as a secretary so I'd better kiss you' attitude?"

The colour drained from her cheeks.

"You do nothing but laugh at me – I hate you."

He drew nearer to her. He was astonished to find how much he wanted to draw her into his arms again and keep her there.

"No, you don't hate me, Christa," he said – "but let's calm down and be rational about this. I don't altogether understand my own feelings. Possibly I had no right —" he stopped, frowning, rubbing the back of his head, as though perplexed. But Christa seized this sign of weakness from him to show her strength.

"I am not going to dress and come down and talk to you. We've got nothing whatsoever to discuss," she said and marched toward the door.

"Look here – wait —"

But she broke in:

"And my letter holds good. I'm still leaving Parfum Joyeux."

"Hang on – wait a moment," he said indignantly. "You can't be all sweet and responsive to me one minute and then behave as though I've insulted you."

She swung round.

"I – I didn't find it insulting. I enjoyed kissing you very much, thank you." she said with rather absurd dignity. "Good night."

"You —" He got no further. For once in Stephen Harrimay's life he was absolutely nonplussed. He couldn't begin to make her out and already he was beginning to wish he had never lost his head and allowed that moment of passion to take place. At the same time he was sure he didn't want to lose her – whatever happened.

He would like to have a further argument or at least get things put back on to a footing that would make the atmosphere less impossible.

But the door had closed firmly behind the slender figure in blue.

"Oh, damn everything," said Stephen under his breath, picked up his stump of cigar and jammed the head fiercely into the ashtray. Then he poured himself out a glassful of the Evian which stood in a bucket of ice on the bed-table, and gulped it thirstily to the last drop.

17

IT took some courage for Christa to go down and meet her employer in the lounge at ten o'clock that next morning as arranged earlier. *Much* earlier she told herself grimacing. Before *all that* had happened.

The lounge was deserted. Only a few early would-be shoppers were up and out on the terrace.

It was a glorious fresh morning with the same peerless sky of yesterday, and brilliantly sunny. The green palm trees and the blue sea outside looked most tempting but Christa barely saw them. She had slept only in snatches after leaving Stephen's suite. She was very much on edge and her eyes were heavy. But she did not feel tired. She was in a strangely exalted state of mind. She had lain awake until at eight o'clock hunger and thirst drove her to ring for her *café complet*. For hours her state of mind had been chaotic. Her reasoning powers seemed to be bogged down by an emotional avalanche. The memories of those few minutes in Stephen's arms, when she gave him kiss for kiss . . . mad delirious kisses . . . swept all other thoughts away. As long as she lived she would have those kisses to remember. To help her maintain sanity in the bleak days that lay ahead (or would they on the contrary drive her insane, she kept asking herself).

She re-lived it all – to the smallest detail. The increasing pressure of his embrace, the warmth of his hand against her throat at one time, while he caressed her, the clean masculine cigar odour of his jacket when she pressed her face against it. He had covered that face with such burning kisses. (Her lips were still sore, yet she loved the soreness just as she loved the memory of his passion.) Mad, bad, it might all be and a great mistake, but she could not be sorry that he had lost his control. After all it was vastly flattering to her feminine ego. She had never really before imagined herself attractive. Not so that she could have such an effect upon Stephen. But what really upset her was the futility of it all. She could be quite sure it was only that he had been physically stirred by her – as any man might be by a girl who wasn't bad-looking – and in her dressing-gown! Yet she refused to regard it as a kind of naughty French farce; that would degrade the whole thing and she did not want it degraded. She wanted it to remain on a pedestal – as something lofty and wonderful. *Stephen Harrimay once made love to Christa Coombe.*

Naturally by now *he* would have forgotten – or regretted it. Barbara had so often preached to Christa that men were like that – and that one couldn't take them too seriously. Besides – she blamed herself. She had allowed him to find her in his bedroom at two o'clock in the morning.

But how heavenly his kisses had been and how exciting! How marvellous his eyes had looked just before his lips came down upon hers. How utterly devastating he was. And what on earth would Barbara say if she knew? She must never know. It would mean the absolute end between Barby and herself if she even hinted that Stephen had kissed her. Barbara would be sure Christa had deliberately manœuvred it all and tried to put her, Barby, right out of the picture.

Other more unattractive thoughts pursued Christa this morning. Stephen might despise her now and feel only too glad that she was leaving the firm.

She was no fool, and hoped she was not a silly prude, either. She knew that all kinds of relationships could exist between men and women in this life. Between a man and his secretary, for instance. But she wan't going to allow any such situation to arise between Stephen and herself. She loved him too much. She wanted him always to respect her. Anyway she thought, as she continued to turn over things in her mind, he'd be glad to see the back of her. He might think she 'was getting ideas'. She couldn't forget that he had – even though good-humouredly – *reminded* her afterwards that she had kissed him back.

"*I thought it pretty marvellous!*" he had said.

Oh, she had thought so too! She loved him so much. It was rotten to think that a man could kiss you that way and *not* be in love with you. But some girls were the same. Some had quite a masculine outlook on sex. She'd heard all about that. They'd told her stories. *She* felt differently – that was all.

Christa began to walk up and down the deserted lounge trying to rehearse what she would say once Stephen appeared.

But he did not come. At first she did not care because she imagined he was probably sleeping late, but after an hour passed she began to feel worried. She knew they were due back for the final conference at the factory at Grasse at midday.

She walked to the Reception Bureau and asked the *concierge* if she might speak to Mr. Harrimay on the telephone.

"One moment, please," he said, smiling at the pretty young English lady. When he returned it was with an envelope which he handed her. "You are Ma'mselle Coombe, eh?"

Christa's heart missed a beat as she saw Stephen's familiar handwriting. Slowly she took the envelope.

"Yes," she nodded.

"Monsieur Harrimay received an urgent telephone call at eight o'clock this morning, Mademoiselle. He left the hotel for the airport at Nice soon afterwards."

Christa's heart sank to its lowest depths. He had gone. *He had gone.* She ought of course to be glad that there would be be no embarrassing meeting, yet the thought that he had left Cannes and that she might never see him again, filled her with darkest despair. She walked away from the reception bureau, tore open the envelope and sat down at a table. Her knees were shaking.

The letter was brief. Stephen's handwriting was always rather small and somewhat illegible. She used to find it difficult at first to decipher his corrections on documents and letters, but she had grown used to it. Now fairly quickly she read what he had written.

Dear Christa,

Let's forget what is best forgotten. And please do not allow it or anything to interfere with the job which you are doing so well for Parfum Joyeux.

I shall expect you to go to the meeting at Grasse, take the notes and bring them to me in London. My sister rang me from the Dinards' villa with the news that there has been a fire in the Hanover Square office. Not catastrophic but unfortunately my office and yours got the worst of it. I reckon there'll be the devil of a lot of searching and sorting to be done and your assistance will be invaluable. Take the Caravelle to Paris this afternoon, please, and then on to London. I'll book your seat when I'm at the airport. As soon as you reach town, report to me.

Yours,

S.H.

The letter almost dropped from Christa's fingers. Her pulses jerked. Here was an unexpected development. And now all personal feelings were replaced by her genuine concern for the firm and Stephen's welfare. *How simply awful* that there should have been a fire while they were away. Stephen gave no details but she supposed the trouble must have started during the night. Perhaps it was that silly office boy, Billy, who was always picking up fag-ends and lighting them and then after smoking them, throwing the ends back into wastepaper baskets. She had caught him at it more than once and warned him one day that he might start a fire. Possibly he had left a basket smouldering, but it hadn't really broken out until everyone had left.

Once again Christa read through Stephen's letter. And now her thoughts returned to the more personal side. Those words ... *"Let's forget what is best forgotten"* ... were cryptic but significant. She knew exactly to what he referred. It was as she imagined; he wanted the passionate interlude of last night forgotten.

At least, she thought, rising to her feet and with an ironic smile, he had given her an outlet for her own pride. He had made it possible for her to overlook last night (not that she could ever forget it in this life or the next). She must never refer to it. He wanted her to go back to the office and help him. Well, of course she would. And it was a glorious relief to know that she *would* see him again – that wonderful expressive face – hear that deep authoritative voice – feel that she was to be of some use, some value, to him.

Her next action was to telephone Madame Roché.

"Yes, isn't it all sickening," said Julia. "If you'll be outside the Majestic, I'll call for you in my car, Christa."

Christa drove with the Rochés to Grasse, carried out the

work expected of her, had lunch and then returned to Cannes and packed her things. She was in Paris late that afternoon and in London by seven. Once at the Airport she telephoned the office. The circuit was still working anyhow, because Pat Westerham answered her.

"Oh hello, Miss Coombe, isn't it gruesome – our room's blackened right out. It was a miracle the typewriters escaped but some of the papers were destroyed and everything's *ruined* by water. It's the water that did most of the damage, they say. We're still here trying to help clear up."

"Is the Boss in?"

"Yes – he's been at it for hours. He's been smashing to us. He said we were all very helpful."

"And Mrs. Jacobs?"

Pat giggled.

"Jolly lucky for us, she's laid up with the flu and didn't turn up this morning. See you later. Ta-ta."

Christa was full of impatience and could hardly wait for the bus to deliver her at the terminal. Then there was the taxi ride to Hanover Square. She jumped out and rushed into the building. At least, she thought, the lift was working. Things seemed normal until she got up to the floor occupied by Parfum Joyeux. There, instead of the usual sweet pervading smell of perfume, was a strong odour of burnt paper and charred wood which made her wrinkle her nose. She could soon see that a great deal of damage had been done to the décor. Curtains and carpets were ruined. The firemen had certainly done their job.

It was now long past eight. Everybody must have gone home. Christa walked slowly into her own office. Here, it was pretty much a mess, she thought sadly. A quick look at her desk and table showed a confusion of charred, half-destroyed boxes, papers and files. Slowly Christa peeled off her gloves. As she did so the glass panelled door on the other side of the room was pushed open.

Stephen walked in.

He looked more tired and haggard than she had ever seen him and – unusual for him – he was dirty and untidy. Shirt and cuffs grimy – like his hands. There were dark shadows under his eyes and he had an exhausted air. But as he saw Christa, his whole face lit up with a spontaneity which warmed her right through like a darting flame.

"Oh, hul*lo*, so you've turned up!" he said.

"Of course. Didn't you think I would?"

He gave a short laugh, produced a packet of cigarettes and held it out to her.

"I didn't know. Have one?"

She shook her head and pulled off hat and coat.

As she smoothed back her hair, his gaze was caught by the lustre of it under the strong fluorescent light above her desk. (At least the lights were on again.) He could never, he thought a trifle wryly, look unmoved upon Christa's beautiful hair. Besides, he had an astonishingly vivid memory of it in the early hours of this morning falling across her flushed cheeks, and of the sweet fine-cut lips he had kissed so passionately.

Then he decided that this was neither the time nor the place to give way to such memories. He spoke in a deliberately hearty sort of way.

"Well, so here we are – in a ruddy fine mess due to this ruddy fire. The staff have been marvellous. We've been at it all day. Salvaged quite a bit, but there are still your papers and files I want us to go through and see if you can get a line on what is missing. The inspector from the fire station thinks it all started in that room where the staff make tea."

"Exactly – where young Bill empties the baskets," thought Christa her lips tightening. "I'll lay ten to one it was that little idiot."

Now that the awkward moment of meeting her employer was over, she spoke as cheerfully as he did.

"I'll soon get down to things. Glad they aren't worse. I suppose every one *has* gone home?"

"Yep . . ." He sat on the edge of her desk, lit his own cigarette and mopped his face with a grubby handkerchief. Somehow it smote her to the heart to see him like this – so fatigued – and dirty. It gave her an extraordinary feeling of tenderness – of wanting to mother him. Impulsively she said:

"Has everything been burned out in that staff-room or can I make you a cup of tea? You look all-in."

He laughed.

"Oh, there was no tea-making possible today. But I'm fine. Only in need of sleep. I shall turn in early tonight. Do you realize that we were still up, you and I, talking at three this morning? It's been the hell of a long day and I expect you're tired, too."

But she was flushed, bright-eyed and alert. Very flushed at the recollection of three o'clock this morning. She said:

"I'm all ready for work."

"Then you can make yourself *un*ready, my child. Put on your hat again. I'm taking you out for dinner."

"Oh, but I'd like to get down to this job —"

"Don't be silly," he interrupted. "It's seven – no, good God, much later than that. I thought I was getting mighty hungry, and you must be famished."

"But I ought to give you the Minutes from Grasse."

"I'm in no mood for Minutes. Take an order, Miss Coombe – on with your jacket and beret. I'll ring for the car and we'll go along to 'Prunier's' which is practically next door to my flat. I'll have a quick wash and brush up. Then we'll get a table and talk."

Christa only hesitated for a moment. She was but human. In spite of all the complications, she longed to be with Stephen again. She even thought forlornly that if she could establish a cool yet friendly atmosphere between Stephen and herself, she would feel the happier for it.

But the dinner at Prunier's did not go that way. After his wash and brush-up, a *Homard Cardinale* and an excellent bottle of Chablis, Stephen relaxed. He felt much better now after the grim day.

He was positively shaken by his own sensation of happiness at being with this girl again; he could not look at her without remembering the sweetness of her lips and the strangely wild hungry kisses they had exchanged. He could not restore within himself any real balance or sanity. He was, as he afterwards described it, in a 'hell of a state' about Chris. She 'did something' to him – and what it was he could not imagine. But it was extraordinarily dangerous, and incomprehensible to himself. For him, the confirmed bachelor, the man who boasted that he never allowed sentiment to interfere with the practical side of his life, to be *this way* about his secretary!

What way?

Flying back to London via Paris early this morning, he had decided that it was all a question of propinquity and controlled passion. Then he decided that it wasn't. The idea of losing her – letting her go right out of his life was so awful that he just couldn't 'take it'. Something would have to be done – something drastic.

While they ate their meal, the two of them talked in a rather pseudo, cheerful, chatty manner; about Grasse, about Paris, about the office fire – keeping up appearances to each other.

At the coffee stage, Christa pulled herself out of this pleasant silly cuckoo world and planted her feet firmly on the ground.

"You must go to bed, Stephen. You look all in, and I'm tired too."

He had just lit a cigar. He examined the end, then glanced at her, chewing his lips with a nervousness he hadn't felt since he was a young boy. (Since Dorella left him, in fact.)

"Look here, my dear," he said, "all that nonsense about you quitting – you're not going to stick to that, are you?"

Equally nervous, she fumbled in her bag for a compact, glanced in the mirror and dabbed the corners of her lips with her handkerchief. Her pulse-rate was going up and up. She felt that she was facing another crisis.

"Yes, I must leave, Stephen."

"You still refuse to tell me why."

"Please don't ask questions. Just let me go."

"No," he said quietly. "I'm not going to."

Her head shot up. The pale grey eyes which he found so fascinating – so luminous – held a startled expression.

"Why? You know I'll stay on until the papers are all sorted out and – until you get someone in my place. I would not let you down, but after that —" she broke off.

Then suddenly Stephen unlocked in his heart and his mind all that had been shut away for so many years. On an impulse that sprang from the deepest source of self-revelation, and his over-powering need of this girl, the answer came.

"*Because I want to marry you!*"

If a bomb had dropped outside 'Prunier's' and shattered the big glass windows into fragments at her feet, Christa could not have been more startled. She felt as though a great wave of warmth, of the most thrilling happiness she had ever known, rushed over her – suffocated her. She could hardly breathe. Then she said, in a whisper:

"You are pulling my leg, of course."

That made him laugh. It was so naïve, so typical of her humility.

"Am I? I don't go round proposing to girls just for a leg-pull, you know."

"You *can't* want to marry me."

"I'm warning you," he said with a twist of the lips and a

twinkle in the eye, "that I'm not prepared to sit here and listen to a lot of modest reasons why you're not worthy of a proposal from the great Mr. Harrimay. Oh, my *goodness*, girl, you're a bore when you start that!"

"Then you can't want to marry a bore," she flashed indignantly.

"We've all got our faults, darling. I'll cure you of that one."

Still she gasped for breath, trying to swim to the surface. She stared at his smiling, handsome attractive face. This did not make sense to her yet, but *The Boss had asked her to marry him*. First, it was Tam Davis. Now Stephen. Why – *why*? She wasn't anything *like* as attractive as Felise, or Barbara, or hundreds of the girls she saw every day.

He noticed the shadow that flickered across her face, and help up a warning finger.

"Don't forget – the inferiotity complex is banned."

So she broke into speech, leaning her elbows on the table. clasping her fingers together in an agony of indecision and amazement.

"But why, why *me*, Stephen?"

"My dear adorable Christa, do stop dissecting and analysing. You women are all the same. I refuse to go into the whys and wherefores. I don't altogether understand them myself. Two people who fall in love suddenly, hardly ever do understand why, do they? It's just the look in the eyes – that electric *something* that sparks as the wires meet. Then you've 'had it'. Beauty or brains, or charm, may be contributing factors but the thing remains incomprehensible. It's witchcraft. *You're* a witch. I refuse to probe any further. It's happened. And I think you must admit that – last night (I mean this morning) was proof of it."

She shook her head.

"You don't admit it?" he asked anxiously.

She opened her eyes wide. They were sparkling.

"Yes, yes, of course I do."

"It *was* marvellous – I told you so at the time."

"Of course it was. I nearly died!" she said wildly.

"Do you love me?" he asked with deep tenderness.

She experienced one more moment of indecision. There was nothing she wanted more in the whole wide world than to love and be loved by this man, but she would have to go back and tell Barbara, and that would seem almost like an act of betrayal. Besides, Stephen might very quickly live to regret it. He might get tired of her.

As though reading her thoughts, he leaned across the table and took her hand.

"My adorable Christa, stop looking so panic-stricken and answer me calmly. *Do you love me?*"

"Yes!" she said, with the colour flaming into her cheeks. "Yes, yes, *yes*! You *know* that I do."

He gave a sigh of relief and pressed her fingers hard.

"Good. Well – yes –I had some idea – but why you've been so reluctant to admit it to me you little noodle, I don't know."

"You're always calling me 'a little noodle'. You can't be in love with me."

"Now, now!" Up went the warning hand again.

She surrendered.

"All right, I'll never say anything like that again. You do love me, you must; or you wouldn't want to marry me and I adore you – every hair of your head. I've worshipped you ever since I first saw you."

Stephen dropped her hand, and sat back in his chair. He took a puff at his cigar. His own heart was beating fast and he realized suddenly that he felt as happy as a boy who had just made a promising date with his first girl-friend.

"You're certainly a spell-binder, whatever your charm may be, my darling," he sighed, "I wish to God we weren't in a public restaurant. I'd like to repeat our moment of love in Suite number – oh, I can't remember – whatever it was!"

"*I* remember," she said proudly and repeated the number.

He grimaced at the flushed, excited young face.

"You're too damned efficient. I suppose I'm really marrying you in order to keep you as a secretary."

"Now you're being beastly."

He grew serious.

"You know I'm crazy about you, Christa; quite hopelessly in love. And you won't be allowed to go on working for me, anyhow. I'll have to find another secretary."

"I'll be terribly jealous. I'd much rather go on working for you."

"Nothing doing, my sweet. Once you're Mrs. Stephen Harrimay you'll be too busy looking after our home. Now take some notes, Miss Coombe, some of the last I'll dictate. Take them into your efficient little brain since you have neither pencil nor pad."

"But I have both!" she said and pulled them out of her bag. He covered his eyes with his hand.

"I shall soon be thinking you're too damned efficient, and I shan't be able to live up to you, as a husband."

"You know that isn't true."

He knew. He knew all about her frailties and sweet shyness, and the love and loyalty of her, and all the other endearing qualities that had made him want her for ever. He knew perfectly well the sort of reception he'd get from Julia, too, when he phoned to tell her about his sudden decision to get married to Christa. How unpopular he'd be with Felise, too. (Barbara of course didn't come into his reckoning. He had no real idea of the state of affairs at Wood Green.)

He grinned at Christa.

"Well, as you've got that pen, you can take down the following notes: *Phone all the best agents and ask where there's a Penthouse for sale. I want us to live at the very top of one of these marvellous blocks of flats so that we can stand on the balcony and survey the commercial empire. Then book two seats on a mid-December flight to the West Indies where we'll begin our honeymoon. And we might go on round the Caribbean.*"

"Stephen, stop —" she broke in appealingly. "It's too much and too marvellous. You're just lifting me right off my feet. I feel as though I'm floating."

"Oh, my darling!" he said. "Float on! I'm going to be so much in love with my absurd small wife."

That sort of conversation went on for quite a time. It had a positively stunning effect upon Christa; yet every nerve in her was alive and responsive to the magic of it all.

There was no early bed for Stephen, as he had prophesied.

He drove Christa in his own car down to the Embankment – along the river to the far end of Chelsea. One hand on the wheel, the other folded over hers on his knee.

On the left of them lay the might of the new South Bank buildings, the fantastic beauty and brightness of the great skyscrapers, floodlit, splendid. And through the dusky blue shadows, the Power House, smoke belching magnificently into the sky. Past the beautiful bridges; through the busy traffic; then to a quiet place where for a moment he switched off the engine, took her in his arms and kissed her on lips and throat. He told her again and again how much he loved her. He revived for her all the passionate thrill she had known in his arms in Cannes.

Later he drove her back to her digs in Wood Green. He was sweet, she thought, about Aunt Cath's little house which she pointed out as they passed it, and said how much he wanted to meet her. He was no snob – no, not a bit like Julia who was rather class-conscious.

And she knew that Aunt Cath would adore him.

"I'll see you tomorrow at the office, my love," he said when he kissed her good night. "We'll discuss our future again then. Good night, and thank you for loving me. I think you're absolutely sweet, and exactly what I've always wanted. It's just that it's taken me a bit of time to realize it."

18

IT wasn't until late the next day that Christa saw Barbara and Aunt Cath again.

She had left her digs for the office early that morning and was involved most of the day with the other girls, helping to clear the débris, and repair some of the damage the fire had caused. All she had time to do before leaving home was to write a short note to Barbara and slip it through Aunt Cath's letter box, telling Barby that she was back in London because of the fire and would be along as usual after lunch this afternoon — it being a Saturday.

She was already tired when she started the day's work. She had been too excited to sleep properly last night. Even when she first saw Stephen again and he snatched a quick warm kiss after she entered his office, she could not believe this thing had really happened, or feel absolutely confident of herself or him.

He was involved with a business lunch. He could not take her out, for which she was thankful. She wanted time in which to readjust herself. But she soon found that when Stephen Harrimay fell in love he did not do so lightly and his were what she called 'hurricane' methods. Once again he swept her off her feet, and took command of her actions.

"You are coming out with me tonight. I shall send the chauffeur for you and arrange something attractive," he said.

"We have got so many more plans to make – we'll avoid theatre and dancing tonight, if you don't mind."

When she started to say it might be best for them to wait, he broke in:

"I shall send for you. I can't get away early so I won't come myself, but tell your aunt I'll see her on Sunday. She is your only so-called relative, isn't she? – other than the beautiful Barbara, of course."

It was the 'beautiful Barbara' of whom Christa was afraid. The very memory of her and what she had asked Christa to do, filled Christa with dreadful misgivings and an undeserved guilt complex.

When she finally reached home she found Aunt Cath alone, reading the morning paper. She received a warm kiss and welcome.

"Oh, I'm glad to see you back, ducks. I thought you'd be away from us all week-end. But I'm sorry your holiday was cut so short. Barby and I read about that fire in Hanover Square. Was there much damage?"

Over a cup of tea, the two discussed the fire rather than Stephen. Christa kept putting off the moment when she must tell Mrs. Lane about the incredible and wonderful thing that had happened to her. She wished passionately that Barby were not so infatuated with Stephen. It did spoil everything to know that she must deliver a mortal blow to the girl who had been not only like a friend to her but a sister all these years.

Mrs. Lane glanced at Christa and thought that her face looked exhausted. Her eyes were shadowed.

"I can't say all this rushing around the Continent has done *you* much good!" sniffed Aunt Cath. "But I suppose it was too hectic. You had no time to enjoy a bit of peace in the sun."

"No. I didn't. But it was very fascinating while it lasted."

"How did Mr. Harrimay take the fire?"

"Oh, all right. He can cope with anything. But naturally it's a blow. But there is more surface damage than anything and a lot more was caused by water than fire. Eventually it'll dry and it will be a question of re-decoration then. The store room where all our stuff is kept was fortunately untouched, so it won't stop us carrying on the business."

Mrs. Lane, lighting her usual cigarette, stretched out her legs, smiled at the young girl, and wanted to know all about

Paris, and the South of France. Before Christa could tell her much they heard a footstep. Barbara was back. Christa felt positively sick. Now for the fireworks! She dreaded telling Barby her good news.

Barbara rushed in. She was looking most attractive, more colour than usual in her face. She dashed up to Christa, and gave her a hug and a kiss.

"Thanks for your note, honey. You must have passed our door darned early this morning. I suppose you were rushing down to see what damage there was in Hanover Square. Fancy it bringing you back from Cannes. A shame! Oh, I've been longing to see you and hear . . . *you know what* . . ." she ended with a meaning little laugh, tucked an arm through Christa's and led her out of the kitchen. "Come along and sit on the end of my bed while I change into my slacks. We'll have a good gossip."

Christa went unwillingly. Mrs. Lane called after her daughter:

"Mr. Jorgensen telephoned, Barby pet, and left a message for you to ring him this afternoon."

Barbara tossed her magnificent head and giggled.

"The Dane is quite smitten. I'll phone later" – and to Christa – "I want to hear about *Him*. Did you do the good work for me? Is he going to see me again? Have you fixed some sort of contact? I can't *wait* to hear."

Christa turned red then white. She seated herself on Barbara's bed and looked miserably around her. This was the front room. Mrs. Lane had insisted on giving her difficult daughter the best. It had the cupboards Barbara needed for all her clothes and it had been attractively papered and furnished, as far as their income would allow. But no one was ever allowed to come in here and 'tidy'. There was a wild confusion always, which Christa was accustomed to although it jarred on her more orderly mind. She had never known anybody to be so untidy as Barby. Yet she was so scrupulous in her personal appearance. But her dressing-table was littered with cosmetics, bottles, jars, tubes, brushes and combs and hair-curlers. Doors half open; tissues, handkerchiefs, scarves, gloves, half hanging out. Sweaters, skirts, coats and a variety of gossamer lingerie flung over chairs and on the carpet, along with dozens of shoes. Barbara would say:

"Oh, you people with tidy habits give me the willies.

Don't *please* put my things away. I know where to find what I want, when I want it. Leave my room alone."

Then, she, herself, would have a tremendous day of tidying up, after which the wild disorder would start all over again. Examining it all this afternoon, Christa decided that you might well tell people's characters by the way in which they leave their bedrooms. Barbara mentally was 'untidy' and her emotions all over the place.

"Lord," thought Christa, "how am I going to tell her about Stephen?"

Barbara was standing in a slip now, graceful, voluptuous. She pulled a jersey from a jumble of woollies on one of the shelves, shook it out, then smiled at Christa.

"What's up with you? You're very quiet and you look as peeky as hell. Did the Great Man work you to death, poor poppet?"

"No," replied Christa in a low voice.

"Did you see that snooty party, Madame Roché in Paris?'

"She isn't snooty at all, really," Christa was urged to say out of a sudden sense of loyalty to the woman who might well become her sister-in-law. Incredible thought!

"What was it like on the Côte d'Azur?" continued Barbara, "How I envied you! Rotten shame you had to come back. But now do tell me what you said to *Him* and what He said to you, about me."

Christa decided that it was no good being a coward. Pressing both hands down on either side of her and with very little colour in her cheeks, she looked up at her friend.

"Barby this is going to be a shock to you, I'm afraid," she began.

Barbara pulled the sweater over her head; when her face emerged through the collar it was unsmiling.

"So you didn't get any response from him?"

Christa moistened lips that felt dry.

"No. But I – I did try —"

"You made him realize how much I want to see him again? You did interest him in me not only as a model but as a girl who has a definite 'thing' about him?"

"Oh, Barby, please —"

"Now don't start lecturing me about throwing myself at a man's head," broke in Barbara crossly. "I know you think I do, but some men have to have the idea planted in their minds. Stephen is obviously one of that kind as he has been so slow in the uptake so far."

"Barbara, he never gave you the slighest reason to suppose he liked you in that sort of way," Christa said in a voice that almost matched Barbara's for irritability.

Barbara flung some laundry into a corner of her room then turned a flushed angry face to Christa.

"All right – so what? You've let me down, I suppose. You didn't really try. Well, all I can say is that you'll jolly well have to try again or I won't think much of your affection for me. Now that you're Stephen's personal secretary you could manœuvre it if you were anxious to bring us together – I'm dead sure."

Christa felt so tensed up that suddenly she sprang to her feet.

"Well, I'm *not* anxious – at least, not now. I did try at first but everything has changed and the sooner you know about it the better."

"Know about what?"

Christa's eyes were very bright and exceedingly troubled but she faced up to the inevitable storm.

"You've got to believe this happened without any manœuvring from me. It was the last thing that entered my head, I swear. It just *happened*."

Barbara pushed up both sleeves of her jersey and hooked her slacks around her slim waist. Her lips were thin and compressed.

"Just what are you trying to tell me, Christa."

"Stephen has asked me to marry him," Christa broke out.

She felt as though she had fired a shot into that small bedroom.

She hated doing it but now it was done and she had no thought for herself. She was completely concerned with Barbara's feelings, and wishing she had not had to hurt her. Even though Barbara had no right to be hurt, it was a bad business. Barbara certainly looked as though she had been hit. For an instant Christa thought that she was going to faint. She held out a hand.

"Darling, please – don't think I *tried* to get Stephen. I hadn't the slightest notion he could ever fall in love with me. Not the very, very slightest. You know I have no great opinion of myself. It's been a shock to me. But he does seem to want me and that is all there is about it. He's asked me to marry him almost at once."

Still silence from Barbara.

Christa's heart sank. She could see one of Barby's worst storms brewing. She wished Stephen were here beside her, holding her hand, ready to defend her. It was all so silly and yet so sad. *And* so nerve-racking when one had to deal with a person like Barby. Any hopes that she might have taken it well and been generous and decent, faded. Barbara hurled the next words at Christa in a truly melodramatic fashion:

"*Traitor!*"

Christa went scarlet.

"Barby, for heaven's sake —"

"You beastly sneaky little traitor!"

"You haven't any right to say that. I didn't betray you. I swear to God, I tried as soon as we got into the plane, after leaving London Airport, to make Stephen see you were fond of him. But he shut me up."

"Or did you forget what I asked and go all out to get him for yourself?"

"I won't have you say such a thing. It just isn't true."

"I'm not taking your word for that."

"How unjust and rotten of you!"

"*You*'re the rotten one!"

Barbara spoke on a rising note of hysteria, her magnificent eyes blazing at Christa, "I repeat, you're a sneaky little traitor and I'll never forgive you for this as long as I live."

"Barby, I couldn't help it. How can you help it if a man falls in love with you?"

"You egged him on from the beginning. You double-crossed me right from the word 'go'. That's obvious."

"I won't have you say that because it is a lie. I did my best for you but it happens that Stephen wants to marry *me*. I never dreamt of trying to be competitive. You know how I feel about you. I've always taken second place to you whenever we've met any men, and been willing to let you take all the limelight. *I've* taken it for granted that you were the one with the looks and the glamour. I'm as amazed as you are that Stephen fell for me."

Barbara gave Christa a cruel unflattering look.

"I'm certainly amazed. The man must be out of his mind. As if you could possibly make a suitable wife for him!"

Christa felt a little sick. She sank back on the edge of

the bed and lifted her hands up to her cheeks. They were flaming.

"You're spoiling everything for me. You're being hateful, Barby."

"What did you expect me to do — offer you my hearty congratulations?"

"Oh, Barby, won't you *please* believe I didn't mean this to happen. It's tragic for me that you feel as you do about Stephen."

"Don't be a hypocrite. You've been after him all this time, sneaking your way into his affections. After all ..." Barbara gave a short high laugh ... "some men have very odd taste and I suppose he's one. You had all the luck being in close touch with him, and you've brought it off. I certainly congratulate you on your brilliant success; poaching on your best friend's preserves."

Christa raised her head and protested:

"How many more times am I going to tell you that I *didn't* poach. He never belonged to you. I fell in love with him at the same time you did, but I kept it a secret and I said nothing, not even to you, because I thought it would be absurd and presumptious of me to imagine he'd ever get fond of me."

Barbara gave her another nasty look. Her voice took on a sneering note:

"And might I ask when this fantastically idiotic marriage is to be?"

But Christa did not reply. She felt she had had enough. She was loyal and devoted and despite all the temperamental difficulties, Barbara had been a good friend, and they had had some very happy times together. Christa did not want to feel in any way responsible for bringing Barby unhappiness. But she would not stand here and be accused of doing ugly things she hadn't done. She started to walk toward the door.

"I'm terribly sorry you feel this way. Maybe we'd better stop talking. Or maybe you'd rather I say good-bye to you and Aunt Cath and don't come here any more."

"That's right. Marry your wealthy Boss and get everything that you have worked for, then chuck Mummy and me on one side. That would be in keeping with what you have done to me!" shouted Barbara.

"*Barby!*" exclaimed Christa, appalled.

Now Mrs. Lane came running up the stairs. She had

listened long enough to her daughter's shrill raised voice. She opened the bedroom door.

"Barby ducks, for God's sake what's this all in aid of? Everybody in the street will hear you —" she began.

Barbara, shaking, in the grip of hysteria, pointed a finger in Christa's direction.

"*Congratulate her* – go on! Give her a big kiss. Your dear sweet good little Christa – you've always set her up as an example to naughty Barbara. Well, she's been jolly decent to me. She's sneaked in and taken away the only man I ever really wanted. I hate her. I hate *him*. I hate you all. *I wish I were dead!*"

She burst into floods of tears, staggered to the bed and flung herself face downwards, clawing at the pillow.

Catherine Lane looked with dismay at her beautiful daughter's writhing figure, then up at Christa, who stood by, white and trembling.

"What on earth's it all about, Chris? Who does she mean? Which man is she talking about?"

"Ask her. *Ask her!*" screamed Barbara pounding her fist against the bed-head until it creaked ominously.

"Oh, dear," said Mrs. Lane, bringing her attention for an instant to practical matters. "Do mind that head-board, Barby. We've only just re-covered it. You'll smash it, ducks."

"Aunt Cath – let me explain —" began Christa.

"I shall kill myself," broke in Barbara. "I've got a whole bottle of aspirins and I'll swallow them. I swear I won't live to see Christa become Mrs. Stephen Harrimay. I swear it."

Mrs. Lane turned quite pale. She took off her glasses.

"Christa, what does she mean? *Are* you going to marry Mr. Harrimay?"

"Well, I can't say it sounds a very happy affair, after all this," said Christa in a low voice. "But the fact is, Aunt Cath, that Stephen asked me to marry him last night. Yes, he did. I had no idea he was in love with me but it seems he was. I couldn't help it. I adore him and always have done. But believe me, I didn't try and take him from Barby. He didn't see much of her. She has built this all up out of one or two sittings in his studio, in Paris, and over here, and the one evening they spent together in Paris," Christa added gloomily.

Mrs. Lane shook her head. She felt a bit confused. Only one thing was clear; her daughter was being utterly unreasonable and hysterical again.

Mrs. Lane was convinced that Christa was no traitor. It was not in her character to betray. Secretly Catherine Lane was delighted that such a wonderful thing had happened to the dear little soul. She deserved happiness if any girl did. For years she had done everything she could to return the hospitality and affection she had received in this house. She had always been a marvellous pal to Barby. Mrs. Lane knew well how often Christa had sunk her own wishes in deference to Barbara's. She had crtainly never taken anything from Barby in the past. On the contrary she had always *given*. It was most unfortunate that the two girls should have fallen for the same man. But of course Mr. Harrimay had never encouraged Barbara. It was one of Barbara's wild fantasies. She never did plant her feet firmly on the ground, thought the mother sadly. This sort of thing was bound to happen.

She looked from one girl to the other and found herself wishing, despite all her natural affection for her own daughter, that she could throw her arms around Christa and tell her how happy she was for her. Just think! Christa to marry the great Mr. Harrimay, and such a man from all accounts. But Mrs. Lane dared not utter one word of congratulation – with Barbara present. So she sat down on the bed and put an arm around her daughter.

"Ssh, ssh, don't cry like this, duckie. You've probably been a bit mistaken about what you imagined Mr. Harrimay felt for you. And don't you think we owe it to Chris to say we're glad she has found such happiness?"

Barbara shoved her mother away. She sat up and glared at Christa, her face distorted, wet with her wild tears:

"I warn you – if you marry Stephen Harrimay – I'll commit suicide!"

Christa did not know what to reply. She stood there silently, shocked and miserable. The happiness she had just found so unexpectedly was melting away. Barbara's passionate resentment and Auth Cath's difficulties, over-rode all else.

"Oh, Barby," she said, "whatever you feel now, I know you'll calm down and realize that I didn't deliberately let this happen just to spite you. How could you imagine it? I keep telling you, I had no idea Stephen would ever so much as *look* at me. Do please try to understand, darling. And don't threaten suicide. I just couldn't bear it."

Barbara refused to answer. She fell back on her pillows and began to cry again.

Mrs. Lane and her adopted niece exchanged miserable glances, then Mrs. Lane got up and drew Christa out of the room. Outside on the landing she said:

"Leave her to me, Chris. She'll come round. Don't worry too much. She won't kill herself. It's just sheer hysteria. You know how she dramatizes herself. She'll be telling you how sorry she is, later on. Switch on the kettle, ducks, and make some tea. I'll take it up to her and try to make her lie down."

"Please, Aunt Cath, believe I never meant to hurt her. It's so terribly unfortunate she set her cap at Stephen. It's put me in an awful position for a long time."

"Of course, Chris, and it's not in you to be as bitchy as Barby makes out. I'm so glad for you – bless you, dear."

And Mrs. Lane kissed the girl on both cheeks and hugged her.

"When Barby is better you must tell us all about it. Are you going out with him tonight?"

"Yes."

"Then enjoy yourself and don't let this weigh on your mind. And tell Mr. Harrimay one day I'd like to meet him."

"He wants to come and see you. But you know this business of Barby does spoil things a bit. I've been dreading telling her. I knew she'd turn against me. But I do understand poor Barby. I don't really take umbrage at the things she says to me in a temper."

"Just as well neither of us does," said Mrs. Lane with a short laugh. "She does lose her control. So like her sainted father – it's uncanny, dear. But like him, she's got a warm lovable side which kept *me* my husband's slave to the end."

Christa sighed and went downstairs to make the tea. While she waited for the kettle to boil she tried to forget all the awful things Barby had said, and in particular that threat of suicide. It would be too awful if anything happened to Barby because of her. And yet she couldn't contemplate going to Stephen now and saying: " I can't marry you because of Barby."

It would be absurd and unfair both to Stephen and herself. Much as she loved Barby, she was not prepared to sacrifice herself to that extent. And as Aunt Cath said, Barby would never take an overdose. But it was a horrid thought. It spoiled even the memory of Stephen's kisses, and of the future, which last night had seemed to Christa so dazzling.

At moments it was hard for her to believe that it was true and not a fantasy of her imagination.

Inevitably the echo of some of the things that Barbara had said crept into Christa's consciousness. Particularly those words: *"The man must be out of his mind. As if you could possibly make a suitable wife for him."*

Would she be more of a liability than an asset to Stephen, she asked herself. *Was* she incapable of making a man like Stephen happy for any length of time? Wouldn't his sister be on Barbara's side? Oughtn't he to have chosen a talented, highly-cultured girl like Felise?

Doubts . . . worries . . . fears . . . all kinds of unhappy thoughts began to cloud the horizon for Christa and over-shadow this moment which should have been so infinitely sweet.

It was a subdued Christa who went to her meeting with Stephen later on that night.

He had sent the big car and the chauffeur for her because he was going to be late after a business engagement, and would only have time to go back to his flat and bath and change before dinner. Christa had not encouraged him to fetch her himself. She had been so sure the result of telling Barbara the truth would be catastrophic. It was certainly not the night to introduce Stephen to the family.

While she was being driven out of the suburbs toward the West End in the beautiful Rolls, Christa couldn't even enjoy the luxury of it, nor glory in the notion that this was to be her way of life from now onward. No more queueing for buses or strap-hanging in the underground. She would always have a Rolls, and everything else she wanted, as the wife of the Director of Parfum Joyeux. She would adore her husband, too. But just supposing for one moment that Barby was right and that it was not the best thing for Stephen.

This idea thrust itself like a dagger into Christa's heart.

19

IF there was one thing that Christa wanted it was that there should be no secrets between her and Stephen. But she found this difficult. She felt that she just could not tell him about Barbara's mad passion for him and the way she had turned against her, Christa. Men were different from women – more rational and broad-minded, and so much more interested in life as a whole – not in petty personal feelings. Possibly Stephen would be understanding but rather scornful, and this, Christa would have hated. So she said nothing about home when she met Stephen for dinner at the 'Mirabelle'. Another new exciting West End restaurant to open Christa's eyes to the wonderful meals that could be eaten in luxurious settings, and by the smart crowd who seemed to have a lot of money to spend.

Once she was with Stephen, she felt better able to forget the unpleasant scene with Barbara and to enjoy the thrill of being engaged. He had the facility for putting her at her ease. He became quite a new figure to her, too. Not the Big Man inaccessible as the stars and up on a pedestal, to be worshipped and somewhat feared. But a very human Stephen, simple, close to her. She couldn't possibly be afraid of him. He made her feel confident of his love. He almost convinced her that she had been put into this world especially for him, and that he couldn't do without her. He had touched the peaks of success, he said. Now he wished to dedicate his life also to a woman – his wife. The future mother of his children.

While they drank their coffee, he sat back and looked at her in a dreamy speculative fashion. His eyes seemed to her both tender and passionate. He managed to absorb her, she thought – to draw her into himself like a strong magnet until she became part of him. She, too, ceased to be the little nervous modest Christa and expanded in this new warmth and happiness. She showed a new side to Stephen. He found that she could be quite witty and amusing when she wanted. She always had been a good listener, and he liked that. Every man likes to talk about himself. She had a perceptive mind, too. An intriguing habit that amused him, of watching people, criticizing them, and being uncannily right about them. He knew several couples who came into the 'Mirabelle' for dinner that night. Without hesitation, he introduced Christa to them as his fiancée – this gave her an extraordinary thrill. After they had gone she would give him her opinion of them.

"I'm sure he's either a doctor or in the law – he has a sort of legal face . . ." or:

"She looks rather frightening. Terribly beautiful but cold as ice . . ." or:

"Those two seem very much in love and always will be, I'm sure."

All correct surmises. He even began to tease her and call her his little witch.

"You must look into the future for the two of us. What do you see, my little crystal-gazer?"

"Unbelievable happiness for me, Stephen. A good fortune which I still cannot really understand."

"I'm unbelievably happy, too, darling. The more I see of you the more I like you. And that's *something*. One wants to *like* the person one marries as well as make love to them."

The colour rushed into her face. He loved the way he could always bring it there. Her sensibility never failed to charm him.

For the first time since he had loved Dorella, Stephen Harrimay felt entirely fulfilled. He knew that this small sweet unsophisticated girl Christa was all that he had needed in a life which up till now seemed full enough. But there had been a missing link in the charmed circle. Christa was that link.

He was so contented, so boyishly in love now, that he cared nothing for the dark hints as to future disaster received from his sister over the telephone. (He had phoned Paris earlier this evening.)

"I hope you know what you are doing, Stephen."

"My darling Julia, you know me. I generally know what I am doing."

"Sure it isn't an infatuation? *Must* you marry her?"

He had tried not to be angry when he answered:

"That's not very flattering to Christa. But I know you are thinking of my good, so I'll excuse it. Do stop being so gloomy, my dear. I have known Christa for some time now. I've worked in close association with her. I am sure she is the one person who can make me happy even though she appears to you rather ordinary. But she is very extraordinary really. I'm sorry you are disappointed it wasn't Felise. But she just didn't appeal to me in that way."

"Well, if you are sure Christa will make you happy, you know I'll welcome her into the family," came reluctantly from Julia, showing her good sense and her good breeding.

"You're a dear, Julia. And I shan't forget how nice you were to Christa when I first brought her to your apartment."

"It will be a frightful blow to Felise," sighed Julia.

"Felise will find someone else. And I have always told you I never mentioned marriage to Felise."

Julia had then congratulated him and told him she would write to Christa and (as Stephen now repeated to Christa), Julia announced her intention of flying over to London with Claude for a celebration of the engagement as soon as it was announced.

"We'll stick it in *The Times* and *Telegraph* on Monday," said Stephen.

"I'm sure Madame Roché can't really be pleased!" said Christa.

Stephen's warning finger went up.

"Forbidden, my darling. No inferiority complex!"

"Oh, Stephen, I don't think I'll ever get used to knowing that you have chosen me."

He began to sing in a low voice, an old popular song, grinning at her.

"They'll never believe me ... they'll never believe me! That from this great big world you've chosen me!"

"Now you're teasing me," she said, with a grimace.

"On Monday," he said, "we'll also go and choose the engagement ring. And tomorrow I'll drive to Wood Green if I may, and take you and Mrs. Lane and Barbara," he added hastily if reluctantly, "out to lunch."

She nodded. But her mind turned uncomfortably to the friend who was now so much more of an enemy.

"Not Barbara," she thought, "Oh, my goodness *not her*."

It was her habit on a Sunday to go and have breakfast with Aunt Cath. Barbara always stayed in bed on that morning until midday.

More often than not it was Christa who fried bacon and eggs and made tea for Aunt Cath, in order to give her a longer rest.

When she let herself into the house this Sunday, with the key that she had been given years ago, she still felt as though she trod on air. All night she had kept waking up remembering Stephen and every word he had said: the way he had introduced her so proudly to his friends: how charming they had been when they congratulated her. They really seemed so pleased Stephen was going to get married – and to her. They said:

"She's adorable."

"You do look adorable and I am sure they meant it," Stephen told her.

But even Stephen, with all his will-power and determination could not with one blow destroy Christa's lifetime lack of confidence. She was still somewhat worried as to whether she would really make him happy.

And she was still worried to death about Barbara.

New trouble awaited her.

Aunt Cath lifted a cheek to be kissed but did not kiss Christa in return. Her nice kind face seemed suddenly to have frozen – like her manner. She has changed overnight.

"I hope you had a good evening," she said politely.

Christa bit her lip.

"Very, thanks. Why did you get up, Aunt Cath? I meant to bring you your breakfast."

"I didn't think Mr. Harrimay's future wife would want to come in and act cook for the Lanes."

"*Aunt Cath!*" exclaimed Christa. "How *can* you say such a thing?"

Mrs. Lane, cigarette between her lips, bent over the gas-stove and stirred the scrambled egg that she had been making.

"Never mind. It's your life, and I don't question your right to lead it as you think best."

Christa looked miserably at her adopted aunt. She was amazed by this change of attitude after the warm understanding and congratulations she had received last night.

"What's happened?" she asked quietly. "What have I done, Aunt Cath?"

Mrs. Lane did not answer for a moment. She was genuinely devoted to Christa but she had had a ghastly night with Barby – the worst in her memory. It had left a mark. She wanted to be fair to both girls – and naturally, Barby was her own flesh and blood – Oliver's child.

She said:

"Well, Christa, I haven't been to bed if you want to know

I have been sitting up all night beside Barby. I've been absolutely terrified."

Christa turned cold.

"Aunt Cath you were so sure before I left last night that there was nothing to worry about."

"Well, I thought so then, but she carried on so alarmingly. I began to get worried. I wouldn't leave her even though she fell asleep. She said some terrible things."

"About me, you mean," said Christa in a low voice.

"Yes," nodded Mrs. Lane without looking at her.

Christa felt her nerves tauten. The cold feeling spread. She began to shiver.

"Aunt Cath, are you blaming me now because Stephen wants to marry me, and not Barbara?"

"No, not exactly. But Barbara feels that you did rather steal a march on her. She said he was very keen on her until you became his secretary and so on. And you did promise faithfully to help her when you went to Paris. Then you come back engaged – it is a bit of a turnabout – a tremendous shock for poor Barby."

Silence. Then Christa said in a low voice:

"I see. Well, it isn't true. It's quite wrong and unfair. I did promise to talk to him about Barbara. I did it – but he wouldn't listen. I have absolutely nothing to reproach myself with. But Aunt Cath, do believe me – right from the beginning Stephen was attracted to Barby only because of her beauty as a model. She didn't have anything else for him. The fact that I did, may surprise you, but it surprised me, too. And I did not manœuvre it. He isn't the sort of man to be led, I assure you. He makes his own decisions."

Mrs. Lane remained silent. In the depths of her heart she believed what Christa was saying but her loyalties were divided. She was not a very strong-minded woman and she had not been able to stand up to the mental battering that her daughter had given her last night. She drew a long sigh and finally she said:

"Well, it's no good us going over it all again. We'll have to leave things as they are. You'll be getting married quite soon. You said so. Then you'll go out of our lives and Barby will just have to learn to accept it."

Christa looked at her with despair. All her passionate adoration for Stephen could not wipe out the very real affection and gratitude she had felt for these people in this little house for so long. They had become her people, and this her home. She felt suddenly heartbroken and burst into tears.

At once Catherine Lane, who was a kind-hearted creature, put down her cigarette and took the girl in her arms.

"Don't cry, duckie. I'm sorry this has happened. Don't cry, please. You ought to be very happy now."

Christa hid her face in her hands.

"But it's all spoiled. You and Barby mean so much to me. I can't bear us to be alienated. I can't *bear* you to think I took Stephen from Barbara, either. I didn't, *I didn't*! I swear it by all that is holy, Aunt Cath."

Mrs. Lane was crying, too. She was tired and thoroughly upset.

"Well, I'll try to believe you but Barby never will."

"Oh, she must!" exclaimed Christa raising her head. "*She must*! She can't be so unjust. Oh, Aunt Cath, you must make her see that it wasn't deliberate on my part."

Mrs. Lane moved away from the girl back to her stove.

"Now, I've burnt the eggs."

Christa wiped away her tears and took off her jacket.

"Let me help."

Mrs. Lane shook her head. Christa went on.

"Aunt Cath, no matter how happily married I'll be or how rich, I shall always love you and this house. I want us to go on being close to each other and for you to share my good luck and everything."

"Well, I want it, too," sighed Mrs. Lane, "but Barby —"

"I'll go and see her immediately after breakfast," said Christa. "I'll make her see sense. I've always been able to do so in the past."

"Well, I wish you luck," said Mrs. Lane gloomily. "She won't listen to me. She was awake just now when I took her a cup of tea, just staring into space and mumbling about life not being worth living. Of course I know it is a very wrong, selfish attitude. I tried to make her come along to church with me this morning. But she won't. She hasn't even got religion to help her, Christa – in spite of her upbringing. And I'm afraid that what so many young people lack today, is Faith. If she went to church and had a few more Christian beliefs like me and my mother and *her* mother before that, there'd be a bit more decency and discipline in the world."

Having delivered this short homily, Mrs. Lane went back to the stove to scrape the burnt eggs from the saucepan.

Then the telephone bell rang. For a moment Christa thought it might be Stephen. She had asked him to ring her here and find out if he could do what he wanted and book a table for lunch for her and the family. Of course now she would have to tell him that Aunt Cath and Barbara wouldn't be available. Soon she would have to tell him the truth; the incredible fact that they might never wish to see him at all.

"*It's grim to be made to feel so guilty for a crime you haven't committed,*" Christa thought.

The call was not from Stephen, however; it was from Henrik Jorgensen. The Danish sculptor was still in pursuit of the beautiful Barbara, no doubt piqued by her apparent indifference.

Mrs. Lane asked Christa to speak. Jorgensen began by heartily congratulating her on the engagement.

"Stephen has told me. I haven't met you yet but I'm longing to do so. He says you are like a little Tanagra figure and that your hair is like wheat with the sun on it, which sounds exquisite."

"Thank you," said Christa, trying to sound cheerful.

"Please will you induce that gorgeous creature, who I believe is a sort of cousin of yours, to speak to me. I want to take her out – down to Brighton for the day, perhaps."

Christa asked him to hold the line.

When she told Aunt Cath about Henrik Jorgensen's invitation, the older woman lifted her brows and sighed:

"Well, I'll tell Barby but I doubt if she'll go."

When she came downstairs again from her daughter's bedroom, however, Mrs. Lane looked slightly less worried.

"As a matter of fact she is just getting up and she says she will come down and speak to Mr. Jorgensen; that looks more hopeful."

Christa, whose knees had been feeling weak, suddenly sat down and put her hand to her forehead.

"Oh, I do hope so. It's all so awful! I hate being made to feel it's all my fault and I hate you being worried like this."

Everything that anybody said in this small house could be heard through the thin walls. Mrs. Lane and Christa now heard Barbara plainly when she answered the telephone. She was using what Christa used to call her strawberries-and-cream voice – rich and velvety.

"Nice of you to suggest it, Mr. Jorgensen . . . oh, all right, if you insist, *Henrik*! . . . No, I can't say I often go down to

Brighton but Mummy and I did once spend a week there with an old aunt who is now dead ... oh, yes, it can be lovely ... marvellous air ... No, I haven't seen the new Casino. Or eaten in the 'Starlit'. They say it's gorgeous up there in the Penthouse Restaurant ... I don't really *want* to, Henrik ..." Then they heard her give a little ironic laugh ... "Well, you wouldn't say so if you could see me. I've got a touch of sinus. I look grim." Then in a better pleased voice: "What rubbish, I'm sure there are far more beautiful girls than me in Copenhagen."

Mrs. Lane and Christa eyed each other hopefully. Christa found herself praying:

"Oh, God, do let Henrik persuade her to go. Do make her go to Brighton ... Do let things be all right. I want to be happy but I want *her* and Aunt Cath to be happy, too!"

Mr. Jorgensen seemed to do most of the talking from then onwards. Then the telephone gave a 'ting' and Barbara swept into the kitchen. She had on a white bathrobe but her face had been made-up and her hair dressed, in a Cleopatra style. Christa made a timid movement toward her. Barbara turned her face in the opposite direction and spoke to her mother.

"I shall be out to lunch, Mummy."

"Oh, darling, I am glad because last night —" began Mrs. Lane. But Barbara interrupted, keeping her back turned rigidly upon Christa:

"Now don't let's have any post-mortems about how I felt last night. If you want to know, I jolly nearly did kill myself, then I decided that neither Stephen Harrimay nor Christa – certainly not Miss Christa Coombe – are worth it. Henrik wants to give me a good time and I might as well take it. He's very handsome and – I understand he comes from quite a well-known family just outside Copenhagen. He's already mentioned asking me over to meet his old father. I may chuck Golling & Nash and go to Denmark. I'm sick of Gollings and this house and everybody in it."

"Very well, dear. I shan't interfere with you," said Mrs. Lane looking very hurt. And as she lit a cigarette, the mother thought cynically of the past. She could almost hear her daughter's unkind words as a painful echo of that past. Oliver – looking at her with those same bitter beautiful eyes, saying "*I'm sick of this house and everyone in it*" — Yes, he often said it – just to hurt her. They were tarred with the same brush, those two. And yet she'd given her life to both of them!

Barbara swept out of the kitchen like a tragedy queen. Christa looked at her adopted aunt and saw her smoking furiously while the tears poured down her haggard face. She immediately went to her and cradled her in her arms.

"Darling Auntie Cath, don't be sad. Barby didn't mean half she said. You know you're always telling me she never really means it. Just be glad she is going out with Mr. Jorgensen. I am. I think it is a good sign. *Don't* be unhappy, dear Aunt Cath. Barby really loves you and so do I. It's just that she feels thwarted somehow, and she needs something to fill her life. A man to adore her. Maybe Mr. Jorgensen will be the one. Who knows? She's behaving as though I don't exist but in time she'll forgive me. Whether I have done anything that really needs her forgiveness or not," she added with a twisted smile.

Mrs. Lane drew away from the warm young arms, sniffed into her handkerchief, then shoved it into her overall pocket. She was never going to get on with this breakfast.

She said in a choked voice:

"Make the tea, lovie, and a bit of toast. Don't let's cook. And forgive me if I was rotten to you when you first came in this morning. I'd had a pretty grim night. But I'm myself again. Don't worry. And you're so sweet to me."

Christa made the tea. They drank it together in silence. Christa could hear Barbara's footsteps overhead. She hated this open enmity between herself and her old friend. But it *was* a good sign that Barby had agreed to lunch with the Dane. Her threats of suicide had been sheer hysteria and self-dramatization, after all.

Then Barbara came down. So well made up, so elegant in her dark charcoal grey wool suit with a fringed matching scarf, a white floppy felt hat on her dark graceful head; white gloves and bag and high-heeled shoes. Big twisted gold and pearl ear-rings. The glamorous model complete.

"I say – Elizabeth Taylor herself, ducks," said her mother admiringly.

Barbara gave a superior smile.

Then Christa got up and held out a hand to her.

"You really do look absolutely lovely, Barby. Won't you shake hands and let's be friends?"

Rather rudely, Barbara turned her back in stony silence. But with sudden confidence, Christa persisted:

"Now look – you know I've never willingly tried to hurt

you, Barby. You know it. Stephen is coming later on to take me out, and he did want you and Aunt Cath to join us. Couldn't we all, including Henrik, make up a party and be really happy?"

Again silence. Barbara was busy drawing on her doeskin gloves.

Mrs. Lane intervened:

"Come on, Barby love – it would be so much nicer if we could all be pals again."

Barbara turned round. Her wonderful eyes looked Christa scathingly up and down.

"Some pal Christa's been! And she thinks a nice little lunch party with all of us would be agreeable to *me*. Me, watching Stephen hold her hand."

Mrs. Lane now put in a tactless but well-meaning comment.

"Well, after all, ducks, Mr. Jorgensen might be holding *yours*."

Barbara said angrily:

"I'm sure that's what you both hope for. It would salve Christa's conscience if she could get me off with Henrik."

Now Christa stood up for herself.

"You're determined to be beastly and unfair. I don't want to get you off with anybody. I just want you to be as happy as I am."

"Your sweetness is out of this world," drawled Barbara in a sneering voice.

Christa made a movement as though to pick up her jacket and leave the house. Her heart beat fast. She felt angry now, out of patience with this completely egotistical and cruel girl. She was not going to let Barbara's jealousy and spite spoil yet another day with Stephen. But she didn't want to leave the house because she could see Aunt Cath's face – rather crumpled and forlorn. She couldn't abandon her today. She was going to make her dress up and come out with Stephen. She said:

"I can't take any more of you, Barbara; it's all too unpleasant for Aunt Cath who's had nothing whatsoever to do with the whole unfortunate business. I'd better keep away, at least while you're at home. You know how I feel about you and always will. But if you will go on hating me and being so ridiculous, you must do so."

"Thanks for the permission," said Barbara and walked out of the kitchen.

She was not in a suicidal mood any longer, but as self-centred and difficult as ever. After Henrik Jorgensen had driven up to the little house in his rather striking-looking Mercedes-Benz, and the couple left, some of the tension in the Lanes' house slackened.

"I must say my daughter is a one!" grumbled Mrs. Lane, looking rather pathetic.

"Now you're going to change, Aunt Cath, and I'll do your hair and find your favourite hat and you're coming out with Stephen and me," said Christa.

But Mrs. Lane resisted all the girl's blandishments or entreaties. Nothing would induce her to go out with them, she said. She looked a wreck today and felt one and she wouldn't even consent to *meet* Mr. Harrimay. Not today. Some other time. But she felt so very tired after last night. Tomorrow, yes, she'd feel better. And perhaps Barby would be better, too. She'd had other rows and created other scenes. She'd refused to speak to anyone for twenty-four hours or even longer. But she always came round in the end. Her mother was sure she'd come round again tonight. She'd be quite different after her day out in Brighton with an attractive rich young man who was keen on her.

So Christa was left to welcome Stephen alone.

From the upstairs window, half hidden by a curtain, Mrs. Lane watched them get into the car. My word, *what* a car, she thought. And what a fine looking young man, Stephen Harrimay. No wonder he had caused all this havoc. Not that he knew it, poor boy! And *fancy*, little Christa was going to marry him! Bless her! Mrs. Lane was filled with all the old affection and tenderness towards her adopted niece. It even brought the romantic tears to her eyes to see the way Stephen Harrimay looked at his fiancée as he got into the car beside her. He kissed her hand in a Continental sort of way. Very sweet, thought Catherine Lane. Long may it last. But there quickly followed a less romantic thought. Ages and ages ago (so it seemed) Barby's handsome father had kissed *her* hand like that. And look how he turned out! But some girls were lucky. All their swans didn't turn to geese. Neither did they all taste the bitterness of disillusion. From what Mrs. Lane had heard of young Harrimay, she was sure Christa was to be one of the lucky ones. She would not be disappointed.

20

CHRISTA felt a trifle cowardly. She did not tell Stephen what had happened between Barbara and herself. First of all she did not want to disparage Barbara and secondly because she was still pursued by the feeling of guilt.

She made a suitable excuse for Mrs. Lane and explained that Barby was lunching with Henrik, which appeared to amuse Stephen.

"Old Henrik seems quite smitten with your gorgeous model-girl-friend."

"I'm surprised *you* weren't!" said Christa impulsively and quite sincerely. She was rewarded by one of Stephen's fingers being put against her lips, and a vigorous shake of the handsome head. After which no further reference was made to Barbara. There were far too many other things for them to talk about.

Stephen drove her down to Bray, where they lunched at the Hind's Head which was a particular favourite of his even in cold wet weather. And cold and wet it was. But they had drinks by a big fire, and a very good meal, and the time flew by on those magical wings which seemed to grow upon the shoulders of lovers.

Stephen was full of plans for the future. Christa by the end of that afternoon was more than ever in love. And a final seal was set on her happiness when he gave her a small locket containing a delicately-coloured miniature of his own mother.

A charming jewelled piece in a frame of tiny emeralds, it had been painted in Paris fifty years ago, Stephen told her. Now he wished her to have it. It was for his future wife.

Christa flushed with pleasure. She looked at the miniature long and earnestly. He could see that the value of it was of no interest to her whatsoever. She could talk only of 'the honour' of receiving such a treasure; and of the likeness between him and his mother, who was in her twenties when this had been painted. They had the same brilliant searching eyes with arched brows, and the same colouring and rather determined lips and chin.

"You're very like her," Christa said in a hushed voice, "I *wish* I could have known her."

"She would have loved you," said Stephen. "She died many years ago. Julia and I were orphaned when we were both in our teens. I must have been still at Oxford. I can remember her saying to me: '*The two most dangerous assets a woman can possess are beauty and charm.* If you want to be happily married, my son, choose a girl who is just a lovable human being, with the three qualities of generosity, integrity and sweetness.' Well, Christa, my darling, she could not have more clearly described you."

Christa pressed the hand Stephen held out and answered him, her voice full of emotion.

"I really do believe you feel like that. You really love me. It's terribly, *terribly* marvellous and exciting."

Then he laughed at her exaggerated choice of superlatives and lit a cigarette for her. The emotional tension relaxed, but from then onward the miniature of Stephanie Harrimay – Stephen's mother – remained Christa's dearest and most-prized possession.

Barbara continued to be unforgiving with strong obstinacy during those next few weeks.

November came. Christa felt rather uncomfortable about going to the Lanes' house now. She believed it might be more helpful if she kept away, much as she longed to see Aunt Cath and spoke to her only when Barby was out. In any case Stephen occupied most of Christa's time. She had to face up to a series of lunches and dinners in order to meet his various friends. In particular two cousins on his father's side – elderly maiden ladies who lived in Bromley. These two received their young cousin Stephen and his fiancée with delight and each sent her away with a little present. From Aunt Olive, a fine gold chain which would be perfect for the miniature of Stephanie. From Aunt Maggie, a glorious veil of Limerick lace. This had been worn by Stephen's paternal grandmother and kept by the aunts for Stephen's future bride.

From now on Christa began to feel much more at ease and to accept her new position without constant self-analysis.

At times she still wondered why Stephen loved her but he, personally, never allowed the question to arise. He just loved her. For him that was enough and he told her that it must be so for her as well.

In the office, of course, things changed. Inevitably the junior members of the staff retreated into a shell and no longer looked upon Miss Coombe, the Boss's fiancée, as 'one of them'. They treated her with new reserve. But she had to admit they had all congratulated her warmly on her engagement. Young Pat had made one of her usual flippant jokes.

"'She Married Her Boss' – *M'm*, I always imagined that was fiction but here it is fact – and the best of luck to you, Christa."

Olga Jacobs herself, when she recovered from flu and returned to the office, shook hands with Christa. She was full of superlatives.

"How simply *marvellous*! I *do* congratulate you!"

But she could not resist one or two veiled allusions as to the unsuitability of the match.

"It just never entered my *head* . . . Such a fantastic surprise . . . you and Mr. Harrimay . . . My *dear*!"

All of which made Christa feel that it really *was* fantastic. And that not only Olga Jacobs would open their eyes wide. But she was very quickly made to forget what Olga said and thought. She was far too happy. There came the thrill of the newspaper announcements of the engagement – then the ring. Christa was told she must choose her own and was forbidden to be price-conscious. That was something Stephen wanted her to stop feeling, although he knew it would be difficult after a lifetime of economy.

It was not to be emeralds, sapphires or rubies for Christa. Her favourite stone had always been an aquamarine. It looked well on her small narrow hand. So they found an exquisite square-cut stone set in brilliants – a flawless aquamarine, so transparent that it looked like blue-green ice with the sun on it. The ring had to be made a little smaller to fit her finger. When she finally got it, Stephen put it on – kissed first the stone and then her lips. He said:

"Always remember that I love you very much and that whatever you may think, I don't want anyone but you, and I never shall. Neither shall I ever change. I'm that sort of a chap."

She believed him, just as she believed that she, herself, would never change. And for the time being she was allowed the delight of working for and with him at Parfum Joyeux. He found her an immense help during the difficult days of expansion and reorganization, both in France and England,

and the disaster of the fire. Finally it was agreed she should go with him to Edinburgh. He wanted to see Tam Davis and the new Princes Street offices.

He had laughed as they made the arrangements.

"I suppose there are still a lot of old crows about who might mutter if I took you up to Scotland alone, so we'll wait and go when Julia's here. I know she'd like to see the Edinburgh office. We can leave Claude here to catch up with the English business."

The Rochés flew in from Paris. That night all went to the much talked-of celebration dinner. Secretly, Christa dreaded her first meeting with the woman who was to be her sister-in-law and whom she felt must deplore the step that her brother had taken.

But she need not have been so worried. Stephen exerted his right to spend money on his fiancée in whatever way he wanted, and insisted that Christa should find herself something really lovely to wear, at his expense. At the same time he took her to 'Chiberta' in Berkeley Street where a very charming man whom he had known for many years (in the fur trade) had made a sable-jacket for Christa. It was a secret Stephen had kept until the jacket was ready. He had shown Michel a photograph of Christa and the rest had been done without the usual fitting.

"I want something worthy of my attractive future wife, Michel," Stephen had said. And Michel, the expert, had produced it.

Christa gasped when she first put on that warm soft jacket tailored to suit her petite figure. This was really intoxicating. Sable – the most beautiful of all furs – and every woman's idea of glamour. Stephen looked at her with that half-amused wholly-tender smile which he reserved especially for Christa these days. He said approvingly:

"You look one hundred per cent, my darling. And now that Michel has done so well for you, you must go off and find the right dress to wear under that jacket tonight. We'll make old Julia's eyes open wide, won't we? You can also wear your sable when you go up to cold, cold Edinburgh."

"I feel quite marvellous and crazy!" sighed Christa twirling herself around and looking in the mirrors of Michel's handsome *salon*. And the handsome Michel smiled back at her. He thought her delightful.

She did find the right thing to wear under that gorgeous

jacket – quite alone, without guidance from Stephen. A silver-grey brocade evening suit which was plain yet chic, and perfect under the rich dark fur.

On the night of the celebration dinner she wore her silver suit and her sable, the jewelled locket with the miniature round her throat and her engagement ring.

Julia Roché had to admit that she was startled when she first saw the small elegant figure walk beside her brother into the lounge of the Dorchester when they all met that night.

If she had ever said anything about Christa being a 'little nonentity', Julia took it back. She never *had* been that, of course. There had always been a unique charm in the young girl which one noticed, not at first necessarily, but gradually. It had certainly eliminated the more blatant glamour of her girl-friend Barbara, completely. But tonight Christa spelt '*glamour*' too.

'And she knows how to dress all of a sudden,' thought Julia as her experienced eye took in the silver suit and jacket. *Sable! Mon Dieu!* Stephen certainly *was* in love.

"*Ravissante*," said Claude Roché and claimed that he now had the right to kiss Christa on both cheeks.

Christa, with fast-beating heart, held out a hand to Julia. There was a mixture of trouble and appeal in those big grey eyes to which Julia responded generously. True, she had had an unpleasant hour with Felise last night, listening to her moans and groans about losing Stephen, and she had thought Stephen a fool. But perhaps he wasn't quite such a fool as he seemed. This child would make a very sweet wife. And a big business man like Stephen needed a calm sensible wife who would adore him and never question his authority. Felise would have been a handful – like all temperamental musicians. Julia also adored Stephen, and she decided to forget all her misgivings. She took Christa in her arms and kissed the girl warmly.

"All my sincere congratulations, darling, and I really mean it."

Christa's cup of happiness seemed to brim over. She could hardly speak as the four of them moved toward the American bar where Stephen ordered champagne. After that in the beautiful restaurant, they had an excellent meal and more champagne, and Stephen was so obviously happy that as the evening went on, Julia became more and more resigned about this engagement.

At one point, Christa said in a low voice to her future sister-in-law:

"I still can't believe it, you know. I don't know *why* he's chosen me."

"Well, I'm beginning to understand why," said Julia smiling. Then with all her sense of feminine attraction alert, she scanned Christa's face and nodded: "Yes, you're beginning to look the cat's whiskers, my dear. Being in love can certainly transform one. I like your make-up – that touch of silver shadow on the eyelids – who taught you that? And that pink lipstick – so effective with your blonde hair!"

Christa blushed.

"I had a make-up – at Arden's."

"It suits you."

Stephen caught the gist of this conversation and put in his spoke.

"Well, I don't want too much of it. I like Christa as God made her. With her Scandinavian colouring she doesn't need too much make-up. I can't wait to get her out in the sun in Jamaica, Julia, and see what that fair hair will look like when she's tanned."

"Lucky you two – to be going to the West Indies. I wish Claude and I could get away but we can't!" sighed Julia.

After that, they began to discuss the wedding plans. It was only at the end of the dinner that Julia suddenly brought up the name that Christa had been trying to forget.

"How's your friend, Barbara?"

"I don't really know. I haven't seen her for a few days. Things are a bit difficult at home," admitted Christa.

"You remember Henrik – Henrik Jorgensen, don't you?" Stephen turned to his sister. "He's rather taken with the beautiful Barbara. He was so jealous of the head I did of her that I think he wants to do one himself, for his Copenhagen show."

Julia, fitting a cigarette into a long holder, leaned back in her seat and smiled at Christa.

"Well, if we're going to be frank, I'm going to say right now, that if Stephen *had* to fall in love with one of you two girls whom he pulled out of that wreck, I'm thankful he didn't choose the beautiful Barbara."

"Heaven forbid," said Stephen.

Claude in the glib flattering way of the Frenchman added: "How could he have chosen anybody but *la petite* Christa!"

They all laughed. Stephen raised his champagne goblet to Christa. She was deeply moved by the look in his eyes. But a sadness crept over her. It was not in her nature to turn her back on the past in an egotistical fashion and be happy because fortune had smiled on her. She was too loyal, too closely tied by the threads of her gratitude to those two in the little Wood Green house which used to be her home.

She was sad because she had not been there lately. Sad because when Aunt Cath spoke to her on the phone — she had telephoned her this morning — she said:

"It's no good you trying to see Barby yet. She seems quite set against you. I just don't understand it."

When Christa had asked what the situation was with Jorgensen, Aunt Cath replied:

"She seems to be going out with him but *you* know Barby. It's a sort of bravado following her breakdown. I think she really was in love with Mr. Harrimay."

Remembering this, Christa could not be entirely happy. Aunt Cath out of her sense of loyalty to her daughter would not even consent for the moment to meet Stephen. Christa had to keep making excuses. Luckily Stephen accepted them. He was too busy to worry much about Christa's adopted relatives.

That next morning, Julia, Christa and Stephen travelled up to Scotland by air.

It was bleak and cold there with an east wind tearing down Princes Street, but Christa in a tweed suit, with her new jacket, felt warm and braced against even that famous fiendish Scottish wind. And she was thrilled by her first glimpse of the beautiful city. It was curiously like a black and white photogravure of the past, with its glorious Squares and terraces of Georgian houses. *And* the Castle, high on the hill with those old grey battlements frowning down upon the City, and beyond, the gentle green slopes of the hills they call Arthur's Seat.

In the newly organized offices of Parfum Joyeux Christa faced another moment of embarrassment, meeting Tam Davis again under these circumstances as Stephen's future wife. It was a bit awkward. Tam had been so nice to her, and he, himself, had proposed. What *would* he think?

Whatever he thought, Tam produced only a beaming smile and a hearty handshake for Christa.

"This *is* a surprise. Or rather *was*, when I first heard it from the London Office. Bless you both! It's quite obvious to me, Christa, the Boss didn't want to lose his secretary because girls like you don't grow on trees, so there he is – leading you to the altar. Good show!"

It was a matter for laughter, for a bottle of champagne which Tam had bought and produced in the office. And the awkward moment for Christa dissolved pleasantly into a charming reception.

Later there was work for the two company directors, and for Tam, and Christa talked to the other girls in the office. After which they went out to lunch at the Caledonian Hotel.

Business over, they said good-bye to Tam and flew back to London.

Driving from the airport to Stephen's flat, Julia generously repeated to Christa one or two pleasant things she had heard in the Edinburgh office.

"Tam's secretary, Miss Mackay, told me she thought you were too sweet for words, Christa. The actual words she used were: *'What I liked was although she's going to marry the Boss, she isn't a bit snooty'*."

Stephen smiled at this.

"One thing Christa could never be is snooty. But what a word!"

They all had a glass of sherry in Stephen's rooms. They were in one of those handsome but dark and dreary apartments, of the old bachelor-chambers' type. Stephen had said several times how glad he would be to get out of it. The hunt for the Penthouse in which he and Christa were to live was already on. They were going tomorrow to see a possible one now being completed in Knightsbridge.

"I'd adore to help with the décor," Julia said suddenly.

"Oh, please, please do," said Christa in an earnest voice. "Your Paris flat is so gorgeous. You've got such wonderful taste."

That pleased Julia. She had been a little anxious in case Stephen's fiancée might resent advice from her and want to do things in her way. But the nicest thing about this girl, Julia decided, was her complete lack of vanity. She admitted that she was inexperienced and that Stephen's home must be perfect. He wouldn't himself have much time to attend to details, and Julia was mad about interior decoration.

So, happy plans were made between Julia and Christa, who

would join forces over the décor and furnishing, once the Penthouse was finally decided upon.

The telephone bell rang just as Stephen was about to drive Christa home.

They heard him say:

"Oh, *hullo,* Henrik . . ."

Christa looked at Julia. Her mind was on the suit she was wearing. She had been examining it in the mirror.

"This skirt must be shortened. I'm livid about it. I must take it back to my couturier as soon as I get to Paris. A skirt must always be frightfully well-made, and not too long; remember that, Christa darling."

Stephen came in from the bedroom where he had been answering the call. His face was grave.

"Christa," he said. "I'm afraid I have bad news for you."

She looked startled.

"Oh, *what?*"

"Jorgensen has just been on. It's your Aunt Catherine – isn't that her name?"

"Aunt Cath – yes – oh, Stephen, what's happened?"

"Henrik was ringing from your aunt's house. Apparently he took Barbara to an Art Exhibition this afternoon and when they got back they found your aunt on the kitchen floor. I honestly don't know anything about it or what was really wrong, but something to do with her heart, I think. Anyhow they had to call an ambulance and Mrs. Lane has been taken to a local hospital. They went with her, but Henrik has just brought Barbara home."

Julia went at once to the younger girl's side. Christa had lost all her colour.

"I'm sorry, dear. You're very fond of your adopted aunt, aren't you?"

"She's been like my own mother," said Christa in a low voice, "I haven't got anybody else in the world." Then she added to Stephen: "Was it Barbara who asked for me, then?"

"Apparently, yes. I'll ring for my car and chauffeur. We'll go straight to Wood Green, shall we, darling?"

Christa was already putting on her jacket and beret.

"Yes – thanks – thanks awfully. I must go at once."

In the car moving slowly through the heavy traffic Christa thought how sad it was – and how ironic – that there was a chance of reconciliation between Barbara and herself only because Aunt Cath was desperately ill. She prayed that dear Aunt Cath would live. She was such a good person in every way. And Christa so longed for Stephen to meet her and for Aunt Cath to get to know him.

She kept saying:

"Oh, dear! Oh, *dear*!"

Stephen's warm hand was strong and reassuring. He comforted her:

"It'll be all right, dearest. Don't worry. I'm sure it'll be all right. Henrik didn't say she was dying or anything. A heart attack is not necessarily fatal. Has she been overdoing it lately?"

Christa felt that she must tell Stephen a few of the facts; reluctant though she was to give the full story of Barbara.

"I've always looked upon Aunt Cath as being strong, but she has had a lot of extra worry lately. I'd better put you in the picture, darling Stephen."

After he had heard a few of the things Christa told him, he looked at her in astonishment.

"But, my dear, I never *was* on those terms with Barbara. You must know that."

"I do know it. She's been out of her mind."

"Very much so," said Stephen grimly. "I think I've always made it abundantly clear to you, anyhow, that I admired Barbara's wonderful head and classic features, but nothing more. Henrik may have different feelings – I think he has – but mine have been purely platonic."

"Yes, I know, but unfortunately she fell in love with you," said Christa sadly.

Stephen shook his head as though mystified. He took a cigar from his pocket and pierced the end.

"What a thing!"

"Don't be cross with her. I think she's really suffered a lot."

"She had absolutely no right to go suffering over me," snapped Stephen.

"Oh, dear!" came from Christa again. "Oh, *dear*!"

Then his brow cleared. He lit the cigar, gave Christa one of his sidelong tender glances and pressed her close to his side.

"My darling tender-hearted little thing, I can see you've been handing out a lot of sympathy where it wasn't due."

"Oh, Stephen, I'm sorry for her. I've had all the luck. You must see how I feel about her."

"Well, it all beats me. You women are odd creatures – damn me!"

"*Don't* be cross."

He took the cigar from his mouth and rubbed his cheek against her soft one.

"As though I could possibly be cross with you."

"Then don't be cross with Barbara either."

"My darling, I can't get up much enthusiasm about the young woman just because she's got me wrong and cherished the idea I was smitten with her. It's been you, and only you, all the time."

"I'm so lucky," she whispered again.

"Well, I promise I won't show her what I feel. But I'll get tough if she does any more snarling at you. She does snarl rather, don't you think? A bit like a handsome leopardess."

"Oh, dear!" exclaimed Christa with a sigh and a laugh. "Poor Barby. She isn't really like a leopardess. She's just a mixed-up kid. She has velvet paws under the claws, I assure you. She can be delightful and was jolly good to me when I was younger. We had an awful lot of fun together – it's just been lately things have gone wrong."

"Are you suggesting I have caused all the trouble, Miss Coombe?"

Christa flushed and moved away. She shook her head at him.

"Now we're arguing – we've never argued before, you and I."

He laughed and pulled her back into his arms. His cigar smoke was pungent and pleasant to her. And he seemed extraordinarily handsome and charming. Her whole heart went out to him as it always did and always would. She said no more but clung to him closely. Their lips met. Then as she drew back again, she reverted to the thought of her adopted aunt. Her mind was full of anxiety again.

Once at the Lanes' house it seemed so natural to her to walk through the front door as she had so often done in the past. It was a cold winter's night with a bitter wind blowing. But it was warm and quite agreeable in Aunt Cath's lounge. Barbara had lit a fire and was entertaining Henrik to a glass of sherry.

As Stephen and Christa walked in, Barbara barely looked at the tall man. He uttered a few polite words of sympathy,

then greeted Henrik. The two men started to talk in under-
tones.

Barbara seemed to go to pieces when she saw Christa and
fell into her outstretched arms. No longer the cold haughty
enemy that she had become, but the old Barbara, warm,
affectionate and reliant upon Christa.

"Oh, Chris! *Chris!*" she said and burst into tears.

"Come upstairs, darling," said Christa and led her friend
up to her bedroom.

First she found a box of matches, set the gas-fire going,
then looked at Barbara who was sitting on the bed with her
head in her hands.

"How is Aunt Cath?"

"I've just been on to the hospital. I left Mum there half
an hour ago. She's conscious again but they say it's a bad
attack."

Christa sat beside her friend and put an arm around her.

"How bad?"

"Well – what they call a coronary thrombosis. I think there
is heart weakness in our family because our grandmother died
in the same way."

This was Barbara, over-emotional, dramatizing herself again,
but Christa was all tenderness and comfort.

"Aunt Cath's far from dead and she isn't going to die.
She's going to get better and be up and about in no time."

Barbara blew her nose.

"Oh, I hope so," she said brokenly.

"Poor darling Barby, I know how you love her. It must
have been a dreadful shock for you finding her there."

Barbara lifted a tragic face. No interest now in her make-
up; running mascara, smudged lipstick, beautiful dark auburn
hair tumbling on to her shoulders. She looked much younger
and quite pathetic this way, Christa thought, and really *much*
nicer than that other Barbara, the vain slinky model-girl.

"I feel ghastly because I know it's been my fault she has
had this attack," moaned Barbara. "When Henrik and I found
her there on the floor I thought I'd die. I've been so awful to
her, as well as you, lately. She's been worried to death and
she hadn't been sleeping – she said so. But she's gone on
working all the time. Then worrying about us. She loves you.
I've been selfish and horrible to you, and now I've killed my
own mother!"

Then Christa actually laughed, even though her own eyes

were full of tears. She hugged her and kissed the beautiful petulant face.

"Oh, you *are* a silly little noodle – that's what Stephen's always calling me. Of course you haven't killed Aunt Cath. I heard Henrik telling Stephen as we left the lounge that her condition was not critical."

Barbara had dissolved into tears again.

"But I've been such a fool and worse than that over you and Stephen. It's affected Mummy."

"Please, darling, forget about it. As long as Aunt Cath gets well again, what's it matter?"

Barbara blew her nose again.

"Well, the Sister and doctor told me it might mean that she'll have to stay put for six to ten weeks but they did say she would recover, only she'll just have to go slower than she has been doing. She's getting older you know, Chris, but she never admits it. She just goes on looking after me and doing everything."

"Darling, we'll both take more care of her when she comes back. Perhaps we can get her into a lovely Convalescent Home somewhere. I know Stephen will help me . . ."

Then she stopped and gave her friend a quick embarrassed look.

"You *will* be friends with me again, and friends with Stephen, too, won't you, Barby?" she added. "You will believe I never meant to hurt you."

Barbara got up and walked away a pace, obviously trying to control herself.

"Yes, I'll try to. I dare say I've been to blame all the way along, but I felt too disappointed and upset to own to it. It was a sort of psychological desire to hurt you because I was hurt."

"Poor Barby! I've missed not seeing you so much. I've hated our falling out – and not coming here."

"I've missed you, too," muttered Barbara.

"Then it's going to be all right again, isn't it?" said Christa joyfully.

Barbara now gave a somewhat weak smile, and sniffed.

"Yes. Of course. And I'm sure it'll cheer Mummy up if we can go to the hospital together tomorrow and see her, and tell her that we've made it up."

Christa sprang to her feet.

"Oh, Barby, you don't know what a relief it is, both to

know that Aunt Cath is out of danger and that you are going to be friends with me again."

"I must say I think you're very forgiving," Barbara admitted. She sat down at her dressing-table and began to clean off her face with a pad of wool soaked in complexion milk. Then she paused, staring at Christa's figure through the reflexion in her mirror.

"My giddy aunt," she exclaimed in a changed voice, "that *jacket!*"

Christa bit her lip. Her eyes were starry.

"Yes. It's sable. Stephen had it made for me as a surprise to celebrate our engagement."

"*Sable!*" repeated Barby in a hushed voice.

"And look at this," Christa held out her left hand proudly.

"Come nearer the light and let me see it properly. Gosh – what a super aquamarine."

"He's been terribly generous. Oh, Barby, he is so wonderful. I can't tell you how thrilled and happy I am. I can't believe yet that I'm actually going to marry our *man* of that Dieppe holiday."

Barbara wasn't listening. Her gaze was once more riveted on the sable jacket; suddenly she dragged it off Christa's shoulders and slid into it, nuzzling her cheek against the rich soft fur.

"It's out of this world! How lucky can you be?"

"I know. And I love him, Barby. I love him."

"I'd love any man who gave me a sable like this," exclaimed Barbara. Then she took it off and put it around Christa again.

"Oh, well, maybe I'll have a decent fur coat of my own soon," she said and twisted her red voluptuous lips at Christa.

"Oh, Barby – do you mean —"

"Yes," broke in Barbara, "Henrik Jorgensen is quite serious about me. I discovered that when we were down in Brighton. He hasn't a big business like Parfum Joyeux or Stephen's wealth. He's a professional sculptor but he also is director of their family business. His father owns a china factory or something – in Copenhagen. We have a lot in common actually. He's really more my type than Stephen. Not so intellectual. He likes dancing with me. In fact he and I have been getting on very well – better than I expected. I don't say I'll find him as attractive as Stephen. But I think I shall get very fond of him soon. He says that I'll cause a terrific stir in Copenhagen and he's always dreamed of a girl with brown eyes and auburn hair . . ." Barbara gave a sly glance at herself in the mirror. "So maybe I'll have an engagement of my own to celebrate before Christmas."

"Oh, Barby, how absolutely splendid! This is all I wanted to make me really happy. I've been miserable over our broken friendship."

Barbara shook her head at the younger girl.

"Have you really bothered to give it a thought while you've been out with a man like Stephen and getting sables and rings and what-not?"

"Of course. I'm devoted to you, Barby. I was miserable because you wouldn't speak to me."

Barbara suddenly melted and gave Christa a quick kiss.

"You're a softie, but I was always very fond of you. We'll go and see Mummy tomorrow and tell her we've made it up. Now just let me put on a bit more make-up and do my hair and we'll go down and have a drink with the boys. That is if you think your Stephen will condescend to speak to me."

"Of course he will. And oh, Barby, we've got so much to discuss next time we're alone. I want to tell you all about our wedding plans and the Penthouse and you'll be my bridesmaid, won't you? And I expect Henrik will be Stephen's best man, and it's all going to be terrific."

"What a romantic little thing you are!"

"No I'm not – I'm just a —"

"Noodle," put in Barbara, grimacing at her.

"A noodle, yes."

They were both laughing as they linked hands and went downstairs together.

THE END

DENISE ROBINS

FORBIDDEN

Two young lovers seeking the atmosphere of peace and tranquillity they were never able to find in London emerge from a car in a sunlit Provencal town square. It was an idyllic setting for a passionately romantic interlude, but the dazzling light and contrasting deep shadows echoed the pattern of their own life, for Nat was a brilliant young surgeon with a professional reputation to uphold and Toni was married to a vindictive business tycoon.

'Rarely has any writer of our times delved so deeply into the secret places of a woman's heart'

Taylor Caldwell

CORONET BOOKS

ALSO BY DENISE ROBINS
IN CORONET BOOKS

All these books are available at your local bookshop or newsagent, or can be ordered direct from the publisher. Just tick the titles you want and fill in the form below.

Prices and availability subject to change without notice.

CORONET BOOKS, P.O. Box 11, Falmouth, Cornwall.
Please send cheque or postal order, and allow the following for postage and packing:
U.K. – One book 18p plus 8p per copy for each additional book ordered, up to a maximum of 66p.
B.F.P.O. and EIRE – 18p for the first book plus 8p per copy for the next 6 books, thereafter 3p per book.

OTHER OVERSEAS CUSTOMERS – 20p for the first book and 10p per copy for each additional book.

Name ....

Address ....

....